JED and the Junkyard War

STEVEN BOHLS

DISNEY • HYPERION
LOS ANGELES   NEW YORK

Copyright © 2016 by Steven Bohls

All rights reserved. Published by Disney • Hyperion, an imprint of Disney Book Group. No part of this book may be reproduced or transmitted in any form or by any means, electronic or mechanical, including photocopying, recording, or by any information storage and retrieval system, without written permission from the publisher. For information address Disney • Hyperion, 125 West End Avenue, New York, New York 10023.

First Hardcover Edition, December 2016
First Paperback Edition, January 2019
1 3 5 7 9 10 8 6 4 2
FAC-025438-18348
Printed in the United States of America

This book is set in 12pt Adobe Caslon Pro/Fontspring; Electra LT Std Display, Times New Roman PS Pro/Monotype; Chisel FS, Columbus MT/Fontspring

Designed by Maria Elias

Library of Congress Cataloging-in-Publication Control Number: 2015042273
ISBN 978-1-4847-3047-8

Visit www.DisneyBooks.com

SUSTAINABLE FORESTRY INITIATIVE

Certified Chain of Custody
Promoting Sustainable Forestry

www.sfiprogram.org
SFI-01054

The SFI label applies to the text stock

To Brandon Sanderson: for your stories of experience,
your devotion to craft, and for teaching me how to be a writer.

J ed eyed the pile of batteries on the far side of the table, calculating if they were worth the challenge.

Probably not.

But for once, the entire crew was smiling at him—cheering for him. It felt good.

On the edge nearest him sat a plum-size gollug slug. Jed poked it. The slug squished under his finger.

"Bite! Bite! Bite! Bite!" the crew chanted.

Shay pushed her way through the group. "Eww! Jed, don't." She leaned closer and whispered, "Besides, you could get *twice* that many batteries, silly mouse." She stepped back and cringed at the slug. "That's disgusting."

Pobble stepped in front of her and slapped Jed's back. "Ah, don't listen to her. It probably tastes like blueberries or something. And just look at all them batteries."

The others nodded.

"Hurry," Sprocket said, "before Captain catches me away from my post."

Jed reached for the slug just as Captain Murdock Bog, a boulder of a man, plowed his way through the crowd. "What's all this?" he shouted, his voice deep and gravelly.

The crew fell silent.

"Well? Answer me."

Sprocket shuffled away, staring at the deck as though suddenly interested in the luster of the copper planks.

Pobble snorted.

Captain Bog glared.

"Sorry, Cap'n," Pobble muttered. "We didn't mean to be lazing around, but Jed was about to eat a bite of a live gollug slug. Found it stuck under the helm."

Captain Bog pointed to the batteries. "And those?"

Pobble nodded. "Only if he swallows a *whole* bite."

Captain Bog shook his head. "You sorry lot ought to be ashamed of yourselves." More of the crew studied the deck. Shay folded her arms and nodded. "Haven't you learned anything since that boy jumped aboard? I expected better from you dimwits."

He turned to Jed. "I'm not letting him walk away with that many batteries for nibbling the backside of a slug." He reached into his pocket, then tossed two batteries onto the pile. "You eat the *whole* thing, or you get nothing."

Shay's mouth dropped open in disbelief.

Cheers erupted.

Jed gripped the slug and pried it from the table. It slurped in its own ooze. His stomach tightened. He met Captain Bog's eyes and wedged the slug into his mouth.

. . .

Jed picked rubbery remains from his teeth with the end of an uncoiled spring. Gollug slugs weren't as slimy as he'd thought—sort of sandy actually. Definitely not worth eighteen batteries, but added to the rest of his stash, it was probably enough to buy a new spatula, a wire whisk, and maybe a bottle of cinnamon.

The slug left an oily taste on his tongue, and he wished he had cinnamon right then. His parents had plenty in their old kitchen—and not just cinnamon. He could almost smell the raw stalks of vanilla, the bitter turmeric, the sweet nigella seed, and saffron . . . *saffron*. Jed inhaled as if he were holding a bottle of it. But the taste of slug pushed the memory away.

Four weeks ago, Jed hadn't known what a gollug slug was. He had never met a scritch, walked through the streets of a floating city, or been caught in a junkstorm. Four weeks ago, Jed had been like any other eleven-year-old. Sort of. If other eleven-year-olds had mothers who drove them (blindfolded) to the middle of Yellowstone National Park and left them with four dollars and a can of orange soda, then, yes, Jed had been *exactly* like other eleven-year-olds.

He could still feel the way his mother's lipstick-slathered kiss had squished onto his forehead.

"Don't get into trouble now," she'd said. "Be safe. And watch out for grizzlies. They'll eat you in two bites."

"I know, Mom."

She clawed the air with a hand and winked. "Rawr!"

Jed rolled his eyes. "Rawr . . ."

"I'm baking lemon cake for your birthday tomorrow," she said. "If you're not home, your father's going to eat the middle and leave you the crust pieces."

"I hate it when he does that! The middle pieces are my favorite!"

"What am I to do?"

"Um . . . don't let him eat it, maybe?"

She sighed and stared dreamily into the treetops. "If only it were that simple. He'll give me one of his irresistible panda-bear pouty faces, and I'll be helpless. Helpless!"

Jed tried to pout.

His mom patted his face. "Not you too! How can I say no to that face? Once again . . . powerless against the wiles of the men in my life." But the surrender in her eyes disappeared, replaced with determined eyebrows and a raised finger. "That's why I'm going to drive away as quickly as I can."

She spun on her glossy red high heels and hopped in the car.

"This is reckless abandonment!" Jed called.

Her window rolled down an inch. "Oh, stop being pouty.

You'll do great. Remember SPLAGHETTI, and I'll see you at home." Her fingers poked out from the open crack and fluttered good-bye as her tires kicked up rocks and pine needles. When the dust around him settled, he was alone. Left in some deserted location with nothing. Again.

"SPLAGHETTI," he mumbled to himself. It seemed like their answer for everything. According to Mom and Dad, SPLAGHETTI was the only survival tool one ever needed: Self-reliance. Perspicacity. Lemons. Artistry. Gregariousness. Heroism. Empathy. Tenacity. Tuxedos. Insanity. He didn't even know what *perspicacity* meant and seriously doubted that lemons or tuxedos would solve his present predicament.

Or *any* predicament.

For *anyone*.

Ever.

He wiped at the lipstick on his forehead. Waxy red streaked over the back of his hand. Dad *never* missed a chance to snarf down the middle of a birthday cake. That much Jed could be sure of. And he wasn't about to let him get away with that sort of blatant thievery.

So, with fresh-baked lemon cake in peril, Jed did what any SPLAGHETTI survivalist would do: he started with self-reliance.

Even if that meant setting a forest fire.

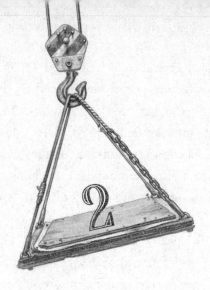

Eleven hours and forty-two minutes later, Jed was standing at his front door.

The knob turned almost as soon as he knocked. "I *told* you!" his father bellowed behind the closed door. "Less than twelve hours! I was right. Wasn't I right? Go on, tell me I was right!"

"Barely," Mom replied.

"A deal's a deal!" Dad said, the door still closed. "You owe me a thirty-minute foot rub and one of those grilled tomato paninis! You know the one—fresh Gouda and basil, yes?"

Mom sighed. "I know the one . . ."

This wasn't the first time they'd placed bets on him: how fast he could climb a sequoia, how close he could swim by the alligators, that sort of thing.

Dad always believed in Jed more than anyone.

And Dad usually won.

The door finally opened. Dad knelt and stretched his arms wide. "Well done, my boy!"

Jed grinned and hugged his dad. Even when he was on his knees, his father's head came nearly to Jed's.

"So?" Dad lifted his eyebrows in a *Tell me the details* way.

"I set a tree on fire."

Dad clapped his hands once. "You didn't!"

"Traded the orange soda mom left me to a hiker for the matches."

"And then?"

"Once the smoke was high enough, the park ranger showed, and I hitched a ride, then hid in the closet of an RV. I hitchhiked from Rock Springs to Boulder, then found that bicycle in a Dumpster."

Dad peeked over Jed's shoulder at a pink bicycle with sparkling tassels on the handlebars.

"Once I fixed the chain, it worked just fine."

Dad nodded. "Stylish."

"Totally. Especially after I popped off the training wheels."

"Dinner's ready!" Mom called from the kitchen. "Caramelized duck."

The smell of honey-crusted duck warmed Jed's nose.

"And cake, too?" he asked.

"Not until midnight. You're still eleven for two and a half hours. Cake at midnight. Presents in the morning. You know the drill."

Eleven somehow seemed so much smaller than twelve—as if midnight would come and he'd somehow feel grown-up.

"Lemon, right?" he asked.

Mom winked. "Of course, dear."

Everything about his last night as an eleven-year-old was rich and bright. Like a page from a magazine: colorful food, openmouthed smiles, and late-night crustless slices of cake.

Late-night turned into later-night.

They ate cake on his parents' bed, telling ghost stories and not caring about getting crumbs on the comforter. It was happiness that made the thought of going to bed seem heart-breaking.

But when later-night and even-later-night were behind them, Jed shuffled to his room and fell asleep to the sounds of his parents washing dishes together . . . splashing each other . . . hushing each other with "Be quiet! You'll wake him!"

Jed's perfect world swirled into perfect dreams.

Those had been some of the best hours of his life.

3

Jed awoke to a silent house.

Excitement buzzed in the air as he opened his bedroom door. It wasn't unusual for Dad to hide behind the sofa, ready to jump up and shout, "Happy birthday!"

Jed tiptoed into the living room and peeked behind the sofa.

No parents.

He crept into the kitchen.

No parents.

He looked in his father's study, the hall closet, the bathrooms, the attic, even under the dining room table.

Not even *one* parent.

He checked their bedroom. Crumbs still speckled the comforter from last night.

Is this another test?

Jed clenched his jaw.

Birthdays are off-limits!

No chores, no homework, and no life-skills tests. It had *always* been that way. He searched every room of the house. When he came to the last unopened door—the hall closet—he bit his lip and flung it open.

Empty.

Hope leaked from his heart like air from an underdone sponge cake.

As he slumped against the wall, the doorbell rang.

Jed scrambled to his feet and yanked open the door. A UPS delivery man in tan shorts two sizes too small stood on the porch.

"Well, hi there," he said, handing Jed a box. Beads of sweat dripped from his face into his mustache. "Hot day, ain't it?" He wiped an open palm across his forehead. With the same hand, he pulled a signature tablet from his front shirt pocket.

"Yeah," Jed said.

"Sign right there." The man squashed a finger against the display, leaving a dot of sweat on the screen.

Jed scrawled his name.

"You look happy," the man said.

"It's my birthday."

"Well, happy birthday!"

Jed returned the tablet and took the package. "Thanks." He shut the door and sat in the entryway. His fingers clawed through layers of packing tape until he managed to pry open the lid.

Heart thumping, he reached inside and pulled out a navy dress trimmed in yellow lace. A gift, but not for him. The box slid from Jed's fingers and hit the floor. He wanted to open the front door and throw the dress on the lawn. He glared at the scattered scraps of tape around his knees.

A sting of worry made his throat feel dry. He called his neighbor to ask if he knew anything.

No answer.

He checked across the street, but no one had seen either Mr. *or* Mrs. Jenkins.

"They'll be here," he heard himself whisper. "Just make some lunch for everyone, and by the time you're done, they'll be home."

He stood and walked to the kitchen.

Lemon-braised halibut, lemon-ricotta fritters, and lemon souf-flé. Mom's favorite meal. She'll love it.

He could imagine Dad's voice, *Smells outstanding, son! Doesn't that smell outstanding, Mary?*

Mom would smile. *Outstanding.*

Soon the tang of citrus diffused through the kitchen in a soothing cloud, blending with the smells of sizzling butter and bubbling sauce.

He set the table and filled tall glasses with tart lemonade.

And then he waited.

And waited.

Jed waited until the air no longer smelled of citrus and oven heat and instead smelled of cold fish and abandonment. He poked his halibut with a fork. He slid the lemon wedge back and forth over the fish. When Jed's legs were too stiff to stay in the wooden chair, he paced the house once more.

Scenes flickered through his mind. His parents were special government agents on a secret mission to save the world. No . . . they were evil scientists, and this was some twisted experiment where they tested his reactions and filmed the whole thing. Kidnapped by the mob. Chasing a mugger through the city. Alien abduction. Maybe they had never existed at all and had been completely imaginary all this time.

Or maybe—

Jed's heart froze. It felt cold. Tangibly, physically cold.

Maybe, all this time, they'd *actually* been trying to get rid of him. Life-skills tests? What sort of eleven-year-old needed to know how to cross high-rise construction scaffolding? Or scale mountains? Or hide from panthers? Or escape quicksand?

Before he could stop himself, the words sprang from his mouth. "They were trying to get rid of me." The cold spread through his chest. Through his arms. To his fingers. "They just wanted me gone. And I kept coming back. So they left."

Fantasies of spies, mobsters, and aliens were replaced with luggage, a taxi ride to the airport, and clinked champagne flutes as a child-free couple flew away forever.

Luggage . . .

They'd need luggage!

On any trip whatsoever, they always took the same

matching suitcases. Brown, brass-cornered boxes that looked a hundred years old.

He flung open their closet doors, and there, next to the family in-case-of-emergency trunk, were two empty spaces where matching luggage had once been.

Gone.

Jed's stomach churned with loneliness, rejection, and hunger. He kicked the in-case-of-emergency trunk, then shuffled to the kitchen and stared at the plates of fish. The empty chairs. The vase of yellow orchids. The—

His gaze paused on the vase—and on the iron key propped against it. The key was as long as a spoon and thick as his finger. Nicks and dents covered the simple, two-pronged device. He picked it up and glanced back toward the bedroom he'd just left. They'd probably waited all day for him to find it. He turned it over in his hand, and warmth rushed back through his heart.

Jed ran back to the in-case-of-emergency trunk. In his twelve years he'd never seen his parents open it. When he'd asked what was inside, Dad had said, *Everything you need in case of an emergency, of course! Why else would I write it there on the top?*

The trunk was caked with dust. Jed held his breath and slid the key into place.

It fit perfectly.

He turned it and felt a satisfying click. The lid squeaked open. Inside, Jed found a folded yellow note and a copper wristwatch.

Our Dearest Jed,

If you're reading this letter, your father and I are in the junkyard. We have likely been kidnapped, imprisoned, or killed.

If this happens, we've made arrangements for you to stay with your grandfather. You left the junkyard as a baby. It was too dangerous to return until we could make sure you were prepared.

Since you are probably not equipped to survive the junkyard, it is imperative that you never tell anyone your last name, that you push every red button you find, and that you keep this key in your shoe at all times.

In this chest is a watch. Put it on and never take it off. Ever. Not when you sleep, not when you bathe. This is our greatest gift to you. I'm sure you have many questions. Grandpa Jenkins will answer them.

Our home has a tunnel to the junkyard through the back of the dishwasher. Use the key to open it. Captain Holiday will meet you at the exit, at twelve noon the day after you read this note, and escort you to Grandpa's steamboat. Take the black emergency pack from our closet. Inside is everything you will need.

Good luck, Son. We love you.
Mom and Dad

A photograph was taped to the paper. A man with a big nose and white mustache.

My grandfather.

The image had lost most of its detail and was small enough to fit in a wallet, but the man sparked a memory in Jed's mind—his *only* memory of his grandfather. A brittle voice. Wrinkled hands buckling blue car-seat straps around Jed. And then Jed was flying.

If this was a test, it wasn't like any before. Words played in his mind: *kidnapped, imprisoned, killed.*

No. They can't be in trouble. It doesn't make sense. They don't get in trouble. They can handle anything—any test.

The wristwatch had four hands too many, and none moved. He rapped it against the trunk as if to jostle the battery. Two black hands pointed to two fifteen. Two copper hands pointed to an *e* and a VII. Two silver hands pointed to symbols Jed didn't recognize.

Why are they doing this?

There was nothing wrong with solving an obscure puzzle, outrunning a tornado, or swimming across a lake of poisonous leeches on an ordinary day, but Jed couldn't remember a birthday when they hadn't been rock climbing in the Himalayas, sailing in the South Pacific, or hang gliding down the Grand Canyon.

We're supposed to be together on birthdays.

He wiped the top of the chest. A layer of dust puffed into the air. Jed had helped set the table the night before, and the key hadn't been there.

A tunnel through the dishwasher? What did that mean? It was crazy. He yanked the key free. *It's ridiculous*, he thought, marching to the kitchen.

He opened the dishwasher, but a cookie sheet blocked his view. He pulled out both racks and piled the dishes in the sink. When he looked inside again, there it was: a keyhole. The words echoed in his mind: *kidnapped . . . imprisoned . . . killed.*

He tapped the key against his chin, then crawled inside the dishwasher and slid the key into the hole. As it turned, he heard a click. The back of the dishwasher swung open.

A tunnel descended into darkness.

Jed backed away from the tunnel. His face was numb and his hands were slick with sweat. No matter how long he stared into the blackness, it didn't get any less black.

He returned to the closet. The emergency bag was a hiking pack stuffed so full the seams were nearly splitting at the zipper.

Why would his parents possibly think he'd need such a pack, when they thought dental floss and a bag of apples were enough to cross the Sumatran freshwater swamps?

He tugged at the zipper. Water bottles and batteries poured out and across the floor. He searched the pack, and found only one other thing: a can opener in a side pocket.

Jed shut his eyes. Fatigue ached behind his lids. None of

this made sense. Bottles and batteries? Tunnels inside dish-washers? It was like a blurry dream. The sort of dream where wallpaper turned into nests of spiders, or the sky swirled like a kaleidoscope.

Sleep.

I just need to sleep. . . .

Things would make more sense in the morning. When he wasn't exhausted.

Wouldn't they?

. . .

In the morning, Jed sat at the kitchen table and stared into the dishwasher once again. The words from the letter played in his mind: *kidnapped, imprisoned,* and *killed.* This darkness wasn't like the tight caves, cold mines, or thick forests he had been in before—it was something else.

He grabbed a flashlight from the utility closet and waited by the dishwasher. The letter said twelve noon, but how long was the tunnel? At ten o'clock, he couldn't wait any longer. Jed put the picture of his grandfather into his pocket, then shoved the pack into the tight space. Holding the flashlight with his teeth, he knelt and began to crawl.

His knee bumped the dishwasher, and something dropped from the counter onto the floor.

A lemon.

Bright and happy. Like his mother's smile. She would pick lemons fresh from their tree, then scratch the rind and breathe

the scent. Jed picked up the lemon and brought it to his nose.

"Just be okay ... please?"

He tucked the fruit into his pocket and continued to crawl.

Inside, the tunnel widened until he was able to stand. He slung the pack around his shoulders. The iron key, tucked into his shoe, pressed uncomfortably against the side of his foot.

No dripping water broke the silence. No scampering mice. No distant creaking. There was only the sound of his footfalls echoing against the walls.

He walked for what felt like an hour when, finally, a pinprick of light glowed in the distance. Jed clicked off the flashlight and slowed. His breath felt tight. The closer he got, the more light illuminated the tunnel.

Sunlight.

He reached the end of the tunnel, but a fat tan barrel blocked his exit. A label on the side read:

MANUFACTURER AFFIRMS THAT THIS WATER HEATER
COMPLIES WITH ASHRAE/IES 90.9221

A water heater.

He pressed against it, but it didn't budge. A wedge of space underneath looked wide enough to crawl through. He shoved the emergency pack through the gap, then wormed his way past the heater into a tight pocket of space, surrounded by clutter: an old mattress to his left, a bookshelf to his right, and a broken ladder ahead.

Sunlight trickled into the narrow space. A warm breeze

drifted over him. The clutter formed a vertical tunnel ending in a circle of blue sky. He gripped the broken ladder with one hand and the pack with the other. Step by step he pulled himself upward.

Soap dispensers, garden tools, telephones, and bowling pins wrapped him in a narrow tube of junk. Jed expected smells of garbage, but this stuff wasn't exactly trash. True, most items were dented, cracked, or completely broken. But some were brand-new. A white sneaker poked out from the heap. Its toe was stuffed with a cardboard insert. It hadn't yet been laced, and it had that leathery, plasticky new-shoe smell.

When the ladder ended, Jed stepped on a plastic bin and grabbed a curtain rod above his head. He wedged his right foot between a tire and a cinder block, then pushed up. As he did, the emergency pack snagged on a broken fish tank.

Ripping sounds cut through the air.

His breath caught, and he froze.

"Steady . . ." he said to the pack. "Don't you tear open on me."

He wiggled the pack back and forth until it pulled free.

"Good job, pack. We've got to stick together, you and me. I need you."

As Jed stepped on the arm of a recliner, the junk around him creaked and moaned. A grandfather clock shifted and fell into a coatrack. The coatrack crashed into a table. The table slipped onto a chair.

It's collapsing.

He scrambled faster. Junk rattled and fell. Something cracked, and the tunnel shook. Faster and faster he climbed, dodging pool balls and shards of glass that cascaded down the tunnel, until he breached the surface—just as the junk crushed in on itself, sealing the tunnel.

Jed stood atop a mountain made entirely from junk. Hundreds of miles of junk covered every inch of the world, as far as he could see.

In front of him, the junk sloped downward to a cliff edge.

Behind him, the junk piled so high into the clouds that Jed couldn't see its peak. The mountain spread endlessly to the left and just as far to the right.

Sunlight reflecting off hunks of metal made the world sparkle. A chill trickled through him. For the first time in a long time, Jed was scared. His feet wobbled on the unsteady surface. Afraid to take a single step, he leaped over a desk, landed on the soft arm of a crooked couch, and slumped into a cushion.

Before his breathing had time to steady, the grinding rattle of an overworked engine roared to life behind him.

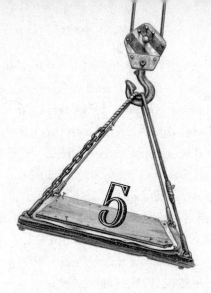

A flying tugboat born of junk drifted closer. Its hull was a patchwork of copper and galvanized steel; sunlight glinted off the polished sheets with a blinding glare. Rubber tires cinched the boat's belly like a belt. Rusty handrails rimmed the deck, and iron grates acted as windows. A plump smokestack, poking up from the top deck, coughed swollen puffs of gray soot.

Three propellers—each like a fifty-foot machete—spun in a ghostly blur at the stern. The engine churned and clanked and rattled and whined.

The ship slowed until it was nearly on top of Jed.

A door opened from the main bridge, and a man in a

rust-colored trench coat stepped from the cabin. Angry slashes crisscrossed the coat's thick leather. The man clomped across the deck, scanning the junk. His heavy coat rocked back and forth as his boots thudded against the deck with purpose. Then he turned, and his eyes locked onto Jed's.

The man's face had more scars than his coat. Some were thin and white, others rough and bumpy, like frayed bits of twine. One scar, as thick as a braid of rope, snarled from above his left ear to below the right side of his jaw.

He moved toward the railing, eyes still on Jed.

"'Hoy there, boy!" he called. "Shout us your name and metal."

"My what?" Jed asked.

"Name and metal. And be quick about it."

"My metal? I don't know what that means."

"Your fleet, boy! Are you dumb? What fleet metal do you hail under?"

"I don't have a fleet. I don't know where I am. I was told to meet Captain Holiday at noon." He looked at the wristwatch, even though its hands still weren't moving. "Is this the right time?"

"I'm Captain Murdock Bog," said the man. "We're filling in for Captain Holiday at the moment—seeing as he's dead."

Another crew member marched next to the captain. He wore a fitted white shirt with sleeves that reached his fingertips. The shirt's buttons and cuff links were a dull silver. He stood stiff and tall and moved like a toy soldier. His face was smooth and pale, ghostly and emotionless, with eyes the color of concrete.

The captain continued. "Kizer here says we're to pick up a short, scrawny boy carrying a backpack. I don't see any back-pack. But you *are* short and scrawny—"

"I do have a backpack!" Jed reached down and lifted the pack. The rip in the pack's belly opened another inch, and a water bottle slipped out.

"What do you have there?" the man asked as Jed picked up the bottle.

"Just water bottles and batteries."

The two men shared a glance.

"Where does a boy like you find a pack full of water and batteries, huh? You steal it from some tinker?"

"I didn't steal anything!"

"Riiiight . . ." Captain Bog muttered. The scars on his face tightened.

"My parents left it for me."

"Sure they did. So where are they? Your parents."

"They're missing."

"And they just 'left you' that pack right before they up and went 'missing'?"

Captain Bog leaned over the ship's railing and stared at him the way Jed's mother would when she knew he was lying. "If you keep spitting out lies, I'll turn right around and leave you where you stand."

"I'm not lying!"

"Did you steal the pack or not?"

"He looks like a thief," Kizer said.

Heat rushed to Jed's cheeks. "I'm not a thief!"

Captain Bog nodded. "Skinny boy like that . . . probably a stowaway. I'd bet a sack of batteries he filched trades from a tinker and jumped ship. Got himself stranded."

Kizer nodded back. "Why else would he be sitting out by the fringe with nothing but batteries and water?"

Jed's skin boiled. Sure, he was a lot of unrespectable things. Reckless? Yup. Impulsive? Definitely. But a thief and a liar? The hot anger prickled his throat. "Either you're here to pick me up or you're not," he said. "But I'm not going to stand around while some guy whose face looks like the bottom of a shoe calls me a thief and a liar!"

Kizer's jaw slackened. His gaze jerked toward the captain.

Captain Bog studied Jed. "The bottom of a shoe?" he said, scratching a thick scar on his chin.

Probably not the best choice of words. This wasn't exactly the sort of place where he could hitch a ride home from a park ranger.

Before Jed could recover with an apology, Captain Bog spoke. "That's maybe the funniest thing I've heard in a week."

Jed waited for him to smile.

But he didn't smile.

And he didn't glare.

In fact, he didn't show *any* expression at all. No red-cheeked insecurity. No playful grin. No *I'm going to grind your skinny body to bits* scowl.

After an uncomfortable silence, the captain turned to Kizer. "Wasn't that funny, Ki?"

"Eh," Kizer mumbled.

"Oh, lighten up, Ki. It was funny." His face was still emotionless as a block of wood. He pointed to his cheek. "You can't get much uglier than the bottom of a shoe, can you?" He rested his elbows on the railing. "You're a funny kid. Now stop lazing about and climb aboard."

He waved his arm, and someone tossed a coiled rope ladder over the edge. It unrolled and snapped into place near Jed.

"Oh," Captain Bog added, "and if you ever say something like that again, I'll strap you to the propellers and run the ship full throttle. Got it?"

Jed touched the rope in front of him. This Murdock Bog had said that Captain Holiday was dead.

What if I'm not supposed to get on this ship?

"Are you coming or not?" Captain Bog called. "Makes no difference to me, so decide. And be quick about it."

The ladder swayed back and forth. He glanced back, searching for the collapsed hole from where he'd crawled.

"So be it," the captain said. "Sprocket, take us about."

"Aye, Cap'n," a woman called from the deck. Her voice was sharp and high and sarcastic all at once.

The engine groaned, and the scent of burning oil filled the air. The hull creaked and began to turn, pulling the rope ladder along with it.

"Wait!" Jed shouted.

Captain Bog shook his head. "I've got a rendezvous to

make, and a dig site to reach. I'm not in a waiting mood. You want on? Get on."

Jed waited for the ship to pause so he could do just that, but it didn't.

"All ahead full!" Captain Bog shouted.

"All ahead full!" Sprocket repeated.

"No!" Jed snatched up the backpack and leaped from the couch. He swiped for the ladder, but his fingers only knocked it away. "Stop!"

He leaped and reached again, but the ladder was even farther away. Jed bounded forward, barely watching the junk underfoot as he barreled toward the ship—toward the sharp cliff edge in front of him.

Jed swung the pack's strap onto one shoulder and bolted. His feet battled with spongy pillows, wobbly dresser drawers, and a pile of scattered golf clubs. He swiped the air again, but the ladder was too high.

"I can't reach it!"

"Probably because you're short and scrawny," Captain Bog called back. "I bet right now you'd rather have a face like mine and a few more inches on your legs than pretty cheeks and those twin twigs."

The ladder dangled tauntingly. The tunnel to home was gone. This was his only hope.

Jed searched the piles, then scooped up an iron. He looped the power cord around his wrist. With a burst of speed he sprang onto an upright refrigerator, then chucked the iron at the rope ladder.

The iron tumbled in the air and flew between two of the rungs. The ship jerked his body from the refrigerator, and something popped in his wrist.

He gripped the cord and flailed in the air.

"Stop!" he yelled, midswing.

A face poked over the railing. "How many times do I have to tell you? We're not going to laze around waiting for you. You want up? Start climbing."

Jed had climbed more mountains than he could name, but the slick, plastic power cord strangled his wrist, and the backpack full of water weighed him down. He flexed, but his body barely raised an inch. He tried again, but the pack was too heavy and his wrist was too weak.

Something above snapped, and his body dropped an inch. The rubber sheath around the iron's cord stretched. The sudden jerk opened the rip in the pack another few inches, and bottles tumbled to the junk below.

"I need help!" he shouted. "Please! I'm going to fall! I'll be cut to pieces!"

"Well, then I won't be the only one with a face that looks like the bottom of a shoe, now, will I?"

The cord was like a noose around his wrist. His knuckles deepened into a bloated purple. A second snap sounded, and the cord pulled another inch from the iron. The weight was too much. It was only a matter of time before the cord broke altogether.

Jed searched the junk below, but they'd flown so high that even the luckiest clump of pillows wouldn't save his life.

His arms shook.

He lifted the pack's strap to his shoulder, then reached back and yanked a flap of fabric in the tear to relieve some weight. The backpack split open. Bottles and batteries tumbled free.

Now get on that ship! he told himself.

But it was too late. The cord creaked again, and Jed knew it was about to snap. Then the ladder began to rise.

"Heave, men," Captain Bog grunted. "Heave."

Jed rose higher and higher.

"That's it, men. Let's pull him in."

A swarm of arms gripped Jed's face, legs, and shirt. They lifted him over the railing and dumped him on the deck. His face hit hard, and he rolled onto his side.

He massaged his wrist, and the color in his hand returned to normal. The deck was a metal collage of steel and copper planks all riveted together.

Kizer loomed over him, amusement tugging at his lips. "'Help, help, pull me in! I can't climb a ladder! I'm going to be cut to bits!' Can you stand up by yourself, or do you need help with that, too?"

Jed shot him a barbed look.

"All right, Kizer," Captain Bog said. "Leave the boy alone. Poor thing can't even climb a ladder."

Jed stumbled to his feet. "I can climb a stupid ladder. I climbed Mount McKinley in the middle of January."

Kizer snorted. "Is that supposed to mean something? I've never even heard of a junk hill called McKinley."

Jed straightened his shirt. "Did I say it was a junk hill? No. I said it was a mountain."

"Settle down there, little tyke," Captain Bog interjected. "No need to get worked up. I'm sure you're a world-class climber."

Jed clamped his teeth together and glared at the deck.

Kizer picked up the empty pack. "Nothing in it. Guess he's no thief after all. Only a liar."

Captain Bog stood over Jed. "Now how about telling us your name and metal."

"My name's Jed. But I don't know what you mean about metal."

"Iron, copper, or rust? It's not a tough question."

The tugboat seemed to have each of those metals. Iron grates, copper planks, and rust covering the edges of them all.

He gave the captain his best puzzled look.

"Stop acting all timid-like. We'd only throw you overboard for one metal, and we both know which one."

"But I don't—"

"Stop blubbering and just tell us. I'm giving you a one-fingered countdown before I toss you over!"

"I don't know."

Captain Bog held up a closed fist.

Kizer had iron buttons, iron cuff links, and iron boot buckles. The captain's coat looked like some mix of rust and mud. And at least half of everything else on the boat was copper. "I'm whatever metal's not going to get me thrown off!"

The captain shook his head and lifted his index finger.

"I don't know!"

"One." The captain began to lower the finger.

"Rust isn't even a metal!" Jed said.

The captain smirked, and the finger paused. "That's certainly true." But before Jed could hope he'd said something right, Captain Bog continued lowering the finger.

"Gold. I'm gold."

Jed waited. Captain Bog's finger froze—curled at its tip as if itching to drop.

"Gold," Jed repeated. "It's a metal."

Captain Bog's face broke into a genuine grin, and he barked two hearty laughs. "Gold *is* a metal! I'll give you that!" He half nodded, half shook his head. "Gold it is." He extended his hand and helped Jed to his feet. He laughed once more, but the emotion was gone. "Looks like we got ourselves a little golden boy. Eh, Ki?"

Kizer smirked.

"Come meet the helmsman, Golden Boy," the captain said. "Sprocket, this is Golden Boy, Golden Boy, this is—"

"Helms*man*?" The sharp voice cut the air like a dagger. A slender woman, arms folded across her chest, sashayed into view. Her body swished like an alley cat. Copper-rimmed goggles hung loose around her neck. She wore a black trench coat with too many copper buttons. It fit snugly over a rust-red top and black pin-striped pants. Leather straps with buckles cinched around her legs and torso, like dozens of little belts. Each housed a different weapon: pistols with intricate gear work and miniature scopes, slick knives, and canisters with fading letters spelling FLAMMABLE GAS. Two loose belts crossed over each other, slouching more on her thighs than on her waist. Bulletlike batteries lined the belts.

Captain Bog rolled his eyes. "Helms*woman*," he amended.

Sprocket nodded, then leaned against the railing. A rifle rocked in its harness on her back. It was unlike any gun Jed had ever seen: at least as tall as him—probably taller—with a double barrel made from twin copper pipes, gears and pistons in a dull copper frame, and a leather grip. Shafts and rods ran parallel to the main barrels, and levers protruded here and there.

"Sprocket's the ship's navigator, mapmaker, and strong arm," the captain explained. "Keeps watch in the stack nest." He jutted his chin toward a lookout perch bolted atop one of the steam stacks. "She and Kizer man the helm."

"I do *what*?" Sprocket asked.

"Oh, settle down. It's a phrase, okay? I've never heard anyone say *she womans the helm.* Have you?"

Sprocket shrugged. "Wouldn't hurt you to start, would it?"

The captain turned to Jed. "She's a bit frosty with strangers aboard. Can't say I blame her. Especially strangers claiming to be gold. And just so you know, she was a copper javelin. In case you get any rabble-rousing ideas."

"What's a copper javelin?" Jed asked.

Sprocket smiled. "Means I don't even need this shatterlance to be dangerous." She pulled a lever on her rifle, and it made a pneumatic hiss. "Means I could storm a dreadnought in the belly of the fog with a half-depleted shatterbox"—she tapped the hilt of one of her pistols—"that doesn't even shoot straight. Means I could—"

"Okay, I get it," Jed said. "Well, sort of. I didn't exactly understand half of what you said, but I get the point. You're tough."

Arms still folded, Sprocket stepped closer. "Where'd you say you port from?"

"Port from?" Jed asked. "I guess I'm from Denver."

"Denver?"

"Yeah."

"I've never heard of that place. And I've heard of *every* place. What township cluster?"

"It's in Colorado, if that's what you mean."

Sprocket looked to the captain. He shrugged.

"Under which sovereignty?" Sprocket asked.

"The . . . United States?"

The captain and Sprocket shared another glance.

"What metal is the United States?"

"The metal thing again? Really?"

The captain squared his gaze to Jed's. "We're not partial to strangers. So how about some answers."

"I'm trying! But I don't know what's going on. I don't even know where I am! I took a tunnel underneath this junk and ended up here. My grandfather's supposed to tell me what's going on, but that's all I know."

"A tunnel? Under the fringe?"

"I don't know what that is."

"The fringe. The border hills. The sky stacks. The yard end. Pick one."

Jed remembered the towering junk that reached into the sky near the tunnel. "The mountains?"

Captain Bog nodded. "Is Denver beyond the mountains?"

Jed's eyes lit up. "Yes! The mountains! The Rocky Mountains! Denver's in the mountains!"

It made a little sense. Not a lot. But it was something.

Silence filled the deck, leaving only the sound of chugging pistons and whirring propellers.

"Let's take a walk," the captain said, turning around. "Kizer, you're with me. Sprocket, take the helm."

Kizer grabbed Jed by the elbow and pulled him toward a square hole in the deck, where stairs led to the lower levels.

They entered a door marked CAPTAIN. Wood slats—some cherry, some walnut—paneled the walls. A pair of brown bookcases stood in the corner. Three paintings hung between them. The first piece was a moonlit forest, the next an ocean sunrise. The last was a woman in a red dress, dancing in the street under a rainstorm.

The captain pointed to a cracked leather sofa. "Sit."

He rubbed his chin and assessed Jed up and down. "Fresh set of jeans, clean face, smooth hands, out in the middle of nowhere up by the fringe. What do you think, Ki?"

"Bunch of glittertales. No ship's been past the fringe. None that I've heard of. Not one scrounger or relic stalker has even *seen* the tip of a sky stack."

"Relic stalker?" Jed asked.

"Quiet, boy," the captain said. "But still . . . if this boy knows of a tunnel . . ." He glanced at one of the bookshelves.

"You actually believe those glittertales?"

Jed squinted at the bindings of the "fantasy" books.

Black Hawk Down.

Tuesdays with Morrie.

The Diary of a Young Girl by Anne Frank.

The *Encyclopaedia Britannica.*

"What is this place?" Jed asked.

"What do you mean?" the captain asked.

"All of it. All of this junk. I've never seen anything like it. Where am I?"

"You're between fog and fringe like every other man alive! What are you playing at? Tell us where you're from!"

"From there." Jed pointed at the painting of the woman in the rain.

Kizer scoffed. "Oh, please . . . You're not from some glitter-tale sovereignty where water falls from the sky."

"You mean rain? Are you saying it doesn't rain here?"

Captain Bog looked at his bookshelf. "I've read about rain."

"He's a liar!" Kizer shouted. "It's all scrap stories! How could anyone live where water fell on top of them all the time? The town motors would be dead in a week!"

"Why would a town need motors?"

"Oh, I see . . . you must use glitter wings to make your township stay in the sky. Yes?"

"The sky? Denver's not in the sky. Why would it be?"

"Maybe so it isn't obliterated during a junkstorm? Or, wait—let me guess—Denver is so special that junk just falls from the sky all around it but never above it."

"Junk doesn't fall from the sky anywhere. Ever."

Kizer made another dismissive noise.

"If it doesn't rain here, where do you get your water?" Jed asked.

"Township pumps, where else?" Kizer said.

"Where do the pumps get it?"

"How am I supposed to know? I'm not a pump engineer. Besides, if water fell from the sky, how would your ships stay dry?"

"We don't have ships, because there's no junk."

"No *junk*?"

"Not like this, at least. Not all over the ground. Nobody uses junk. We bury it."

"Now you *do* have junk but you bury it? Your lies aren't adding up."

"Where do you get food if you don't use junk?" the captain asked. "What do you live in? Where do you find clothes?"

"We make them."

"Out of what?"

"Don't you have any trees?" Jed asked.

Kizer and the captain looked at each other with blank stares.

"We find things called trees and cut them up, then make them into other things. I guess it's kind of like the junk here, because trees are everywhere." Jed pointed to the painting of the moonlit forest. "They grow big and then we cut them apart and make things out of them."

"Grow?" Kizer's voice was dark and accusing.

"Yeah, they're alive." Kizer's eyes narrowed. The look made Jed's skin itch. "They're made out of wood and grow and make things like food. And when they get big enough, we cut them apart and make houses."

"Living junk. That you chop up and make into . . . *things*."

"I—I guess?" Jed said.

Kizer turned to the captain. "Sound familiar?"

The captain rolled his eyes. "That's ridiculous, Ki."

"Did you hear what he just said?"

"Look at him. Scrawny thing like that? Dainty skin and pouty eyes? No."

"What are you talking about?" Jed asked.

Captain Bog held up a hand. "All right, that's enough. From both of you. Story hour's over. Either Golden Boy has answers and won't give them up, or he doesn't know. Either way, this is a waste of time."

"But Captain, he's clearly—"

"Leave it alone, Ki. That's an order." He cupped his hands to his mouth. "Sprocket! Get down here!"

Footsteps pattered above them; then Sprocket entered the cabin.

She gave an exaggerated curtsy. "You called, great and merciful captain of my life?"

"Take care of Golden Boy until we arrive."

"Me? Why me?"

"Take him to the mess and feed him a can. Or half a can. Or whatever's left in the garbage. I don't care. Just take him."

Sprocket folded her arms. "Babysitting? Really? I trained as a copper javelin. I've infiltrated iron prison camps. I could blast a falcon pilot's eyelash off his pretty little face. And you want me to spoon-feed a six-year-old?"

"Now," he said. "That's an order."

Sprocket turned to Kizer. "So it's a 'that's an order' day, is it?"

Kizer gave her a small shrug, though he didn't stop glaring at Jed.

"Oookaaay," Sprocket said. "Well, come on, then, Golden Boy."

Jed tried not to look at Kizer as he followed Sprocket out the door. The man hated him, and Jed had no idea why.

7

The mess was an open room with mismatched chairs around a chalkboard tabletop propped up by four barrels. Shelves packed with hundreds of cans lined the back wall.

A man in a shirt the color of old dishwater sat in the corner, spooning diced pineapple into his mouth. The shirt was three sizes too small, and the man was ten sizes too big. As Sprocket entered, he scrambled upright.

His enormous belly didn't slouch over his belt. Instead he looked like a stiff beach ball, his arms perpetually lifted from his torso. A sparse patch of hair sprouted from his head like the stem of a carrot.

"This is Pobble, the ship's bard," Sprocket said. "He eats and plays fiddle."

"Nah . . ." Pobble said, his head drooping and chin smooshing into his neck. "A knob broke on my fiddle. But Riggs is going to fix it up."

"This is Pobble," Sprocket said again. "He eats."

"I'm Jed."

Pobble's face brightened. "Nice to meet you!"

Pobble grabbed Jed's hand and shook. His palm swallowed Jed's.

"Where do you port from?" Pobble asked.

"I—"

Sprocket held up her hand. "Nope. Don't even get started on that. Let's agree he's from far away. Far, far away."

"Wow . . ." Pobble's eyes glistened like wet Ping-Pong balls. "Sounds exotic. Bet there's neat junk out far, far away."

"Are those all cans of food?" Jed asked, pointing to the shelves.

"Yup." Pobble puffed out his chest with pride. "For the most part. Can't say I consider spinach actual food. You hungry?"

"Do you eat everything from cans?"

Pobble squeaked. "Course we don't! Bowls and plates are over there." He pointed to a china cabinet stocked with dishes and silverware just as mismatched as the chairs.

"No, I mean does all your food come from cans?"

"Where else would it come from?"

Jed eyed the cans. "But how do you find so many in all that junk?"

Pobble assumed his pride pose again. "We're the best scroungers in the yard."

"It's not that hard," Sprocket said. "Look! A can on the ground!" She pretended to see a can at her feet. "I think I'm going to pick it up! Yup. Real tough."

Pobble frowned. But then he smiled at Jed. "How about some chili?"

Jed smiled back. "Sure."

Pobble selected two cans. He pulled a screwdriver from his pocket and began stabbing the can around the rim.

"What are you doing?"

He looked up. "We have to open it. The chili's inside."

"I know how canned food works," Jed said. "Why don't you use this?" He dropped the emergency pack and unzipped the pocket with the can opener.

"What's that?" Pobble asked.

"You've never seen a can opener? How is that possible? You said everything you eat comes from cans!" Jed took the can and wedged the can opener around its rim. As he twisted the handle, Pobble's Ping-Pong ball eyes returned in full force.

Jed popped off the lid and handed the can back to Pobble.

"Can I try?" Pobble asked.

Jed showed him how to fit it on the second can. Pobble twisted until the lid popped free, then handed the chili to Jed.

"Thanks," Jed said.

Pobble spooned a bite into his mouth.

"Do you have a microwave or stove or something?" Jed asked.

"A what?" Bits of chili garbled Pobble's words.

"To heat it up. You don't heat it up?"

"Heat *what* up?"

"The food."

Pobble and Sprocket both looked at the chili.

"Why would I heat up food?" Pobble asked.

"So it's warm," Jed said.

Pobble studied the can.

"Never mind," Jed said. He found a spoon and took a bite of his cold chili.

"So what metal are you?" Pobble asked.

Sprocket snickered. "He says he's gold."

"Ha!" Pobble bellowed. "Good one. Good one. Yeah, me too! I'm gold too!"

"Why does everyone keep asking me what metal I am?" Jed asked. "I don't know what that means."

Pobble stopped laughing. "Really? How far away are you from?"

"Pretty far, I guess," Jed said.

"Come on over here. I'll show you."

Jed tailed Pobble to the left side of the room, where a floor-to-ceiling map covered the wall. In truth, it looked more like a treasure map than a *map* map. At the right edge, there was a solid black vertical strip. At the left edge, there was a solid brown vertical strip. And in the middle, there were large sections shaded in silver, orange, and red.

"Iron, copper, and rust," Pobble said pointing to the splotches of color.

"What metal are you all?"

"Rust!" Pobble said excitedly.

"But rust isn't really a metal, is it?"

"That's the point," Sprocket said. "We don't *belong* to anyone."

"So there's no gold?" Jed asked.

"Not anymore, at least. Have you never heard the story of gold?"

Jed shook his head.

"Well, pull up a seat!"

Pobble pulled out chairs, and they sat around the table.

Sprocket took out her shatterlance and an oily rag. "Might as well do something useful. Our bard has a habit of droning on. And on. And—"

"Once upon a storm . . ." Pobble said, his arms wide and his eyes filled with excitement, "there was a man more golden than the sun. He lived hundreds of years ago—maybe even thousands. Nobody knows for sure."

Sprocket smirked. "That's sort of a big difference, don't you think?"

"How about you let *me* tell the story," Pobble said. He began again. "*Thousands* of years ago, before the yard had junk, before towns flew in the sky, before—"

"Are we almost at the end?" Sprocket asked.

"Don't listen to her," Pobble said to Jed. "She has the attention of a deck slug . . . one without very good attention.

"Thousands of years ago, all the towns were built right on the ground. Golden cities. With cans of food bigger than this tug. And batteries, too. More batteries than a whole town of men could carry."

Sprocket blew on her shatterlance's barrel. "What about a town of women?"

Pobble rolled his eyes. "Still too many."

"What were they using to carry the batteries?" Sprocket asked. "Did everyone have bags? Or did they just use their hands?"

"There were just lots of batteries, okay?" Pobble said. Sprocket winked at Pobble. "The people who lived there were as gold as the town itself."

"So where'd they get all those batteries?" Sprocket asked.

"They probably had giant junk makers or something. I don't know."

Sprocket nodded. "Oh! That makes perfect sense. Sorry for interrupting."

Pobble ignored her. "One day, a disease spread through the town. *The blotch*. Everyone started getting sick . . . coughing and stumbling. Doctors tried patches and medicine, but nothing worked. It was as if the gold itself was diseased. Folk got sicker, until they were so sick, their bodies stopped working right. Arms . . . legs . . . fingers . . . toes . . . all just wilted and died. Like they were dead stumps clinging to nearly dead townsfolk. The dead limbs rotted so badly, they started falling right off. Flopped straight to the ground. Deader than a slug stuck to the bottom of a boot. Townsfolk limped around the streets—some with barely half an arm to drag their own body along. They grew so desperate, they pulled apart machines and sewed scrap parts right to their elbows and knees. But the disease didn't stop. It rotted away gold until there wasn't gold left to rot. The townsfolk replaced so many parts, they became empty. No souls. Just . . . empty inside. And they still crawl the yard today. Flying about in broken ships, making everyone who sees them feel as empty as them, sounding more like clanking metal than people, looking so awful that folk now just call them . . . *dread*."

Jed waited for Pobble to continue, but he didn't. He sat back and released a deep, story-conclusion-style sigh.

"Then what happened?" Jed asked.

"Happened with what?"

"The dread. What's the end of the story?"

Pobble looked from Jed to Sprocket. "That *was* the end. That's the story of where the dread came from."

"You're saying they're real?" Jed asked with a *yeah, right, there's no way I'm believing that* tone.

Pobble laughed once. "Of course they're real! What else do you think lives in the fog?" He pointed a stubby finger at the wall map. Jed eyed the map's wide black edge.

"That story *can't* be true. Those things can't actually exist."

"The dread," Pobble repeated. "You know . . . the *dread*." He hooked his arms together and twisted his expression to look like scrambled eggs.

"The *dread*," Sprocket echoed, as if Jed simply couldn't understand Pobble's accent.

"Yeah, no, I heard that part."

Sprocket interjected, "Denver?"

"Denver."

She stood and motioned for Jed to join her at the map.

She pointed to the far left near the orange border. It read THE FRINGE.

"We picked you up here," she said. "Show me where Denver is."

"I'm from somewhere else. Somewhere not on here."

"Here?" Sprocket walked to the other side and touched the black edge of the map.

Jed shook his head. "Not there, either. I don't think so, at least."

Brown letters inside the black edge read THE FOG.

"I'm from somewhere other than the fringe and the fog. I've never been anywhere on this map. And I've never heard of the dread!"

"You're serious," Sprocket said. "Completely serious?"

"Completely," Jed said. "Do those things—the dread—exist?"

"Let me show you something," Sprocket said, waving Jed to follow. "And you can tell *me* if they exist."

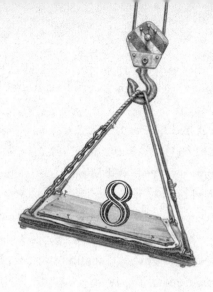

Jed, Sprocket, and Pobble walked to the main deck, near the largest mast. Pobble took a can of diced tomatoes with him and ate as they walked.

"There," Sprocket said.

Halfway up the smokestack, a head sat mounted to a metal plate. The face was a patchwork of bolts and springs. Gears littered the inside of its skull and left cheek. Frayed cables and wires fused patches of leathery skin with scraps of rusted metal.

Where its left eye should have been, there was only a dark hole, its edges withered and wrinkled. In place of its right eye sat a brass spyglass with a cracked lens.

"That thing was a dread?" Jed asked.

Before Sprocket could answer, the gears inside the shriveled head ground to life. Sparks dribbled from the frayed wires, and the face tilted.

Though it had no eyes, Jed knew it was looking straight at him. He could feel it. As if the empty hole wasn't empty at all.

Then it spoke. "Well, well. What have we here . . . ?"

Jed lurched backward.

The gears spun faster, and its ashy lips curled into a grin.

"Here we have Captain Spyglass," Sprocket said as if she were a museum tour guide. "Captain of the smokestack!"

Pobble chuckled.

"It's alive?" Jed said.

"I wouldn't say what that thing is counts as *alive*, exactly," Sprocket said. "It wriggles around and speaks, if that's what you mean."

"Of course I'm alive, little boy. Alive but alone. All alone. I do wish I had a friend. Someone to talk to . . . someone who would hold me . . . someone I could pull apart into little pieces and slurp up for breakfast. Will you be my friend?"

Jed took another step back.

"Charming, isn't he?" Sprocket said.

"Come up here and give me a hug, little boy. You can stand on the fat one there. Jump on him like a trampoline."

Pobble's lower lip scrunched in embarrassed anger.

"Oh, don't look so pouty," the dread said to Pobble. "It makes you look *fat*. Then again, being fat also makes you look fat, I suppose."

"Hey, shut your ugly mouth," Sprocket said. She took Pobble's can of tomatoes and chucked it at the dread. The can smacked it square in the face, but the thing didn't even flinch.

"One of these nights," it said to Sprocket, "when you're sleeping safe and sound, I'm going to find you, and then I'm going to slurp up every last bit of soup you keep inside that soft, pink bag you call skin."

"Sure you will," Sprocket said. "Only one problem: you're a bit short on legs. And arms. And your face is nailed to a smokestack. Oh, and we killed all your buddies. So good luck with that."

The dread dragged its tongue around the rim of its lips. "You'll be the first to go. I won't roast you or boil you like I'll do with the rest of this crew. You, I'll have raw. And next I'll eat *you*," it said, tilting its head toward Pobble. "Though . . . that might take a while."

"Remember the whole 'no legs' thing?" Sprocket said.

"Don't worry about me, dear. I'm patient. So when I *do* get my legs back—because eventually I will—know that I'm coming for you."

"C'mon," Pobble said, "let's go." He and Sprocket turned and began walking away.

But before Jed could follow, the head looked at him again, its empty black socket boring into him as if the cavity itself was staring at him.

It spoke in a voice that was barely a whisper. "Happy birthday."

Cold shuddered through Jed's arms. "What?" he whispered in return.

The spyglass protruded another inch, focusing on Jed's eyes. "Welcome back."

They stared at each other in silence for another moment.

"You okay?" Pobble's voice said right behind him.

Jed recoiled.

"Whoa, there. It's just me. You okay?"

"Huh? Oh, I'm fine. Sorry, you just startled me."

Pobble slapped Jed on the back. "I know what you mean. That creeper makes my stomach feel like leftover green beans."

"Yeah," Jed said, staring back at the dread's now-expressionless face.

Pobble grinned. "You know what always makes that feeling go away?"

"What?"

"Strawberries. I have a secret stash of fruit cans in the mess. How 'bout we share a can later?"

"Save me some peaches and it'll stay a secret stash," Sprocket said.

Pobble smirked. "Yeah, okay."

"Also, would you watch Golden Boy while I check on the nest?"

"How about it, Jed?" Pobble asked. "Want to take a tour?"

Jed nodded. For the first time since he'd been on board, someone had used his actual name. "I'd love to."

"Precious," Sprocket said. "You two go play." She turned to walk away, but paused and added over her shoulder, "Don't touch anything."

Pobble tugged Jed toward a cabin at the front of the ship. "To the helm." He led the way up a back staircase to the bridge. The small cabin door barely fit Pobble's bulk. The room was open, empty, and well lit by huge windows on each wall, which gave a full view of the junkyard.

"This is the helm," Pobble said. "Controls are a bit different, since *Bessie* was a dread tug before we stole her. Snatched her right out of a dread shipyard from under their dread noses!"

Thick bolts anchored a throne in the center of the room. Levers—each at least the height of Jed's waist—shot up from slots in the floor. Some were forward, some back, but each joined to a base. Five pedals, made of pie tins, sat in a half circle around the huge chair. Hoses and pipes snaked from the pedals, through the levers and gears and around the back.

Jed's eyes lingered on the pie tins. Every Saturday Mom made something lemon for dessert: lemon meringue pie, lemon bars, lemon-ginger cheesecake, lemon-coconut cupcakes, lemon pound cake . . . They'd sit together and thumb through their Lemon Anthology—a collection created over the years of the finest lemon desserts.

"Which one for today?" She always let Jed pick. As a result, they'd had lemon poppy-seed doughnuts every Saturday for two months. Lemon poppy-seed doughnuts were *exactly* what he wanted. Right then. Hot icing soaked to the doughnut's core. So soft it would melt between his teeth.

"It's Saturday," he whispered to himself, his tongue tingling.

"It's what?" Pobble asked.

Jed snapped back to the present. "Oh, nothing." His fingers were in his pocket—wrapped around the lemon he'd brought.

"Pretty neat, huh?" Pobble rested his fists on his hips and surveyed the room.

"I've never seen anything like it. But where's the wheel?"

"Wheel?" Pobble looked around.

Jed shook his head. "Never mind."

It was then that he noticed a red button atop one of the levers. His heart jumped. *It is imperative that you push every red button you find.*

Pobble turned to the side and looked out over the junkyard. *He's not looking. Do it. Now.*

Jed reached for the lever. But before his fingers could touch the button, it turned green.

He froze, arm still outstretched.

"Get away from the controls!" a voice shouted. Kizer stood in the doorway, hands clenching the door's frame so tightly, his arms shook.

"Oh—I—uh . . ."

"You were what?" Kizer released the frame and stepped into the room. "I saw you reach for the altitude stick. What were you going to do?"

"I don't know—I—"

Kizer turned to Pobble. "Why did you let that *thing* in here?"

"Just giving a tour of the—"

"Out." He jabbed a finger at the open door.

Pobble waddled away. Jed tried to follow, but Kizer grabbed his shoulder. "Not *you*."

Kizer bent closer until his breath tickled Jed's cheeks. "I know what you are." His words were slow and doused in venom.

"What I *am*?" Jed stepped back, but Kizer closed the gap.

"Let's chat about what you said earlier in the captain's quarters about living junk. You seem to know an awful lot about it."

"I was just trying to explain—"

Kizer grabbed a wad of skin on Jed's arm. "This doesn't fool me."

"Ouch!" Jed yelped.

Kizer pulled the skin to his nose and inhaled. His lower lip jutted out as if he'd just breathed vinegar fumes. "Pretty skin like that? Not a wrinkle. Not a scar. Smells like . . . *soap*."

"Thanks? I—um—shower when I can?" His answers lifted at their ends as if they were questions.

Kizer released the skin. "Under all that sky water? Beyond the fringe? A glittertale place that doesn't exist?"

"What are you accusing me of?"

Kizer pinched some hairs from Jed's head and yanked.

"Ow! Get off me!" He shoved Kizer and backed against one of the windows, rubbing the now-tender patch of scalp.

Kizer studied the hairs, then sprinkled them over the floor. "Don't lie to me. You didn't even feel that! Manipulative parasites like you don't feel anything."

"Manipulative what?"

"We both know you're not from the fringe. You're just a little monster from the fog . . . snuck on board to devour us all."

"The *fog*? Are you serious? How could you even—"

"Where's your beacon?"

"My what?"

"Show me!" Kizer said. He drew a shatterbox. The weapon wasn't elaborate like one of Sprocket's, but Jed guessed it still fired just fine. "I saw you tampering with the altitude controls."

Jed held up his hands and shook his head. "I was just looking around!"

"You're not a very clever dread, are you?"

"Dread?"

Jed glanced out the window behind him. *It's not too high to jump. Not high enough to break my legs, at least.*

Kizer nodded. "Dread."

"How could you possibly think I'm one of those things?"

Kizer pulled the hammer on his shatterbox. It clicked. He curled a finger around the trigger. "You're just wearing somebody else's skin . . . hiding underneath pretty, soaped-clean pink."

"I swear, I'm not a dread! This is my real skin!"

"I was watching you earlier. I saw the way you looked at that stack ornament."

Jed's brain crackled, tingly with guilt over what the dread had said to him.

Jed's voice trembled. "Looked at it how?"

"I know what I saw. You two are planning something, aren't you? Mutiny arrangements? Makeup tips on looking human? Do you even *feel* real emotions? No! You don't! And you're not going to feel anything when I squeeze this trigger, because you're not a real person. You're scrap! So stop acting scared!"

"Would you just listen to me?"

"I'm not going to let you slurp up this crew and turn us into twisted, clicking beetles. Time for you to go."

His finger flexed against the trigger. Jed tensed, ready to jump through the window. The bridge door flung open, and Captain Bog stomped into the room.

"What's going on?" he shouted.

Kizer flinched. "He—"

"He *what*? If you're going to make a mess on my bridge, and if I have to get Pobble up here to scrub pieces of that boy out of the gears, there'd better be a good reason."

"Captain, this boy's a dread. I saw him acting suspicious around the head. I think they're working together to kill us and take the ship."

"What?" Captain Bog asked.

"I saw him reaching for the altitude controls. He's going to crash the ship, then kill us and take our skins, and—"

Jed held his hands higher. "I don't know what he's talking about. I'm not a dread. I'm not trying to kill anyone!"

"Keep your mouth shut until I tell you to open it," Captain Bog said. He rubbed his eyes with his thumb and index finger. "Kizer, is this Henry all over again?"

"I'm telling you: he's full of gears and scrap. That pretty sheet of skin is a disguise! He's a dread, Captain. I know it."

"Gears?" Jed said. "I don't have any gears!" He lifted an arm and poked it to show how squishy it was.

"That's what you said about Henry." Captain Bog's voice was careful and steady.

Kizer shook his head twitchily, as if a fly had landed on his nose. "I'm not crazy."

"That scrawny runt who can't climb a ladder? You think he's a dread? All his parts are matching. I don't see any extra clunk on him. Do you?"

Kizer considered Jed. "He's hiding it."

Captain Bog shook his head. "All the parts match. All in the right spots. You ever seen a dread like that?" Kizer shook his head with a strained motion. "Me neither. Besides, he'll be off in a few hours. Won't be our problem."

"They don't leave." Kizer lowered his shatterbox. "They never leave. He'll find a reason to stay and kill us all."

"All right." Captain Bog patted Kizer's shoulder. "Glad we had this chat." He pointed at Jed. "You. Out."

Jed strode past Kizer.

"You keep riling up my crew," the captain added, "I'll lock you in a closet."

Pobble waited for Jed on the deck. He slapped him on the back with a meaty hand. "Sorry about Kizer. He's been a bit"— he twirled his finger around his ear—"ever since he escaped the fog."

"Escaped?"

"Dread raided his township a while back. Scooped up all the townsfolk and left. Kizer couldn't save no one's skin but his own. Who knows what he went through. Now he thinks every stranger is a dread."

"Like Henry?" Jed recalled the name.

"Henry was lookout before Sprocket. Kizer said he was a dread. Always yelling at him. Accusing him."

"What happened?"

"Poor kid lost his leg in a junkstorm. Since no gears tumbled out, Kizer let it go. Till now, I s'pose."

"Is he going to try to do something to me?" Jed asked. "Like kill me?"

"Nah, Cap'n will set him straight," Pobble said. "Unless you really are a dread."

Jed's gut squished in on itself as he thought of the whispering voice.

"Yup." Jed smiled. "That's me. Jed the dread."

"C'mon, let's—"

A high-pitched whistle sliced through the air.

"Incoming falcon!" Sprocket called from the lookout. "Starboard! Less than a scope and closing!"

The bridge door flung open. Captain Bog cupped his hands and yelled, "Battle stations!"

Pobble grabbed Jed by the elbow. "Get to the shatterkegs!"

"Shatterkegs? What's going on?"

The two paused at a second whistle.

"Looks like more than one!" Sprocket called.

"What's happening?" Jed asked.

Pobble pointed at the black dots in the distance. "Incoming falcons!"

A third whistle.

And then a fourth.

Each time Sprocket opened her mouth to shout, another falcon's whistle blew, until there were too many to count.

"Sprocket?" Captain Bog stared up at her.

She studied the sky. "Could be an entire wing, Captain. Maybe two. Closing fast. Three-quarters of a scope away."

Captain Bog stared at the black dots.

"Who are they?" Jed whispered to Pobble.

Pobble looked at Jed as if he'd forgotten everything Jed had mentioned about living beyond the fringe. "Iron."

"Orders, sir?" Kizer said.

"Cancel battle stations!" Captain Bog called. "Prepare for a duck-and-hide!"

Sprocket scrambled from the stack's nest and leaped to the deck. "I'll prep three cloud bombs and wait for your order."

Captain Bog turned to Kizer. "Tell Riggs to punch all four boosters and burn hot at the first cloud."

Kizer hurried to the staircase.

"Why are the irons after us?" Jed asked.

"Irons think they own the whole yard," Pobble said. "Don't give scrap 'bout junkers like us. They'll strip a ruster ship faster than you could kick a slug from your shoe. Then they'd steal those very same shoes. And your socks too. And anything else they say is property of the Iron Guard. They'd take your fingernail right off your pinky, if they thought it worth half a battery."

"And no one tries to stop them?"

"No one except copper. How we supposed to stop that?" He waved an arm at the dots in the sky, which were getting bigger by the second.

"Three cloud bombs ready for launch," Sprocket called. "But I don't think a dozen would keep even half a wing from finding us."

"Got a better idea?" Captain Bog asked.

"Not really."

"Then let's hope those T-five boosters were worth what we paid. Kizer, take the helm. Everyone, get ready."

The falcons drew closer. Sunlight glinted off their sleek silver hulls.

"There's more than two wings!" Sprocket called. "Looks like a full flock!"

Pobble stood on his toes and squinted at the approaching army. "I ain't never seen a full flock lumped up together like that. Something's going on. Something big."

The falcons kept a tight formation.

"What in the clunk are they all doing?" Captain Bog mumbled.

"Captain?" Sprocket called.

He held up his hand. "Hold. We've only got one shot."

The falcons' whistling deepened into a deck-rattling hum.

"Captain?" Impatience tugged at Sprocket's voice.

"I know what I'm doing. Hold."

The falcons were close enough for Jed to see dents in their metal and letters painted on their noses.

"Now, Sprocket!"

Sprocket ignited a cloud bomb and dropped it into a metal tube. The tube made a whump, and the bomb launched toward the falcons.

When it reached the fleet, it exploded into smoke.

A rich black stained the blue sky like oil.

"Fly straight into the fleet," Captain Bog said to Kizer. "They'll be expecting us to go the other direction and will hopefully pass us straight by."

Kizer jammed the controls and punched a pulsing blue button.

Something popped and hissed in the engine room.

Jed could hear a faint, angry voice through the deck. "Scrap piece of second-rate, cheap gutter clunk!"

"Riiiggs?" the captain called.

"I've got blown batteries all over the control board!" he yelled through the floor. "Boosters are dead!"

"Get us out of here!" Captain Bog yelled back.

"Nothing's responding! We're stuck!"

Silence spread over the crew as the black cloud spilled across the sky.

The first falcon emerged from the smoke. Dozens followed, piercing the cloud like needles.

One by one, until there were hundreds.

Captain Bog sighed. "Scrap."

Sprocket dropped the second cloud bomb to the floor and kicked it. "Scrap."

"Well," the captain said, "enjoy your last ten seconds of life. It's been a pleasure."

He lifted his chin and closed his eyes.

The first falcon reached the tug.

A gust of wind sliced over them as the falcon whooshed by. The next wave of falcons reached them—and flew past. Falcon after falcon. Wing after wing.

And then the whole flock was gone.

Silver dots once again.

"I—I don't understand," Kizer said, joining the captain on deck. "They just . . . *ignored* us."

The captain stared at the fading pinpricks of silver.

"A battle," Sprocket said, joining the others. "It has to be."

Kizer shook his head. "There hasn't been a battle that size for decades."

"War's not over," Captain Bog muttered. "Not for *them*, at least."

Jed turned to Pobble. "War? Who's at war?"

Sprocket folded her arms across her chest. "Everyone's at war, Golden Boy. Even when they're not."

"What do you mean?"

"Everyone wants something. Odds are, if you want it, some*one* else some*where* else wants it too."

Jed pointed to the falcons. "What do *they* want?"

Sprocket winked. "Gold."

"They want relics," Pobble said. "All of them."

Sprocket shook her head. "Just a relic? Iron would've sent one squadron for that—maybe two. A whole flock? No way. This is bigger. My guess? A gilded relic."

"*Gilded* relic?" Kizer said. "There hasn't been talk of a gilded relic for years."

Sprocket nodded. "Exactly."

"What's a gilded relic?" Jed asked.

"Another glittertale . . ." Captain Bog said. He kicked absently at a spot on the deck. "One shiny enough to fuel a war."

When the last of the falcons disappeared, Captain Bog turned to Pobble. "Check on Riggs. See what's wrong with the engine, and report back. Got it?"

"Aye, Captain."

"Kizer, Sprocket, follow me. Make sure every shatterkeg is ready."

Jed tailed Pobble to the engine room. The amber-lit corridor stretched half the length of the ship, but it was barely wide enough for two people to walk side by side—well, even *one* in Pobble's case.

Copper pipes walled the passageway. Loose valves leaked puffs of steam, and hidden pistons chugged in the darkness. They passed dripping oil and hissing gauges.

The engine room was a silver dome. Copper pipes—some thin, some fat—squiggled like veins and arteries all along the curved ceiling and down into the engine. The engine itself stood in the center of the room. It looked alive. Like an angry beast fueled by the wheezing pipes. Lights pulsed on and off: its heart, eyes, and mouth.

"Hey!" a voice said. "What are you doing down here, Pobble? And who's *that*?"

A man at a cluttered workbench stabbed a finger at Jed.

"Jed, meet Riggs," Pobble said. "Our engineer."

Riggs didn't look particularly old, but he had more wrinkles than Captain Bog had scars. Grease seeped into his skin, smeared his coat, and stained his shirt.

Riggs took off his glasses and wiped the lenses. His coat had dozens of pockets sewn on haphazardly. Riggs placed the glasses in an empty pocket, then retrieved a different pair and put them on his nose.

"I'm Jed."

"Do I look like I care?" He lifted a crate of batteries onto his workbench, then began plugging them into slots on the engine. "What are you doing here?"

"Cap'n wanted to know what was going on with the engine," Pobble said.

"Oh, did he?" Riggs said. "Well maybe you could remind him that if he doesn't want to *crash* and *die* in a fireball of regret, he might want to get that defluxor core sooner than later."

"Sure thing," Pobble said. "Fireball . . . death . . . regret . . . fluxa-der-something core. Got it."

"A core he promised me last month."

"I'll pass him the message—"

"Death. And regret," Riggs said again.

"Death and regret. I'll pass it along." Pobble turned to Jed. "Good-looking engine, huh?" he said cheerfully, as though he hadn't heard the bite in Riggs's voice. "Oh, Riggs! You won't believe what Jed here's got!" Pobble asked Jed for the can opener and handed it to Riggs. "It's a can slicer! Opens them faster than slug spit!"

Riggs pinched it between two fingers like it was a dirty sock. "How . . . *cute*," he said, handing it back to Jed.

"Riggs is great with tools," Pobble continued. "Builds all sorts of things." He pointed to the workbench. Riggs side-stepped in front of them, folding his arms across his chest as if daring Jed to take a step closer.

"It looks great," Jed said. "The engine, it's . . . nice . . . and . . ."

"And what?" Riggs said. "What does some stray know about four-valve combustion counterflow engine boosters and lead-weighted compound stabilizers?"

Jed didn't respond.

"Nothing," Riggs said. "Because I just said a bunch of scrap nonsense. But you didn't know that, did you?"

"I'm sorry," Jed said, holding up his hands. "I didn't mean to offend you. I was just making conversation."

"You know what, stray?" Riggs started. "I think—" His eyes paused on Jed's wrist. He removed his spectacles and took a third pair from yet another pocket and adjusted them on his nose. "That watch," he said, the knife-edge tone melting into curiosity. "Give me your watch." His fingers curled into a beckoning motion.

Jed touched the copper band and fiddled with the clasp.

The letter. It said to never take off the watch. Ever.

"Um, well, the clasp is broken and I can't really get it to . . ." He pretended to struggle with the band.

Riggs smiled. "It's my job to fix things. I'll have it off before you can say no."

"No," Jed blurted. "I mean, no thanks. I'd rather not take it off. It's kind of important to me."

Riggs smiled again, but darkness lurked behind the grin. "Oh? Then I'll only look. One quick peek?"

Jed forced a shrug.

The engineer walked forward until he was so close that Jed could smell the grease in his frizzy hair. Riggs rubbed the spectacles, then swapped them for yet another pair.

Who carries that many pairs of glasses?

"Just don't touch it," Jed said as Riggs's nose nearly pressed into the copper.

The man held up his hands, then put them behind his back. He hovered near Jed like a mosquito. Hunched over Jed's wrist, he studied the timepiece.

"Hmm," he said with a nod. "Hmm. I see . . . interesting. Yes . . ."

"What's interesting?" Jed asked.

Riggs stood upright. "Where did you say you found this?"

"I didn't say."

"Hmm," Riggs said, stroking his chin.

Would you stop muttering "hmm" and just say something already?

"Well, where *did* you find it?"

Jed shifted his weight, trying to inch away from Riggs's snooping spectacles. "It was a gift."

"From?"

"Just a gift."

"Ah." Riggs nodded. "*Just a gift.* And does the owner know that they gave you such a gift?"

Jed's eyes narrowed. "Are you saying I stole it?"

"I didn't say anything of the sort. But you're so defensive that it almost makes a man wonder."

Jed clenched his jaw. "I'm not a thief. This is *mine*. It doesn't belong to anyone else, and nobody is missing it. Understand?"

Riggs's smile widened, turning the wrinkles in his cheeks into half moons. "Oh, I bet I understand more than *you*. But don't worry"—he stole another glance at the watch—"I'll keep your secret."

"What are you talking about? I'm not keeping any secrets!"

"Of course not," Riggs said. "The rest of the crew doesn't need to know." Pobble stared at the pipes along the wall as if oblivious to the conversation. Riggs patted Pobble on the shoulder. "Pobble here won't say a word. Will you? Not if you want me to fix your fiddle."

Pobble met Riggs's gaze. "Not a word."

"There is no secret!" Jed snapped. "I'm not lying about anything! I didn't steal this!"

"Hmm . . ." Riggs said. "Good to know. Because if someone informed the captain about what's on your scrawny wrist, things might get *uncomfortable*."

"Are you blackmailing me? Because I don't even know what you're trying to blackmail me for!"

Riggs shook his head. "Blackmail implies that I'm exploiting you for my own gain. We haven't reached that point yet, have we? We're just talking. Let's not make this into something that it isn't."

"That *what* isn't?"

"Exactly," Riggs said, moving back to his workbench. "I won't say anything if you don't." He picked up a hammer and began flattening a sheet of metal. "Oh, and stray"—he didn't look up—"I'm ready to talk when you are. But don't wait too long."

11

Pobble took Jed to the mess to share his promised can of strawberries. But before they'd finished half the can, Sprocket called from the stack, "Steamboat ahead! Half a scope and closing!"

Jed dropped his strawberry and smiled at Pobble. "My grandfather's ship!" He ran to the top deck. Black smoke snaked up from the junk ahead and swirled with white clouds above. The stench of scorched metal stung his chest.

He walked to the railing, squinting at the wreckage. A graveyard of ships littered a blackened field of smoldering junk. Decimated parts lay in heaps. Ashy flakes of debris fluttered in the breeze.

The falcons from earlier—hundreds of them—lay like

shreds of twisted paper. More ships were strewn beside them in broken bits. In the center of the wreckage lay a massive steamboat.

Fear pulsed through Jed.

"Looks like we found where the falcons went," Captain Bog said. "Sprocket," he called. "Report. What sort of clunk are we looking at?"

"Copper, iron, dread . . . they all showed up for the party. Can't say who won, though—or if anyone did."

"Risk of entry?"

She shrugged. "I can't see any movement, but I suppose there's always risk of dread. I'd say risk is low to moderate."

Captain Bog nodded. "Take us in, then."

Jed's voice felt unsteady. "What . . . what happened here?"

"What do you *think*?" Captain Bog said. "Bunch of birds squawked at each other for a spell, then decided to all take a little nap together under an ash blanket."

"But my grandfather. Where is he? He's—" Jed scanned the ravaged steamboat. "This isn't how it's supposed to be . . ."

Captain Bog shrugged. "Piles of dead iron, copper, and dread is *exactly* how it's supposed to be, if you ask me."

Jed clamped his teeth. "I didn't."

"You didn't what?"

"Ask you."

"No need for temperament. Just making an observation."

Jed searched the heaps for anything still alive. "I was supposed to meet my grandfather. What if he's . . . dead? What do I do?"

Captain Bog looked up as if trying to recall something. "Well, the particulars of this contract were a bit . . . *thin*. Bring one passenger *here*. That's all. I don't recall any what-ifs. Now, I could be wrong, but the thing is, I'm never wrong. So the logic doesn't really check out."

"What about Captain Holiday?"

"The dead man whose contract we took? *That* Captain Holiday?"

"Yes. Where's his ship? Maybe you could bring me there if everyone here is . . ." The word caught in his throat as he looked at the approaching debris. "If everyone's *dead*."

"Listen." Captain Bog rested a hand on Jed's shoulder. "I don't mean to sound like I don't care about your situation, but"—he paused, deciding on his next words—"well, I just don't care."

Jed opened his mouth but didn't know what to say.

"We'll make certain you reach the steamboat safely like the contract states. Sound good?" Before Jed could respond, the captain patted his shoulder. "Excellent. Sprocket! Take us down."

"Aye, Cap'n!"

"What if nobody's there?" Jed asked. "You can't just leave me to die!"

Captain Bog thought for a moment. He tugged a cable bolted to the smokestack. He studied the helm. "Kizer, has Riggs reported more engine problems?"

"Other than the defluxor core he keeps whining about?"

"Yup. Other than that."

"No."

Captain Bog nodded half a dozen times, then turned to Jed. "Ship's in working order, so I'll have to strongly disagree. I *can*, in fact, leave you to die."

"But—"

"Yes?"

Jed paused. Sob stories wouldn't change the captain's mind. This wasn't a man who brought flowers to hospitals or adopted three-legged puppies.

No. This was the time to be resourceful. His parents hadn't raised him to complain when he found himself in uncomfortable situations. They'd taught him SPLAGHETTI for a reason.

"I just figured you were tired of opening cans with your teeth is all." The captain raised an eyebrow. "A man such as you might like one of these." He held up the can opener.

"And that is?"

"Get me a can and I'll show you."

"Someone get me a pineapple juice!" Captain Bog hollered.

Pobble trotted over with a can. Jed clamped the tool to its rim, then sliced off the lid.

"Where did you—" Captain Bog's jaw slackened, but he stiffened before too much excitement could creep into his face.

"You like it?"

"Fine. Give me your little toy and my crew will search the ship for survivors. Two hours. That's my offer. We've got two hundred scopes to cover in two days. If we miss our rendezvous with the tinker and Riggs doesn't get his defluxor core, I'll have mutiny on board. Is that clear?"

"But what if we don't find anyone on the steamboat?"

Captain Bog shrugged. "It's all I can offer. Take it or leave it. This boat's not a transport, and it sure isn't some scrap orphanage. So unless you've got a pocket full of batteries I don't know about, that's the deal."

"If no one is aboard the steamboat, I'll need a ride."

"Nope. Out of the question. We'll barely catch the tinker as is. And then we've got a dig site in Skova a hundred scopes from there. I won't miss either for some can slicer."

Jed nodded. He knew when people were willing to give, but he also knew when they weren't.

"Give me three days on board. Lock me in a closet if you want. You don't even have to feed me." Jed winced as the words left his mouth. Captain Bog seemed the type to hold to such agreements. But Jed didn't offer something he couldn't handle. He'd gone four days without food in Kenya. With water, three was easy. "You can drop me at the nearest town when you're ready."

Captain Bog studied Jed. "No food, huh?"

Jed cringed. He'd hoped the captain would take his offer just for the sake of entertainment.

"And three days in a closet?"

"That's right."

Captain Bog stepped forward. "I'll drop you at a township, but here's the new deal. No closet nonsense. Each day when we land, you'll have two hours to hunt for twenty-one cans to feed the crew. Twenty-one cans. No less. You find the cans, you buy a day's passage. You're one can short, don't bother trying to board. No amount of blubbering will convince me otherwise. And if you want food for yourself, find more than twenty-one cans, or expect to live on cloudy mop water."

Captain Bog snatched the can opener from Jed, then walked away.

The faint scent of blackened wood and melted metal made Jed's throat feel smaller. If the steamboat was empty, then he was alone in the world.

12

The tug approached the charred steamboat. A low buzz hummed from its hull, and a flash of activity caught Jed's eye.

"Wasp!" Sprocket shouted.

Captain Bog followed her gaze. "Ready weapons!"

"Aye!" Kizer yelled, punching buttons on the bridge.

A small brassy device wobbled inside the steamboat's cargo bay. It rose and swayed unsteadily in the air.

"Lock shatterkegs," the captain said. "If it takes aggressive posture, fire."

"Aye," Kizer called.

The wasp was barely able to fly. It turned toward the tug, then drifted backward.

"Run away, little copper," Captain Bog mumbled. "Don't make me blow you to bits."

As if it heard the captain, the wasp's engines flared; then it spun and rocketed away.

Captain Bog nodded. "Stay sharp down there," he said to Kizer, "in case there are any more stragglers."

"Aye, sir."

"Rear up. Raise the sky propeller."

"Rear prop up," Kizer responded. "Sky prop engaged."

Thin shadows moved across the deck at Jed's feet. Fastened to the top of the smokestack, five blades lifted into place. As the hum of the tail propellers faded, the sky prop began to spin until it was a blur. Violent wind from the whirling metal gusted down against Jed, nearly knocking him off-balance.

"Set us down on the main deck," the captain said.

"Aye!" Kizer shouted over the noise.

The tug hovered over the steamboat and began to lower. The deck of the steamboat dwarfed the tug.

The tugboat's engine sputtered to a stop.

Sprocket hopped down from the stack's nest and tossed a rope ladder overboard.

One by one they climbed down the ladder to the wide, empty steamboat deck.

"Let's look around, shall we?" Captain Bog said.

Before Jed could follow the others to explore the ship, Riggs put a hand on his shoulder. "Given any more thought to our conversation?"

"I don't know what you want me to say. I didn't steal it. It was—"

"A gift. Right. Sooner or later you'll cooperate." He motioned to the deserted ship. "We both know everyone here is dead. I'm guessing we're about to find out you're all alone. You might need a friend—especially considering Kizer's opinion of you."

The sick, lonely fear punched at Jed's gut again.

Riggs's dark grin widened. "Captain told us about your little can-scrounging deal. We're taking bets on how many you'll find. Most said under five. Pobble must like you, because he guessed all the way up to *nine*. We all know you're not making it back on board. You're going to die here."

"Why are you saying this?"

"Tell me about that watch and I might remember a secret passage through the ship that leads to a stowaway cabin hidden under the mess. Access to food and barrels of water . . . I'll even throw in a blanket." Riggs outlined the square edges of a panel in the tug's hull with his finger. "What do you say?"

The captain wouldn't show leniency if Jed couldn't find the cans, but Jed couldn't offer information he didn't have.

"I swear. I don't know anything about this watch. If you could just tell me why it's so important, maybe I could help."

Riggs scratched his wrinkled forehead. "Listen. I wouldn't be surprised if you didn't know how to use relic junk. I'd even believe that you don't know what it does. I'm willing to negotiate. Tell me who you stole it from and we have a deal."

"I didn't steal it! You want the truth? My parents gave it to me. Okay?"

"Ah . . . your *parents*. Why not mention it earlier? It's a simple enough answer."

"Maybe I don't trust you."

"Then where are your parents?"

"They're missing. This watch is the only piece I have left of them."

"Convenient."

"No, actually, it's not convenient. I'm stuck on this scrap tugboat, and now I find out that my grandpa—the last person who can help me—is probably dead. What about that sounds convenient to you?"

"The part where you're lying about all of it."

"Whatever. I don't care anymore. I can't help you if you won't believe me."

Riggs continued as if he hadn't heard a word Jed had said. "If you won't tell me who, then tell me where. What township cluster? Did anyone else have watches, or was there only one? Did they know how to make them work? Give me something, Jed. Anything. I'm quite reasonable. But I need to know that you're willing to talk."

"If I knew anything else, I'd tell you. But I don't."

"What about your parents? Who are they? What are their names?"

Jed thought about the letter telling him not to mention his last name. "I—I can't tell you their names."

"That's what I thought. Tough to come up with names on the spot for imaginary parents."

"Why do you care? It doesn't even work." He tapped the glass face and showed Riggs the unmoving hands.

"Maybe you don't know how to use it."

"And you do? Then tell me what it does. Because it seems useless."

"Useless?" Riggs smiled. "Look around! You're in the middle of a war zone. How many ships do you think are lying in pieces around us? Two hundred? Three? All for pieces of scrap that are just as *useless* as the one you're wearing. I know people who would kill a ship full of men just for a peek at that scrap on your wrist."

"It sounds like you should know different people," Jed said.

Riggs nearly laughed. Nearly. "Probably true. But if you don't tell me the truth about where you found it, I'll tell Sprocket what you have, and after we've left, she'll return for the answers. With a bit more *coercion*."

"First you accuse me of stealing it, then you blackmail me, and now you're just going to torture and rob me?"

"Who said anything about robbing?" Riggs said. "The captain doesn't tolerate stealing. Not one bit. I'm perfectly happy with you keeping what you've rightfully . . . *acquired*. I'm not interested in one little trinket. But a shiny piece like that has brothers and sisters. . . ."

"Well, good luck with that. Nothing I say is going to help. I didn't even find this in the junkyard."

"I thought someone gave it to you. Now you *found* it?"

Jed rolled his eyes. "You know what I mean. . . . I didn't *get* it from the junkyard."

Riggs smiled. "Oh. That's right. You're from the fringe. You must have gotten it from your glittertale home. Clearly. Listen, if you won't respond to reason, I guess I'll wish you luck when Sprocket returns. And don't try to sneak in here." He patted the stowaway panel. "I'll have my eyes on you the whole time. And you have cans to find."

Jed's stomach swirled at the mention of cans. He wondered if what Riggs had said was true. Had they really bet on how many cans he'd find? The charred junk blended together in a sea of black. Finding even five cans was going to take a miracle.

"Jackpot!" Pobble shouted. The crew swarmed around him.

"We got ourselves a caseful!" Sprocket whooped, drew a shatterbox, and fired a shot in the air.

"Pobble, grab that end," Captain Bog said. "Riggs, help him." They gripped the edges of a plastic crate, then shuffled closer. Jed peeked into the crate at more than a hundred cans. When they passed, he pulled the captain aside. "Is this why you wanted to 'help' search? To scavenge for supplies?"

"A man's gotta eat. Besides, no harm in poking around while we look for a crew that doesn't seem to exist anymore." He took a swig of pineapple juice from a yellow can. "But you should get started hunting. Twenty-one cans is a tall order."

"Twenty-one cans? What do you mean? You just found a whole crateful."

"Exactly. *We* found them."

"Only because of me. Those should count!"

"Did you find them?"

"It's the same thing."

The captain shook his head. "A deal's a deal. I'd get started, if I were you. Wasting time running your mouth."

"But what about my grandfather? You haven't even looked!"

"I'm a man of my word. The crew will search every room of this scrap of charcoal. I doubt they'll find more than a pock-etful of batteries and a nest of gollug slugs, but they'll do it all the same."

"A nest of what?"

"Time's running out. Twenty-one cans. Two hours." Jed glared at the captain. "Oh, I'm sorry. Where are my manners?" He held up the pineapple juice. "Sip?"

Jed pointed to the wreckage. "What about the dread?"

"What about them?"

"Sprocket said there could maybe be dread down there."

Captain Bog patted Jed on the back. "Don't worry. They're more scared of you than you are of them. Or maybe I'm think-ing of slugs. Yup, that's right. Dread will slurp you up and wear your nose before you can spit. But good luck trying to spit, because they'll be wearing your lips too. Tick-tock."

Jed stalked off to the lower decks. The ship was an eviscer-ated corpse of shredded steel and splintered wood. He leaped over a broken pipe and a twisted shoot of rebar. *Always watch your feet,* his dad had warned him once after they'd set a half dozen traps around their campsite.

"Watch your feet," he whispered to himself.

The captain was probably right. The empty ship was a skeleton in a graveyard. If anyone *had* survived, they were long gone. Or worse.

No bodies.

No voices.

Nothing.

A porthole led to the junkyard floor. Out of reflex, he glanced at the broken watch on his wrist. *Two hours.*

He lifted a metal grate and began searching. He stacked a shovel and a basketball on the top of a barbecue, then tossed a checkered sweater over his shoulder. As he pulled a lawn chair free, his heart leaped. The first can. It couldn't have been more than a minute and he was already one can closer. He brushed the smoky black from its surface. *Kidney beans.*

He pulled a plastic crate from the junk and tossed the first can inside. Water chestnuts and diced peaches quickly followed.

Three cans in less than ten minutes. If I keep this up, I'll be back on the ship in an hour.

And then . . . nothing.

Jed searched under a cast-iron bathtub, in a hand-carved wardrobe, around a dusty chimney. His heart beat faster as the minutes passed. He slipped on a red pool ball and rammed his knee into a bedpost. He swore, then grabbed a fire poker and slammed it into junk. Bits of plastic from a sewing machine scattered around him. He whacked the junk until the pain in his knee dulled.

Focus. You can do this.

As he stared at his feet, a dark shape moved under the gaps in the junk. He scrambled backward and fell.

He hadn't actually seen anything.

Had he?

Jed curled up and inched forward. He studied each dark cavity.

And then he saw it.

A dozen layers deep.

A dread. It had one eye and one empty socket. Crooked wires fused the eye to a mechanical face patched with dead, leathery skin.

Jed stood there, frozen, as the dread watched him. Still and ready like a spider.

A red light appeared on the side of its head and began to pulse.

"Slippery boy," it said through the junk. "Tucked away in secret places. Secrets, secrets, secrets! You're Secret Boy, aren't you? I can smell it. I can taste your secrets!"

Jed stepped back.

It skittered through the junk underneath him like a shark circling a defenseless boat. It crawled through impossible crevices, twisting its body this way and that.

"You smell soft and frightened. Frightened makes soup drizzly. I like drizzly. I want to slurp drizzly from your belly and play scratch with your bones."

Jed backed away, but the dread followed beneath him.

He picked up a baseball and chucked it into one of the gaps. "Get away from me!"

The dread slipped to the side of the ball. And then it began to make its way upward.

Jed scrambled back, but he was too slow.

The dread surfaced from the junk. Its legs were bars of iron, and its rotting chest was held together with swatches of chain-link fence. One arm limp—almost dead—flopped at its side. The other was outstretched and clawed at the air in anticipation. "Father says no slurp up Secret Boy! Secret Boy off-limits. But I want Secret Boy. Secret boys taste like winning and defiance!"

"Get away from me!" Jed yelled again.

He ran.

The dread skittered forward, its metal legs clacking unevenly against the junk.

When its twisted shadow had nearly reached Jed's, a crack filled the air, and the dread burst into a clatter of metal parts.

A cobalt-colored trail of smoke stretched from the dread to the end of Sprocket's shatterlance. She gave Jed a fluttery wave with her fingers, then scrawled her signature in the smoke.

Jed slumped to the pile and gave Sprocket a thank-you wave.

The metal pieces of the dread were still. All except for the green eye, which still rotated on its gear, blinking and watching him.

"If you're going to find twenty-one cans," Captain Bog called from the ship, "you should probably spend less time frolicking around with those things and more time searching the piles."

Jed sucked in a deep breath. "Thanks," he called back, his voice shaking. "Appreciate the concern. Really thoughtful of you."

"That's what I'm known for," the captain said. "Thoughtfulness. That and warm hugs."

Jed stood and limped over a pair of garden gnomes and a dentist's chair. His muscles jittered and his knee throbbed. The more he walked, the more the key in his shoe pressed into his foot.

Don't think about the dread. Just find cans.

He studied the junk, soaking in the scene, and managed to scrounge four more cans from the pile.

"One hour!" the captain called. "Then we're gone!"

Jed's heart banged against his ribs. He scrambled around and found a can of lima beans, three cans of soup, and a can of tomato paste.

Ten more, he thought. *Only ten more.*

He glanced back at the steamboat, realizing for the first time how far he'd ventured. The farther he walked, the farther he'd have to walk *back*.

But with still ten cans to go, he didn't have a choice. Captain Bog's voice burned in his ears: *One can short, don't bother trying to board.*

As he scampered up yet another pile, he was grateful for every Himalayan rock-climbing trip his parents had forced him on. The crew couldn't have known he had that kind of experience—especially with their low guesses. Jed spotted another few cans and added them to the crate. He smiled. He would make it. The look on Captain Bog's face would make every cut and scrape worth it. The thought gave him the boost of energy he needed to lift a small airplane wing and snatch a hidden can of asparagus.

He plowed through a wheelbarrow, an electrical box, and a trampoline, finding several more. Minutes sped by. He raced faster, tearing his palms on loose nails and fractured concrete.

"Ten minutes!" Captain Bog yelled.

The voice was too quiet. Too far away. Jed dropped the bicycle seat he was holding and looked in horror at the distant steamboat. He studied the milk crate. *One . . . two . . . three . . . four . . . five . . . six . . . Wait, no . . . four . . . five . . . six . . . no!* His hands shook as he shoved cans from side to side. Counting . . . recounting. He tilted the crate to dump it out, but hesitated, eyeing the gaps in the junk.

He counted again. *Twenty-one.* Again. *Nineteen.* Again. *Twenty.*

"Nine!" Captain Bog bellowed.

No more counting. Just go!

He bolted toward the steamboat, scanning for any cans he could have missed.

"Eight!"

He leaped over a motorcycle, but his toe nicked the seat. His body crashed into a lawn mower, and his arms flew apart. The milk crate tumbled free, and cans scattered in every direction.

"Seven!"

He pushed himself up and grabbed cans as fast as his arms would allow.

"Six!"

When the crate was filled, Jed knew it felt lighter. He scoured the junk again.

"Five!"

"Shut up!" Jed yelled back.

He saw the water chestnuts under a crumpled rug. He scooped the can up and found the asparagus hiding too. Hope swelled in his chest. He threw the cans in and ran.

"Four!"

The crate barely fit through the porthole as he scrambled into the steamboat. "I'm here!" His voice echoed in the empty space. The ladder to the main deck somehow looked more rickety than when he'd used it two hours earlier, and the crate suddenly felt twice as heavy.

"Three!"

"I'm right here! But I can't climb the ladder with all this food!"

"Not my problem," Captain Bog called. "We're leaving in three minutes whether you're here or not. You should have worked on your ladder-climbing issues earlier instead of lazing about, touching altitude controls."

Jed unfastened his belt and whipped it free. The leather band flapped as it passed each belt loop. He coiled it through the handles of the crate and cinched it tight. Gripping the belt in the middle with one hand, he tested the weight.

"Two!"

Jed planted his foot on the ladder. The rungs creaked.

He climbed, sweaty fingers clenching the cool metal. *Step . . . step . . . step . . .*

As his foot pressed into the next rung, the bar snapped. The crate pitched backward, and the green beans wobbled on the stack, threatening to dive free. He glared at the can. *Don't. You. Dare!*

"One minute, Golden Boy."

He grabbed the next rung.

Then the next.

Then the next.

As his head breached the top deck, he swung the crate onto solid planks and jumped beside it. Lifting it in both arms, he ran until *Bessie's* smokestack peeked into view.

"Well," Captain Bog called, "your time's—"

"I'm here!" Jed's voice cracked with dry rasps. "I'm here."

He stumbled forward and released the crate. It thunked against the floor at Murdock Bog's feet.

"You sound out of breath," the captain said.

Jed collapsed. Only then did he see blood. Deep red seeped through his pants around his knee. As his adrenaline faded, pain charged over him. The joint felt swollen—like his knee was covered in barely heated wax.

Did I break something?

He'd never broken a bone before. He bent his knee back and forth.

Bruised? Definitely. Broken? Probably not.

"You all right?" Captain Bog asked.

"Oh, I'm terrific . . ." Jed mumbled.

"Let's see . . ." Captain Bog turned his attention to the cans. One by one he lined them in stacks of four. After the fifth stack, the crate was empty. "Where's the last can?"

The pain in Jed's knee—in his hands—in his head—all disappeared at once. "There are twenty-one. I know there are." The words tripped from his mouth. His mind pulled him back to the junk piles, to his hurried counting, to his splayed fall . . . "There have to be twenty-one . . ." He spoke more to himself than to the captain.

There have to be.

Captain Bog slowly shook his head, fidgeting with one of the torn labels. "Twenty."

"Count again."

"Look for yourself." He nudged the five stacks of four with his boot.

"But—"

Captain Bog shrugged. "No cans, no ride."

"You can't be serious."

Captain Bog fixed his eyes on Jed's. "In the short time you've known me, do I strike you as someone who 'can't be serious'?"

"You found a whole case of cans on the steamboat! And I brought you twenty more! This is ridiculous!"

"It's unfortunate, I'll give you that."

"Unfortunate? It's a joke!"

"You were the one eager to make the deal. What kind of

captain would I be if I let people slide whenever they whined?" He cocked his head.

"You're making a mistake."

Captain Bog shook his head. "I really don't think so. Never had much luck taking on stragglers. You're not the first stray I've dealt with."

With that the captain turned and climbed the rope ladder back into the tug. "Engage the sky prop!"

"Aye, Cap'n!" Sprocket called.

"Stop!" Jed yelled.

Captain Bog peeked over the railing. "Haven't you learned that telling me to stop doesn't work?"

"I'll find more cans. Twenty-one more!"

"You couldn't find twenty-one to begin with. That's not much of a deal. Besides, I don't have the time to wait while you prance through piles. Take us away, Sprocket."

"Aye, aye, Cap'n."

Bessie lifted from the deck of the steamboat.

"Wait!" Jed yelled. "I have another offer!"

Captain Bog held up a finger. The tug paused, a few feet in the air. The captain focused on Jed and leaned over the railing. "You have ten more seconds of my time, and then we're gone forever. Choose your words delicately."

And in that moment Jed realized why his parents had made *tuxedo* a part of SPLAGHETTI.

Spectacle. Put on a show. A magic show if you have to.

"I can make your food taste better."

The captain lifted his chin. Intrigue swirled in his eyes.

Not enough. He's going to say no.

"I'll make meals every day. They'll all be something you've never tasted before."

Captain Bog stared for another five and a half seconds.

"Time's up!" He lowered his hand. "All I hear is a bunch of scrap. Guess Kizer's right about you being a liar. I always thought you were just, you know, *misunderstood*."

The tug lifted another few feet.

Jed's face burned with heat, but he restrained his tongue. "I'm not lying."

"Easy for you to say down there."

Jed needed to add another ruffle to the tuxedo. "If the crew doesn't think my food's good enough, you can throw me overboard while the ship's in the air."

Captain Bog held up his finger again, and the sky prop slowed. He leaned against the railing with both elbows. "Is that so?" A devious grin crossed his face. "Careful what you offer. I'm not the sort of man who lets particulars of a contract slide. As I'm sure you understand."

"I'm not the type of kid who offers such particulars lightly."

"Five crew members—including myself. One vote each. You lose the vote, we toss you overboard. No matter what. No whining and squealing."

Jed's voice was steady. "No whining and squealing."

Captain Bog gave a single nod. "Toss him the ladder!" he said to no one in particular. The rope fell against the side of the ship. "Can you climb up on your own?"

Jed gathered the cans he'd collected and dumped them back into the crate. Gripping the belt loop in one hand, he climbed from the deck of the steamboat into the tug.

As his feet hit the deck, a shadow loomed over him. Kizer's face was nearly an inch from his own. The man's breaths were quick and shallow.

"I told you . . ." Kizer glared at the captain. "I said he wouldn't leave, and look. Here he is. That *freak* is a machine. Can't you see it?"

The crew looked away, pretending to be occupied with something else.

They do that a lot, Jed thought, watching Sprocket polish the tip of her shatterlance and Pobble kick absently at a bolt in the deck.

"Kizer . . ." Captain Bog rubbed his eyes. "Look at the scrape." He pointed to Jed's knee. "Bleeding like a stuck slug."

"That's not blood! It's—it's—machine oil! Colored red to trick us! He's taking us for fools! Cut deeper. You'll find gears."

"You're a good crewmate, Ki—one of the best. But you've got to drop this. That stick of a boy isn't a dread. If *that*"—he waved at Jed—"is the dread's secret weapon, then the world's in a tizzy over nothing."

"He makes you see what he wants you to see. That conniving monster isn't the helpless weakling he claims to be."

"Um . . ." Jed raised a hand. "I didn't exactly claim to be a—"

"That helpless weakling might not be here as long as you think," Captain Bog said. "He says he can win over the crew by mashing together cans and making a proper meal, or some such nonsense. We'll vote. If we like it, he stays. If we don't, we toss him overboard. Sound all right?"

"You want my vote?" Kizer asked. "I think his food tastes like scrap! And any of you who say differently will clean toilets for a month! With your tongues!"

Jed looked from Kizer to the captain. "Wait. That's not fair."

The captain shrugged. "Kizer schedules toilet duty. If he wants them to use their tongues, we'll just find breath mints next salvage. Besides, I thought we agreed—no whining, no squealing."

"But—" Before more words escaped his mouth, Jed closed his mouth. "You're right. No whining. No squealing."

For the first time ever, Captain Bog gave Jed a certain genuine nod that said something Jed could only interpret as *Well done.*

Captain Bog told Jed to wait until *Bessie* was "good and high" before he started. Riggs flooded the turbines with extra push to propel them above the white puffs of clouds.

"Until I say otherwise," Captain Bog announced, "the mess is closed. I've graciously granted Jed the opportunity to dumbfound us with something we've supposedly never tasted before. Made from cans we've all tasted before. Can't say I understand, but he's so insistent, he's bet his scrap life. I don't know about the rest of you, but it's been a while since we've had the treat of watching a man thrown overboard." The crew shouted a single cheer. "Whatever the outcome, we all win. Either this boy makes something extraordinary, or he's the evening entertainment. Sounds like a fair deal. What do you say?"

More cheers.

Captain Bog patted Jed's shoulder. "I want this runt to have all the help he needs. Plank walkers deserve a proper send-off. Let's make this a funeral party to remember!"

Jed cleared his throat. "Um . . . thanks?"

Captain Bog patted his shoulder again. "Thoughtfulness and warm hugs. Just like I said. Let's get to work! Pobble, how about a song?" He clapped his hands twice.

"I know just the tune!" Pobble said. He scurried off and returned a moment later with his fiddle. Its knob was still broken, so half the notes wobbled.

Oh, once a day or three ago, our Bessie *ran the yard,*
She found a scrawny, wimpy boy with mind to feed this
bard.

Oh, ohhhhhh!

We ate and ate and ate some more until the pot was bare,
When then he added shredded beef, potatoes, and a pear.

He filled the pot and mashed the cans and stirred them all
about,
Until the food was ready, and the men began to shout.

Oh, ohhhhhh!

We ate and ate and ate some more until the pot was dry,
Then threw the boy right to his death—and watched him
try to fly.

Sprocket clapped to the beat, and Captain Bog tapped his foot. "Now what would you like help with?" he said with enthusiasm.

Jed rolled his eyes. "Take me to the mess."

The men followed. Pobble tailed, belting out his song. At each chorus, the crew joined in—"Ohhh, we ate and ate and ate some more until the pot was bare"—then Pobble finished with a new line.

In the mess, Jed studied the cans. "How are they organized?"

"Celebration cans here"—Pobble pointed to the top shelf, with applesauce, gooseberries, cranberry sauce, mandarin oranges, maraschino cherries, and sugarcane syrup. "Cans for when you're hungry here"—he pointed to canned meats, canned beans, tuna, and chili. "Cans to eat when there's no other cans to eat"—he pointed to green chilies, tomato sauce, jalapeños, and mushrooms. "And cans you only eat in an emergency"—he indicated the artichoke hearts, spinach, anchovies, and asparagus.

If there was one word Jed loved in SPLAGHETTI, it was *artistry*.

"Get me sliced mushrooms, red peppers in oil, spinach, fire-roasted tomato halves, tomato sauce, and canned chicken."

Pobble picked up a can of spinach and cringed as if Jed had just asked him to eat it right then. "You sure? Don't you want cans off *this* shelf?" He patted the shelf of fruit and syrup.

Jed smiled. "Not today. But I'll need a frying pan."

"What's that?" Pobble asked.

"It's made of metal. About this big." Jed made a circle with his hands. "And it has a handle."

"Would a shatterkeg lid work?" Sprocket asked.

"Show me."

Sprocket took Jed to a shatterkeg porthole and rolled the gun into the ship. The shatterkeg looked like a giant-size version of Sprocket's shatterlance—with wheels. Sure enough, when the shatterkeg was inside, a black frying pan flopped closed, covering the porthole.

"Perfect," Jed said. "Now I'll need to build a fire."

"A *what*?" Captain Bog snapped. "*Fire?* On *my* ship?"

"I told you!" Kizer said. "He'll burn us to ash!"

Jed met the captain's gaze squarely. "If I don't get to whine and complain, then neither do you. I need a fire."

The crew stared at the captain. "If you say you need a fire, we'll make you a fire. But"—he held up a finger—"you try anything funny and Sprocket will put three rounds through your head before you can blink. Got it?"

"Got it," Jed said.

Sprocket cocked her shatterlance and winked at Jed. "Got it."

"Good. Riggs, make the boy a fire."

"Do you have *any* idea how hard I work *not* to make fires on this ship?"

"Make the fire," Captain Bog said. "Keep it contained."

Riggs stalked to the engine room. When he returned, he held a contraption that looked like a toaster with two bent prongs sticking out of the top. He flipped a switch, and electricity zapped between the prongs.

"I'll need something flammable," Riggs said, the words stiff in his mouth. "I don't keep flammables on board as a rule...."

"We'll hook something for you," Captain Bog said. "Sprocket, take us to hook range."

"Aye, Cap'n. Hook height it is."

They returned to the main deck, and Sprocket entered the bridge.

Jed's stomach lurched as the tugboat dropped altitude.

"I don't want this getting out of control, you hear?" the captain said.

Jed nodded. "It doesn't need to be a big fire, but I'll need it to burn for at least an hour."

"Sounds reasonable enough." The captain took a spyglass from his tattered coat, then adjusted its length and peered over the edge. "Nine degrees starboard and release the hook!"

"Releasing the hook," Sprocket said.

Something clunked below them, and a heavy chain rattled.

"Two degrees port," Captain Bog called. The tug turned. "And slow ..."

"Ready to scoop," Sprocket said.

"Open the hook. Scoop me that bathtub a quarter of a klick north, and everything around it."

"Aye, aye."

"A bathtub?" Jed asked. The chain clinked lower, and a

hydraulic opening sound filled the air. When the hook reached the bathtub, the ship jolted as hook and chain crunched into junk.

"Sprocket," Captain Bog said, folding the spyglass in on itself, "load the tub into the cargo hold and dump any scrap that won't burn."

"Yes, sir."

Jed and the others followed Sprocket to the cargo hold at the rear of the boat. The chamber was empty but for a massive five-pronged claw attached to metal links as thick as summer sausages. A wad of scooped-up junk sat clenched in its grip. The porcelain bathtub was wedged between a sofa and a phone booth.

A control box hung near Jed at the end of a cable. It had three buttons.

And one of them was red.

Not now . . . he thought, his skin prickling with sweat. *Not now* . . . He reached into his pocket and touched the lemon. *They know what they're doing. They wouldn't tell me to do this if it wasn't important.* He sucked in a breath for courage and stepped forward to grab the control box.

"Stop! Don't touch that!" Sprocket shouted.

Jed reached for the red button, but Kizer plowed into him. Jed's finger missed and squashed a black one instead.

Amber lights pulsed and sirens squealed. The cargo room floor shuddered and began to sink. Cracks of light glinted from the edges of the room, and the floor tilted—preparing to dump them from the ship into the junk below.

Sprocket bolted forward and snatched the control box. She jammed her thumb into a yellow button. The siren faded with a whine, and the floor settled back into place. "What do you think you're doing?" she yelled. "Trying to kill us?"

Pobble and Riggs stared at Jed, eyes wide as if Jed were about to lunge at them with a knife.

"I—I'm sorry. I didn't mean to."

"Do. Not. Touch things. On this ship," Sprocket said.

"I won't," Jed said. "I'm sorry."

Sprocket sighed and her shoulders relaxed. "It's fine. You just startled me. Forget about it and get your junk."

"Forget about it?" Kizer said. His voice screeched. "He just tried to kill us!"

"He would have died too, Kizer," Sprocket said. "That'd be a pretty dumb plan."

"Why would he care? His dread buddies would patch him up good as new."

Sprocket pressed a blue button on the control box. A depressurized sound filled the room, and the claw released its treasures. "Riggs, Pobble, help me with this tub," she said, pushing past Kizer, who stood waiting for a response. "We'll grab that sofa once we get this to the main deck."

Riggs and Pobble avoided Jed's eyes. *Great . . . an hour before they vote whether to throw me overboard, and everyone thinks I'm trying to kill them.*

The control box swayed on its chain, red button smiling at Jed. *Push me . . . push me,* it taunted.

Yeah, well, I tried.

Even if he went for it again, Kizer would probably shoot him over another tackle.

"You coming or what?" Pobble asked.

"Yeah." Jed pried his eyes away from the unpressed button and followed.

He hurried to the front to avoid Kizer's cold stare.

When the tub and couch were on the deck, Captain Bog pointed to the tub. "This is where you're going to build your fire."

"You want me to cook inside a bathtub?"

"Do whatever you want in it, but the fire isn't going anywhere else."

"Fine."

Captain Bog ripped off a piece of fabric from the couch and gave it to Riggs. Riggs flipped on his machine, and electricity crackled between the rods. He dipped the fabric into the arc, and the cloth burst into flames.

"Let's get started," Captain Bog said, tossing a couch cushion into the bathtub. Riggs added the burning swatch, and the cushion ignited.

Jed gathered the cooking supplies. "Do you have any salt?"

"Salt?" Sprocket said. "What do you need salt for?"

"I got some," Pobble chirped in. "Cap'n had me spray the stack for slugs two nights ago." He grabbed a leaf blower from a supply cupboard. The machine had a canister strapped to its handle. Copper hoses looped through the canister and blower.

"What is that?" Jed asked.

Pobble aimed the blower at the deck and flipped a switch.

A fan hummed, and salt sprayed from the nozzle. "Pipe cleaner. Kills slugs clogging the tubes." He reached into the canister and removed a blue container with the words MORTON IODIZED SALT over a picture of a girl in a yellow raincoat holding a white umbrella.

Jed took the canister and shook some salt into his hand. He sprinkled it over the frying pan.

"Whoa!" Kizer rushed forward to block the pan from the white crystals. "What are you doing dumping that scrap in our food?"

Jed smiled. "You're scared of a little salt?" He waggled the can.

Kizer's eyes darkened. "You think we'll let you add slug poison to our meal? I'm not stupid."

Jed pinched some grains and tossed them into his mouth. "Happy?"

"That doesn't prove anything," he said. "Your stomach's full of gears and scrap."

Pobble took the salt and poured a pile into his hand, then licked the white grains. His face contorted, and he spit onto the floor. "Uuarahahag!" He scraped his tongue with his fingernails.

Kizer's eyes went wide, and blood drained from his cheeks. "I knew it! Poison! Poison!"

"It ain't poison," Pobble said, wiping the sleeve of his shirt against his tongue. "It's disgusting!" He spit again, then shuddered. "Why you putting that in food?"

Jed turned to Kizer. "Happy?"

"I won't be happy until I watch your flailing body hit the junk!"

Jed picked up the frying pan. "Fair enough." He turned to Captain Bog. "Would you start opening cans with the tool I gave you?"

Captain Bog pulled the can opener from his pocket.

"Great. Open the red peppers in oil and the canned chicken." Captain Bog opened the cans and handed them to Jed. "I need more fuel for the fire." Riggs sliced another chunk of fabric from the couch and tossed it on the flames. "Use the couch's frame instead," Jed said. "Too much smoke with the fabric. It'll ruin the taste."

He waited for the crew to break apart the couch and add slats of wood. When the planks were crackling and the black smoke was gone, he emptied the chicken into the pan and added the red peppers and oil, making sure to coat the chunks of chicken in oil.

As he set the pan atop the flames, Pobble gasped. "You're burning our food!"

The crew stared at the flames dancing under the iron pan.

Jed grinned. "It'll be just fine."

"If you burn a dozen cans of food," the captain said, "I'll let Kizer take a few whacks at you with that pan before I toss your corpse overboard."

"What happened to no whining, no squealing?" Jed said.

Captain Bog smirked. "I suppose this is *your* funeral party. Burn away."

When the oil started to sizzle, Jed swirled the chicken until its edges were crispy and brown. "Now hand me mushrooms, spinach, and fire-roasted tomato halves."

Captain Bog sliced off the lids and gave him the cans. Jed added a quarter of the spinach, half the mushrooms, and all the tomatoes. When all the contents were finely seared, he poured in the tomato sauce and waited for it to bubble.

The crew watched in horror as Jed stirred the contents. "Does anyone have a spoon?" he asked.

Sprocket fetched a spoon, and Jed tasted the mix. He motioned for the salt and added three more pinches. When he tasted it again, he nodded.

"Is it ready?" Pobble asked, confused.

"As ready as it can be, I guess." His stomach clenched as he watched the appalled expressions. This wasn't playing out the way it had in his mind. The crew was supposed to take one whiff of the cooking food and suddenly realize how tragic their every meal had been up until this point. Probably too much to ask, but at least they weren't supposed to be so disgusted just by the preparation. A sick sensation jabbed at his stomach. He glanced at the tug's railing and pictured himself tipping over it. Falling . . . falling . . . until—

"I'll get some plates," Pobble said.

"Yeah, okay. Thanks," Jed said.

When Pobble returned, Jed scooped out a portion and handed it to Captain Bog. "Give it a try."

The captain looked confused. He opened his mouth, but no words ventured free.

"What's wrong?"

The captain eyed the wisps of steam as if they were sway-ing cobras. "It's—well—it's been in the fire. It'll burn in my mouth. I can't eat that right now."

Jed scooped a bite off the captain's plate and ate. "See? I didn't get burned. And I'm just a scrawny wimp, remember?"

The captain offered a sly smirk, then scooped up a bite of his own. He looked at each crew member, then put the spoon in his mouth and chewed.

He gazed into the sky, chewing . . . chewing. "Hmm . . ." he said finally.

Hmm? And?

Jed waited, but the captain didn't elaborate. At this, the crew lined up and shoved their plates toward the pan. As Jed served them, his heart felt like an angry lion trapped in the cage of his chest. He'd expected the captain to smile or gri-mace, or anything except *Hmm* . . .

What was it with these people and *hmm* . . . ?

Kizer refused to take a bite. Pobble shoveled food into his cheeks as fast as it would go. Sprocket poked tentatively at the chicken before testing small bits. And Riggs ate at a steady pace that didn't hint at anything.

Silence filled the deck, bothered only by clinking silver-ware and the rattling engine. Riggs spoke first. "Is there any more?" He held up an empty plate. Relief burst through Jed. He grinned and piled seconds onto the plate.

When the plates were clean, Captain Bog stood and addressed the crew. "It's time we put this to a vote."

Kizer—plate still untouched—stood. He turned the dish

vertical. Food slid to the deck, splashing at his feet. "Tastes like scrap. I vote no."

"Riggs?" Captain Bog said.

Riggs licked the rim of his plate. "Whew, I'm stuffed," he said, patting his belly. "Can't remember the last time I ate so much in one sitting."

"So is that a yes?" Captain Bog asked.

"Course not!" Riggs said, dragging his thumb along the last spot of sauce on the plate. Chin lifted and eyes closed, he sucked off the sauce and savored the flavor. "I'm with Kizer. Pile of scrap. Utter waste. Terrible. Toss the kid off the side." He looked at Jed, and his eye twitched in a mischievous wink that Jed interpreted as *This is what happens when you don't do what I ask.*

Captain Bog nodded. "Two for no and—"

"Is there any left?" Riggs asked, smacking his lips extra loud.

Captain Bog peeked inside the pan. "A few bites."

Riggs scampered to the pan and scraped the rest onto his plate.

The captain chuckled and turned to Pobble. "What's your vote?"

Pobble held his plate against his mouth, scooping up the last bits of mushroom and chicken. Tomato sauce streamed down his chin. His cheeks looked like they each held an apple. He opened his mouth, but Kizer hissed. Pobble looked over and Kizer glared, tightening his fist. Threat burned in his eyes, and his head made the slightest of shakes.

"Look at me," Pobble said, sloshing his belly with both

arms. "You think I'd turn down food that good? I'd lick a hundred toilets if I could eat like that every day." He belched, then wiped his mouth and cocked his head. "Even that burp tasted good. My vote's yes."

"Two for no, one for yes," the captain said. "Sprocket?"

She scooped up the last bit of chicken. "Yes," she said, stuffing the food in her mouth. "That's my vote."

Captain Bog nodded. "That makes two for yes and two for no."

Jed's stomach tightened. He stared at the captain, thoughts bouncing around his head like loose springs.

No. Not him. How was it down to him? Riggs was supposed to say yes, but now the captain would chuck him overboard for a bit of "evening entertainment."

Scattered thoughts pulled together in Jed's mind, and he plotted.

Sprocket's shatterbox . . . The sidearm dangled in a holster near her knee. *I can get to it,* he told himself. *Two steps. Maybe three.* He only needed a distraction. The bathtub. He could push it over, and while the crew scrambled to put out the fire, he'd get the weapon. No one would expect it.

"Scrap, huh?" Captain Bog said to no one in particular. "If this is scrap, it's the best scrap I've ever eaten. And I say Jed's sticking around to make more of it!"

14

Jed rested against the ship's railing. Stars glittered overhead. Constellations he'd never seen looped through the dark sky as horned elephants and upside-down bicycles and lemon trees in full bloom. The clean air filled his lungs with cool relief. It smelled like cedar and spot-welded metal. It was a good smell. He was alive, and he would likely stay alive for a few days.

As he gathered the dirty dishes from the bathtub, a soft red light pulsed in the darkness. He walked to the smokestack. Red glowed from the side of Captain Spyglass's head. The empty socket somehow stared at him.

"I know your secret, little boy," it said. "Such a . . . *delicious* secret. Makes you smell . . . *nice*. If Father would let me, I'd slurp up your soup in three slurps."

Jed grabbed a crate and climbed on top of it.

The face followed him.

"What secret? What are you talking about?"

It chewed on its withered lip as if itching for something to taste.

"He wants you all to himself. It's not fair. Not fair at all!"

"Who? Who wants me?"

It was then that Jed noticed that the red light was actually a small button. He reached up and pressed it. The light vanished, but nothing else happened.

"Soon," Spyglass said. "Soon."

"Soon what?" Jed asked.

The head smiled and turned away. Its gears slowed, and it fell silent.

"Hello?" He waited but it didn't look at him again. "Great. Say a bunch of cryptic scrap and then stop working. Perfect. Even some shriveled head seems to know more about me than *me*."

He walked back to the bathtub and continued scrubbing dirty dishes. Thoughts of home crept through him. The key in his shoe suddenly felt twice as irritating. He touched the lemon in his pocket. The rind was starting to stiffen. He pulled it out and scratched it, then breathed in the smell of citrus.

His passage home was buried. Lost. Forever hidden. His mom's flower-spotted aprons, the box of spices his father gave him last year . . . all of it gone. Probably forever. Every memory he had of his parents lost in a covered hole.

He stacked the clean plates and walked to the mess. The crew was asleep, but he preferred things that way. Nighttime solitude was soothing—the feeling that the whole world was sleeping while he was still awake. It felt like freedom and possibility and independence all wrapped up into one.

As he pushed open the mess-hall door with his hip, a faint creak echoed in the room, followed by a soft click. He froze, steadying the dishes so the stack wouldn't wobble. The thought of dread skulking in the darkness made his fingers cold and rigid.

The porthole on the far side of the room cast weak beams of moonlight onto the uneven deck boards. He squinted, but nothing stirred. The empty room stayed quiet as the night.

He inched inside and put the dishes into an empty barrel. When his eyes had adjusted to the darkness, he grabbed a can of black beans from the shelf and stabbed it open with a screwdriver. Black were always the best beans. He scooped out a spoonful, but before he could bring it to his mouth, something creaked below him. *Riggs?* No. Riggs had gone to the engine room.

Another creak—this one fainter than the last. And then another.

Footsteps. Small and soft.

He searched the floor and saw the outline of a trapdoor.

The trapdoor Riggs had mentioned? To the stowaway cabin . . .

The noises were delicate. Too big for rodents. Too soft for dread.

Jed set down his food. He crouched beside the trapdoor and pressed his ear to the wood. The footsteps were gone, replaced by tapping metal.

He gripped the edges of the trapdoor. The wrinkled wood was old and its hinges rusted. *Don't creak*, he begged. He held his breath and flung it open. Quick and silent.

No creak.

He crept down a dusty staircase. A cool draft flowed through the empty shell of the ship. Dim light flickered in the darkness to his right. The yellow glow revealed a crawl space between gears and engine innards.

Jed squeezed into the space. Bent pipes jutted out like ancient bones buried in the hull's mechanical graveyard. He crawled over cracked timing belts and decaying pistons to a small compartment.

The pocket of space was no bigger than his bathroom at home. Black drawings covered the walls in streaked patterns and shapes. Eyeless faces, spindly trees, a grazing rhinoceros . . . and a *lemon*. Most of the drawings were tangled scratches huddled in recognizable patterns, but the lemon was full and rich with detail. Nearly as tall as Jed, it hogged more than its share of wall. The dimpled rind looked real enough to peel.

He stepped forward and peeked inside. The room was empty except for a small girl jabbing a screwdriver against the top of a can. Her clothes were ripped but not tattered or old. Her arms were skinny but not starved, and though they were smudged with black, they weren't particularly dirty, either. A sheet of long hair hid her face. The bright strands were like spools of copper.

A thin stick—probably from a staircase railing—lay beside

her. Its tip was burned charcoal, but most of the black had been rubbed off to make the pictures on the wall.

"Hello?" he whispered.

The girl squeaked and dropped the can. She scrambled to the far corner and clutched the screwdriver with both hands.

"I'm not going to hurt you."

She squinted and cocked her head. "You're that mouse," she said. "The mouse that doesn't belong."

"Doesn't belong?"

"Of course you don't." She lowered the screwdriver and arched an eyebrow. Her face was strangely unreadable as it cycled through expressions: anxiety, suspicion, contempt, deviousness, alarm.

Jed shook his head. "No, I don't belong here. My name's Jed."

"Of course it is."

"How do you know my name?"

She rolled her eyes and released an exaggerated sigh. "I have ears, don't I?" She pinched one as if to make sure it was still there, then pulled on it and turned her head to try to see it.

Jed tried to hold back a chuckle.

"Is something funny?" She released the ear.

"No. Why?"

She tilted her head and leaned forward. "*You* know something special."

"Something special? What do you mean?"

"Of course you do. You do, don't you?"

Jed swallowed. A manic jolt buzzed in her eyes, and the

room felt a bit smaller than it had a moment ago. "What do I know?" He glanced back the way he'd come.

"How am I supposed to know? You wouldn't tell that funny mouse with glasses."

"What funny mouse with glasses? What are you talking about?"

"He told you about the hiding place." She swept her arms about the stowaway cabin. "He said he'd tell you *this* secret if you'd tell him yours. But you *didn't!*" She nearly shouted the last word, and Jed jumped, bumping his head on a pipe.

"Ouch!" He rubbed his scalp.

"So they made you fetch things for them like a dog. Arf! Arf!"

"I didn't have a choice. They wouldn't let me on the ship."

"But you didn't find the cans, did you? Bad dog!"

"What's your name?"

She smiled. "Shay."

"How did you get here?"

"I listened to Glasses Mouse."

"Are you talking about Riggs?"

She nodded. "Glasses Mouse was toooo busy watching you play fetch. So I crawled and snuck and stayed veeeeerrry quiet. . . . *Shh!*" She held her finger to her lips and grinned.

"Where did you come from?"

"The big boat."

"You mean the steamboat?"

"Was it a big boat?" she asked.

Jed nodded. "Well, yes—"

"Then the big boat."

"How long were you there for? Were you there before the dread came?"

"You mean the scritch?"

"The scritch?"

"The spindly mice that look like wicked scratches and make your skin itchy, scrawly, and scritchity!" She shivered and scratched her arms all over.

"Yes. The . . . *scritch*. Were you there before they came?"

"How else would I have gotten there, silly?"

"Then you must have known my grandpa! He was on the boat too! I was supposed to meet him, but the ship was empty. Everyone was gone."

She shook her head. "Not me. I wasn't gone."

"What happened? Did they die?"

"They died. Then they weren't dead. Because scritches *slurped* them up and patched the leftovers into new scritchlings. Then the scritch skittered away. Clickity, scratchity beasties."

Jed tried not to think about his grandfather dead—and then *not*.

So few memories of him.

A blue car seat. His wrinkly hands buckling the straps.

The memory lingered, and more details took shape. His grandfather's brittle voice as he snapped the buckles into place. *Hey there, buddy. Guess what? You're going to take a* very *special trip.* Then he threw Jed in the air, and Jed was falling . . . then floating . . . then falling again. Falling forever, it seemed. Never landing. He struggled to connect the bits of memory. *Floating in a car seat? That doesn't make sense.* They felt like slivers of a dream that seemed so real but disappeared before he could hold on to them. But as the memories trickled away, the sensations remained. Falling ... floating ... falling.

"What was his name?" Shay asked. "Your grandfather."

Her voice shattered the picture in his mind. "Huh? Oh. Um ..." The letter from his parents made him pause. *Never tell anyone your last name.*

He fought to remember Grandpa Jenkins's first name. Something odd. Something ... *"Butterfly,"* he said, remembering.

She sucked in a lungful of air, and her eyes opened wide. Her pupils were the same metallic orange as her hair.

"Captain Butterfly? Hair on his lip. Big nose. Not like you. Your nose is like a mouse's nose." She scrunched her nose together in a surprisingly accurate imitation of a mouse.

"I have a picture!" Jed showed her the photograph.

Her eyes locked onto the image. He held it closer, but she jerked back.

"Did—did you know him?" Jed asked.

Her head cocked to one side, then to the other, her eyes never leaving the image. "I—yes . . . yes. He's not nice. Not nice at all."

Jed turned the picture as if to make sure it was the right one. "What do you mean he's not nice?" The memory flashed again. Falling ... falling ... *Why was I falling?*

"Because he put me in a *tiny* cage and hit me with a pipe." She pinched her fingers together as if to show just how tiny.

A chill rushed under Jed's skin as if he'd been stabbed with an icicle. "He . . . *what?*"

Her eyes were blank as she massaged a muscle on her arm. "Whack!" Her voice snapped like broken glass. "Whack, whack, whack!" Her fists clenched and flinched each time she said the word *whack*. "Whack! Whack!"

"No. He couldn't have done something like that."

She peeked once more at the picture. "Oh yes. That's him. That's the one." Her voice was normal again, as if casually identifying an acquaintance.

"Are—are you sure?"

She studied the face. Her lips pursed, and she scratched her chin. For nearly a minute she sat like a block of stone, eyes fixed on the picture.

"Oh yes. Quite sure. Quite, quite. This one"—she tapped the picture a half-dozen times—"this one right here." A spastic shiver ran over her. "Whack, whack, *whack!*"

"But why would he do something like that?"

Her muscles relaxed, and she released a lungful of air. "To teach me. 'I'm helping you, Shay'—whack! 'This is for your own good, Shay'—whack! 'It's a brutal world, Shay. You better learn your place. Stop acting pathetic. Learn not to cry when I hit you.' Whack, whack!"

Jed's head swam and his skin hurt. He'd never thrown up in his whole life, but at her words, he suddenly wanted to. *It can't be true.*

Maybe she wasn't telling him the whole story. Maybe

she was lying. Why would she lie? Maybe she was confused. Traumatized by the attack. His mind spun. It wasn't true—it couldn't be. She wasn't telling him something. His parents had sent him to find his grandfather. They wouldn't send him to someone like that. If they trusted him, so did Jed. It would have to be enough. At least for now.

"What happened to him? Is he . . . *dead*?" The word stung.

"Not this mouse." She tapped the image. "Nope. Not dead at all. They *took* him!"

"Took him? Who took him?"

"The scritch, silly. Who else? They sometimes take *special* ones."

"Special?"

She nodded.

"Special how?"

"How would I know? I'm not a nasty scritch, silly!"

"What do they do to them? The prisoners."

"Bring them to the scritchity mouse king!"

"Who's the scritchity mouse king?"

She twisted her expression into a sour look. "Mouse king of the junkyard. I don't like him, either. He hurts mice. Flies around in his big, fancy boat and thinks he owns the whole world. Well, he *doesn't*!"

Jed flinched as she yelled the last word. "Shh." He held his finger to his lips. "Why did he take my grandfather and leave everyone else?"

"Why does the mouse king take anyone?"

Jed waited for the answer. "I don't know," he said.

"Hmm," she said. "I don't know either. He didn't take me. He left me. Left me for dead. Left me to get slurped up by wicked little scritchlings."

"But you didn't get slurped up."

Shay checked each arm, then each leg. "Nope."

"How did you escape?"

"Sneaky . . . like a *mouse!*" Shay twirled a piece of copper hair in her finger.

"I need to find him," Jed said. "My grandfather. Do you know where the scritch mouse king is?"

"On his fancy boat, of course. The *Red Galleon.*"

"The *Red Galleon?* Where's that?"

"It's where they took Captain Butterfly."

"Yes, I know—but *how* can I find my grandfather?"

Shay shrugged. "You should ask the scritchity mouse king. I bet he'll know." She nodded to herself. "Because he *took* him!" she added, as if Jed couldn't piece that part together.

"Right. But I don't know where the scritchity mouse king *is.*"

"I already told you, he's on the *Red Galleon.*"

Jed's jaw clenched. He spoke slowly so he wouldn't sound as frustrated as he felt. "But where is the *Red Galleon?* How can I find it?"

She glanced at his hands and curiosity glittered in her eyes. "What's that?" She pointed at his watch.

"What is what?" He turned his wrist to obscure the watch.

"That!" She scampered over on all fours. "That, that!" She

grabbed his wrist. Her skin was cool and soft and hugged the bones in her fingers like a tight sheath. "That, that, that!" She tapped incessantly on the glass face.

"I don't know. It was a gift."

She sucked in a delighted breath and clapped her hands. "I know, I know! I know what it is! You're so lucky. It's so pretty. So, so pretty."

Excitement rushed through Jed. "You know what this is?"

She nodded and didn't stop nodding. "Yes, yes."

"What is it?"

"You don't know?"

"I already told you, *I don't know*." His voice was tight with frustration.

She stopped clapping and scowled. "You don't have to be rude." She folded her arms in front and pouted.

"I'm sorry. I just really need to know. This was the last thing my parents left me. They said it was important."

"Oh, it *is* important. *Very* important. And pretty."

"Can you tell me what it is?"

"Yes, I can."

Jed waited. "Okay, can you tell me now?"

"Yes."

"Soooo . . ."

She smiled at him. "Yes?"

"So, what *is* it?" he asked.

She cupped her hand to her mouth and whispered into his ear. "Relic junk."

Jed nodded. "That's what Riggs said. What is relic junk?"

"Old junk."

"Why is relic junk important?"

"It does things."

"What kind of things?"

"Lots of kinds of things. All different kinds of things."

Jed clenched his fists. Shay was tougher to interrogate than a trained operative. "What specifically?" he said through gritted teeth.

"Well . . ." She cocked her head. "Captain Butterfly had a spyglass that could see lies."

"Lies?" He infused the word with as much skepticism as he could manage.

"Mm-hm." She nodded as if not catching the disbelief in his tone. "And I've seen a music box that can put men to sleep. Wind it, wind it, wind it, then *bam*—asleep."

"That doesn't sound possible."

"Of course it's possible. I saw it with my own two eyes." She touched each of her eyelids.

Jed looked at his watch—at the six unmoving hands. "Then what does this one do?"

Her right eyebrow flicked. A knowing look aged her twenty years. But the look faded as quickly as it had come. "It could make you mouse king of the junkyard. The biggest mouse— bigger mouse than the scritchity mouse king."

15

"**B**efore the steamboat," Jed started, "I heard the crew mention something about gilded relics."

"Ooooh . . ." Shay said. "Yes, yes. The prettiest of *all* the pretties!"

Jed touched the watch. "Is this one of them?"

"Ha!" She giggled uncontrollably for barely a second or two. "Silly mouse! Of course not! It's so small. How could it be when it's so tiny? No, no, no."

"Then how could it make me king of the junkyard?"

"Learn how to read it."

"It doesn't work. None of the hands move."

"Not yet. They move when they're ready."

"When?"

"Look for yourself. They'll tell you when."

Jed stared at the symbols. "I can't read them."

"Then you won't be mouse king, will you?"

"Can *you* tell me?"

She shook her head. "Glasses Mouse can."

"Riggs? How do you know?"

She held her hands to her eyes as if they were spectacles. "Glasses, glasses, everywhere. Only clever mice wear glasses. And he has *lots* of glasses. He must be *extra* clever. But if he finds out what it does, he'll *take* it from you, and Ugly Mouse will be mouse king."

"Ugly Mouse?" Shay screwed up her face and made scratching motions on her cheeks. "Oh." Jed smiled. "Captain Bog?"

She nodded.

"How do you know he'll take it?"

"Because I know what it does."

"Then tell me. How does it make someone mouse king?"

She scrunched her lips and studied Jed. "I don't know what kind of mouse you are. What if you're a bad mouse? If I tell you, you'll be mouse king. I don't want another bad mouse king."

"Another?"

"The scritchling mouse king is a very bad mouse king. He makes disobedient mice drink the same oil his engines drink. And then he watches them gurgle their last squeak."

Jed cringed. "That's horrible." He pictured Shay held prisoner, forced to drink oil.

He studied her. How could he convince her to tell him?

He'd always been skilled at bartering or convincing people to help him, but he didn't understand this girl. Nothing about her made sense. If he pushed too hard, she wouldn't trust him.

"You're right," he said. "I don't want a bad mouse king either. You don't have to tell me yet. You can wait to get to know me."

Her eyes turned suspicious. "Don't try to trick me, little mouse."

The quirkiness that had laced her voice was gone. When she said *little mouse*, she wasn't the odd girl anymore. She was someone in control—threatening, even.

"I wouldn't try to trick you."

"Because I have relics of my own," she said in the same serious voice. "I know when I'm being lied to. Don't lie to me, little mouse."

Jed wanted to back into a corner. "No. Of course not. I won't lie to you."

A sneaky grin crept through her cheeks. "I like you. Maybe you'd make a good mouse king. But we'll have to wait and see, won't we?" She tapped his nose with her index finger.

"Um, okay. Well I should probably let you get to sleep, then. Can I get you anything before I go?"

"Do you have a can slicer?" She raised the dented can she'd been trying to open.

"Fresh out."

"That's okay. Good night, little mouse." She smiled, then picked up the screwdriver and started tapping the lid of the can.

"Good night."

He looked again at the charcoal art on the wall and thought about lemons. He wondered if this one had anything to do with the lemons in SPLAGHETTI.

As he returned to the mess, he realized Captain Bog hadn't told him where to sleep. He wandered the decks, searching for a room. There weren't any, so he returned to the mess and lay on the hard floor.

The evening wasn't cold, but the room was drafty from the cracks in the trapdoor. He wrapped his arms around himself and curled into a ball. He was asleep before he had time to shiver.

. . .

Jed awoke to a rubber sole pressing his cheek into his nose. He pushed Captain Bog's boot away from his face. "Stop kicking me," he said, rubbing his eyes.

"Kicking?" Captain Bog drew back his leg and whacked Jed's sternum.

Air seized in Jed's chest. "What—are—you—doing?" he said between strained breaths.

"Kicking you."

Jed coughed and hunched over. "Why?"

"So you know what kicking's like. You seemed a bit confused about it." The pain trickled away, and Jed glared. "See you found a nice place to set down for the night."

"Yeah." Twinges of pain nipped at Jed's chest. "Thanks for that."

"Where's breakfast?" Captain Bog took his new can slicer from his coat pocket and handed it to Jed.

Jed took the can slicer and gathered peaches, blackberries, and sweetened condensed milk. "I need another fire," he said.

"You going to need one for every meal?"

"Most of the time."

"Hmm."

"Are you hungry or not?"

The captain tapped his chin. "You win. I'll have Riggs scorch up the left arm of that sofa."

Jed searched for the plates he'd washed last night, but they were gone.

The crew was waiting on the top deck around the charred bathtub. Every man but Kizer was holding a plate.

"What are you going to make?" Pobble asked, licking his lips.

Jed held up the berries and sweetened condensed milk. "A little treat."

"Get the bathtub fired up, Riggs," the captain said.

But Riggs was already tossing planks of wood into a pile.

"Not too hot this time," Jed said. He opened the sweetened condensed milk and emptied it into the pan. "Hold this over the heat," he said, handing the pan to Sprocket.

"Umm . . ." Sprocket's arms were stiff and her wide-eyed expression hesitant.

Jed rolled his eyes. "You'll be fine."

She stood as far from the fire as possible while still allowing flames to lick the pan.

Jed stirred the liquid with a spoon. He opened the berries

and drained their syrup into one bowl and added the fruits to another.

"Jed, Jed!" Sprocket called. "Something's happening!"

Bubbles lifted from the basin of the pan and popped at the surface. "I can take over."

Sprocket gave him the pan and relaxed as if her whole body had been flexed.

Jed jiggled the pan. "Oh, it wasn't *that* bad."

Sprocket raised an eyebrow that said, *Yes. Yes it was.*

Jed slowly stirred the milky liquid.

"Nothing's happening," Pobble said.

"It'll take a while. You might want to come back later." But no one left. Everyone stared at the milk as Jed stirred.

Many silent minutes later, the liquid started to brown. Jed lifted the pan and kept stirring.

"What's going on?" Sprocket asked.

"I'm making caramel."

The liquid thickened, and a rich amber bled through its center. Pobble sniffed the air above the pan.

Jed pulled out the spoon, and gooey caramel stretched to its tip. "It's done." He scooped the caramel into a bowl and set it next to the fruit. "Enjoy." He brushed his hands together.

"How do we eat it?" Sprocket asked.

Jed took a blackberry and dipped it into the caramel. He held it for the others to see, then tossed it into his mouth. The crew shuffled forward, snatching berries and dunking them into the creamy pool. Even Captain Bog shouldered his way past Pobble and Riggs to the bowls.

"Hey!" Sprocket shouted. "You're taking too much! You've had plenty."

"No, *you've* had plenty!" Riggs said. "Get out of my way!"

"You keep cooking like this and we'll have a mutiny on our hands," Captain Bog said.

A whisper sounded in Jed's ear. He jumped at its tickle against his skin. "That's exactly what you want, isn't it?" Kizer said.

Jed spun around. "Would you leave me alone already?"

"You want me to leave you alone?" Kizer peeked over the side of the boat. "Then take a dive and I won't say another word."

"I'll pass."

"Thought so."

"Why don't you have some breakfast?" Jed smirked.

Kizer turned and stalked off.

Sprocket reached for another peach slice, and Captain Bog smacked her hand to snatch the fruit away. He tossed it into his mouth and licked his fingers. "Golden Boy, I'm officially promoting you to ship's can masher. Congratulations."

"As long as I am not the only one looking for cans every time we land."

"Don't you mean *find*? Because I'm pretty sure you *looked* for cans last time. We need to work on your *finding* skills. That's why the rest of the crew will look *with* you from now on. Sound reasonable?"

"Sounds reasonable."

Captain Bog gave a small smile and turned back to the bowl of fruit.

Which was now empty.

"Hey, Golden Boy," he said, "what's for lunch?"

"Lunch?"

"Yes. It's the name of a meal. One that comes before dinner and follows breakfast. That's how it works between the fringe and the fog, at least. What about your glittertale Denver? Do folk have lunch there?"

"Thanks for the explanation. I had no idea what *lunch* was. But now that I've had a vocabulary lesson, I feel so much smarter. You realize that, by your definition, *lunch* comes *between* breakfast and dinner, yes? Not right after breakfast."

"Ship's can masher probably wasn't the most accurate title. It probably should be ship's can masher who mashes cans slower than a salted slug with belly rot climbing a frozen wall upside down on its back using only its face."

"That sounds like one pretty incredible slug," Jed said.

"I'm not bad-mouthing our little slug's efforts. It's doing a clunk better job than expected. But by the time our slug scrubs the dishes, washes the deck, cleans the fire tub, and mashes more cans, it'll be time to start again for dinner. What do you think?"

Jed gave the captain a confused look. "Wait a second . . . that slug with belly rot can mash cans? I thought it was just climbing a wall."

The captain laughed once. "And if it doesn't climb fast enough . . . it just might fall off." He picked up a deck rag and tossed it to Jed. "Best get scrubbing."

16

As Jed gathered dishes and returned to the mess, he noticed the red light again, blinking on Spyglass's head.

What are you up to?

Once again he dragged the crate to the stack and pressed the button. The light shut off. Nothing else happened.

He walked into the mess while the crew scrabbled for the last remains of the caramel. He emptied the dishes into a basin and opened the spigot on a water barrel to let them soak.

The cabin below was silent. Shay was perfectly quiet.

Once the crew had returned to their duties, Jed opened the stowaway panel and climbed inside.

Shay was scraping the last of her charcoaled nubs into another picture of a lemon.

"Why the lemons?" Jed asked.

"Lemons are happy. Don't you think?" she said.

"They're actually my favorite."

She paused and looked excitedly at him. "Yes! They should be *everyone's* favorite! I wish I had one right now. No lemons around here."

Jed pulled out the lemon in his pocket.

Shay scrambled over and pressed her nose into the rind. "Mmmmm . . . so nice. So yellow. Yellow smells the best of *all* the colors."

"You've seen one of these before? I thought the junkyard didn't have trees."

She giggled. "Of course I have, silly. It's a rather big mouseyard, wouldn't you say?"

"I wouldn't know. I haven't been to many places."

"Oh, well . . ." She leaned close to his ear as if sharing a secret. "It's a *rather* big mouseyard."

"That must make it hard to find things."

"What things? I'm the best at finding things! What are you looking for?"

"My grandfather."

"That's easy. He's on the *Red Galleon*. It *took* him."

"And if *you* looked for the *Red Galleon*, where would you go?"

"Why would I do that? I don't want to be taken too! That doesn't sound like fun at all. Not at all."

Jed rubbed his eyes. "I know. But I'm trying to find my grandfather. If he's on the *Red Galleon*, that's where I need to look."

"Does he hit you with pipes too?"

Jed winced. "I haven't seen him since I was a baby."

Shay tapped her chin. "Maybe he doesn't hit baby mice with pipes. I've never seen him do it, at least. But you're not a baby anymore, so maybe *now* he'll hit you with a pipe!"

"Maybe he won't. Maybe he'll be nice. But I won't know if I can't find him. So if you could just tell me—"

"Yes!" Shay said, excitement filling her eyes. "If you never find him, you'll never find out! Very well, I agree."

"Agree with what?"

"That we should never, ever, never look for mean mice that hit not-baby mice with pipes."

"No, that's not what I—" Before Jed could finish, footsteps clomped down the steps to the lower decks. "I have to go. Someone's coming. Stay quiet."

"Quiet like a sleepy lemon."

"Exactly."

Jed hurried back to the mess and shut the hatch just as the mess door opened.

Captain Bog eyed the still-dirty plates.

"See? What did I tell you? At the rate you work, you won't have lunch finished until dinner."

"What do you want?" Jed asked.

"Lunch. But that might not happen for another day or two."

"Captain!" Sprocket shouted. "Schooner's one scope and closing!"

He turned around and walked back to the main deck.

Jed followed.

White ship sails sliced through a puffy cloud ahead and turned toward them.

"Riggs!" the captain called.

"Aye, sir?"

"The tinker's schooner is five minutes away. Do you have our inventory log ready?"

"Aye." Riggs removed a leather book from one of his pockets. "Here."

The captain stuffed the log into his own pocket.

"Might I remind you—" Riggs began.

The captain nodded before he could finish. "I know. I know. Defluxor core. Death and regret. Pobble gave me the message."

Jed gripped the tug's railing and squinted at the ship. "What's going on?"

"Kizer," the captain said, "assemble the crew. When we land, scout for cans. Negotiations shouldn't take longer than an hour, but I want everyone back in half that time for loading."

"Loading what?" Jed asked. "Where is everyone going?"

"*You* aren't going anywhere," Captain Bog said. "I want my lunch. Can a salted slug with belly rot make lunch in five minutes?"

"If I remember, the slug was climbing up a wall backward using only its face, right? Compared to that, a five-minute lunch is easy."

"Get it done." He turned to the rest of the crew. "Golden Boy will make the rest of you slugs lunch after we're finished here."

Pobble scowled and held his belly in both arms as if it were a weeping baby.

Jed tapped him on the shoulder. "What's a tinker?"

"He's . . . he's the *tinker*," Pobble said. "You know, for trading goods?"

"Like a store?"

"Sure. Like a store but with better stuff."

Jed hurried to the mess and grabbed ham, hominy, and green chilies. The tub still had coals from the morning, so he heated up the skillet and made a hasty potatoless hash. By the time he finished, the white schooner was almost touching *Bessie*.

The ship had a sleek, expensive look, like the kind of ship the rich hero sails into the sunset at the end of a movie. The triangular sails were clean and bright white. Sunlight glowed against them, giving an angelic touch.

"You're coming with me," Captain Bog said.

Jed thought of Shay. This would be a perfect time to ask her more questions. "Why don't I just get started on dinner for the crew?"

"Ha! You think I'm going to leave a kid *alone* on *my* ship? Especially one who needs just such a ship to stroll around looking for his missing grandpop? I don't think so."

"You think I'd steal the tugboat? I can't even drive a car! What makes you think I can fly a boat using a bicycle handlebar and a wrench?"

"I have no idea what you just said, but it doesn't matter. You're coming with me. End of discussion. And bring my lunch."

Jed followed the captain to the edge of the ship where the schooner approached. Captain Bog tied the boats' railings together.

The captain snatched the plate of food and pointed to the schooner. "After you."

Jed climbed the railing and hopped to the schooner.

Planks of clean wood and metal paneled the deck in a tidy design. It was still a hodgepodge of junk, but each strip of material either matched or complemented the others.

By the time Jed turned around, the captain had finished his food. He tossed the plate overboard and waved Jed forward. "Over here."

The schooner's helm was a four cushion–wide sofa behind polished metal levers and pedals. The white leather cushions looked pristine and even had a new-leather scent.

A man—probably the tinker—stood from the couch. Everything about him was somehow disproportioned. Waist too high. Belly too round. Hands too wide. Arms too thin. Eyes too beady.

"Ah, if it aint the mitey cap'nbog," the tinker said.

The words came out in a jumbled heap.

"Good to see you," Captain Bog said. "Looks like trade's well."

"Bin doonjus fin thankye."

"Good to hear."

"Howstha roadbin longthaway?"

"Fine. Haven't seen trouble since Brillagate."

"Goodgood," the tinker said.

Jed perked up. Something he understood.

"Got meself plintee of chrezures ijus noyool luv."

"Wonderful. Shall we conduct business, then?"

The tinker nodded and waved them to an open staircase. "Goodgood."

The cargo hold wasn't much different from the junkyard. Perhaps more organized. The rows and rows of gears and gadgets made Jed think of the Home Depot. Some looked like they belonged on one of Sprocket's shatterlances; others looked like engine-room parts. There were crates of springs, ball bearings, and sheets of glass.

The tinker babbled on, his lips barely moving as he spoke. Captain Bog nodded and pointed here and there and asked about Riggs's defluxor core.

They talked for nearly a half hour. Well, the captain talked, at least. Jed still didn't know *what* the noises from the tinker were. He picked up a bolt the size of a breadstick.

The tinker glanced at him. He was about to look away when he froze. His too-big eyebrows scrunched into a bush. "Sthat wat ithink itis?" He pointed at Jed's watch.

Jed dropped the bolt. It clanged against the floor. He twisted his wrist to hide the watch's face.

Not again.

Captain Bog rocked back and forth, trying to see.

"Answer the man," he said to Jed.

"Answer him what? I don't know what he said."

"Isthat boy def er sumpin?"

"Nah, not deaf . . ." Captain Bog said. "Just a straggler who can't seem to hear a scrap thing I tell him." He walked over and slapped Jed's shoulder with the crushing weight of his palm.

"Ah itsnot a bituva wury. But ayestill wantano. Wut thatbe theron isrist?"

Captain Bog squeezed. "Start talking."

"I—I can't understand him," Jed whispered.

"You keep acting like a fool, I'll toss you down to the piles. Understand *that*? Tell him what's on your wrist."

Jed squirmed. "Just something my parents gave me."

"Thochu said eewaz a straggler?"

"I *did* say he was a straggler. Found him stranded."

"Thenwats he doon withat?" The tinker poked his finger at Jed's wrist three more times.

"Jed? Tell the tinker what you're doing with whatever you've got there."

"I'm not doing anything with it." He clutched the copper band so tightly it dug into his wrist. "My parents gave it to me."

"You said that already. Bring it over here; let's have a look."

"I—I'd prefer not to."

Captain Bog's eyes burned. He slowly lifted one eyebrow. "Bring. That. Watch. Here. Now. *Please*."

Jed swallowed and stepped forward. The tinker grabbed his arm and yanked him closer. He held Jed's wrist an inch from his eye.

"Whcha wantfer this?"

"It's not mine to offer," Captain Bog said. "I couldn't say a price."

The tinker spoke slowly for the first time. "Try me."

"Ask the boy. It's his," Captain Bog said. "How much you want for that watch?"

"It's not for sale," Jed said.

Captain Bog shrugged. "Guess it's not for sale, then."

The tinker's grip tightened. "But—but—" he stammered. "Lisnere boy. Ilpay ya twntee thowsnd btries."

"Twenty thousand batteries?" Captain Bog's jaw sank. "For *that?*" He snatched Jed's wrist and reached for the clasp.

Jed yanked away. "I said it wasn't for sale." He covered it with his other hand.

"Jed." Captain Bog patted the air with his hands as if Jed were holding a human hostage instead of a wristwatch. "I don't think you heard what he's offering."

"I heard. I don't care. This isn't for sale."

"You don't understand." Captain Bog's breathing turned deep and labored. "Our scrap tug isn't even worth twenty thousand batteries. It's not worth ten!"

"No."

"Thaboy aintno straggler."

"What do you mean he's no straggler?"

"Whakinda straggler walksroundwith a relk?"

"A *what?*" Captain Bog's voice cracked in the air. "A *relic?* You brought a relic onto my ship?" The scars around his eyes drew together. "Who are you and where did you get that?"

"I'm not a thief!" Jed yelled so loud the tinker flinched. "I'm tired of being accused of stuff I didn't do!" He took a breath and started over, lowering his voice. "I'm only going to say this once more. My parents. Gave me. This watch. I didn't steal it. I don't know what it does. They left it for me with a note that said to never take it off. Ever. And now they're gone—lost. I don't know if they're in prison. Or if they're dead. You think I want to be here? I don't!" His voice felt like fire. "This is a nightmare, and there's nothing I can do about it! So, no! I'm not selling the only piece of scrap I have left of my parents!"

Something glinted in Captain Bog's eyes. Something sincere. Empathetic. "I guess that's your answer," he said to the tinker. "The watch is out."

"Jusripitoff isrist antoss himoverboard!" The tinker spit at Jed.

Captain Bog shook his head. "I'm not a thief either. That's not how I do business."

"Idun karbout nonthat! Brinmee that relk—er . . . er . . . er tha deelsoff!" His shiny forehead was slick with sweat and red as a cherry tomato.

"I don't know what to tell you. It's not mine to trade. If the boy won't sell it, there's nothing I can do."

The tinker's cheeks lit up in a splotchy red to match his forehead. He stamped his foot. "Youdont do sumpin bout this, I wontever tradewithyou nevergain! An iltell evry tinkr ta doothasame!"

Captain Bog grabbed the man by his throat. The force

rippled through the tinker as the captain slammed him against the nearest wall. The tinker's belly bobbled up and down. "Do I seem like someone you can threaten?"

The tinker tried to speak, but only squeaks of air escaped. He shook his head.

Captain Bog tossed him to the floor. "I've always been fair with you. Treated you right. Paid more than I should on occasion." He squatted beside the tinker. "You ever threaten me again, I'll burn your ship to scrap. How about you tell the other tinkers *that*?"

The tinker held his throat and stared at the floor.

"Okay, then. Sounds like things are all wrapped up here." He slapped a box of screws off a shelf, sending them sprawling across the floor. "Let's go, Jed. We're done."

They walked up the stairs and hopped back to the tug. The captain unlashed the ropes and shoved the schooner's railing. It floated away lazily.

Jed touched his watch. "Thank you."

Captain Bog lifted an eyebrow. "Thank you? For what? Not smacking around some kid and stealing his toy?"

"Um, I guess?"

Captain Bog released a weary breath. "You realize what just happened?"

"I know. I'm sorry I messed up the trade. I know how important it must have been."

"You do?" The captain folded his arms. "Enlighten me."

"Um, well, I guess you need supplies to fix up the ship and . . ."

"And?"

"I don't know."

"I didn't think so. Remember the defluxor core Riggs was whining about? It's not something you find lying around. And it's not *cheap*. This was the first tinker in a month who had one at a price we could afford. So when we're plummeting in a burning fireball of death and regret, remember who put us there."

"I'm sorry. I wish there was something I could do."

"There is. You're wearing it."

"Oh, right. I mean . . ."

"Stop babbling empty apologies to make this less uncomfortable. It's uncomfortable. *Very* uncomfortable. And how comfortable will it get when the crew hears? How about when falcons and wasps are hunting this scrap tug because some petty tinker told them what we had on board?"

Jed looked at the deck. "I don't know what to say."

"You say, 'Sorry I'm a scrawny, incompetent fool, Captain,' and then shut up."

"I'm sorry I'm a scrawny, incompetent fool, Captain."

The captain knocked the side of Jed's head with his palm.

"You and I aren't done. I can't just unhear what I heard back there."

"I know."

"And if the crew finds out? Well . . . I might be able to stop a weak, lazy tinker, but I wouldn't bet half a battery on your life against my crew. You understanding what I'm saying?"

"Yes."

"Good. When we get going again, we're having a little chat. And bring that fancy clunk with you."

The crew was lined up on the deck, awaiting direction.

Kizer clasped his hands behind his back. "The storeroom's cleared out, ready for supplies. Sprocket and I will load trades to the schooner while Pobble and Riggs haul in the new cargo. Let's be quick and efficient. No mistakes this time. We don't have time to waste."

Pobble stood on his toes and stared over Kizer's shoulder. "Uh, where's the tinker going?"

The others turned.

"Stop!" Kizer shouted. "What is the tinker doing?"

Captain Bog cleared his throat. "Deal didn't go through."

"What do you mean it didn't go through?" Kizer asked.

"No trades today." The captain tossed the supply-list book back to Riggs.

Riggs thumbed through the pages. "But—but what about my list?" he said. "What about the defluxor core? And I need a half-dozen capacitors, steel bulkhead paneling, microgenerators, and copper tubing!"

"I'm aware of that, Riggs."

"We're running an illegal T-five engine block! We can't just shop for those parts at a township! We won't see another tinker for a month—at least!"

"Then keep our girl flying for another month."

"That's what you said last month. And the month before that. And—"

"And look how good a job you're doing. Sprocket," the

captain said, dismissing Riggs's frantic eyes, "get *Bessie* moving. Everyone else, back to whatever you should be doing. I need to speak to Jed in my quarters. We're not to be disturbed."

"*You!*" Kizer jabbed a finger at Jed. "This is *your* fault? You slimy little scab-faced slug! I'm going to tear your scrap skin from those scrawny limbs and boil it in your own blood!"

"Enough, Ki," Captain Bog said, though the words sounded less than halfhearted. "Jed, with me. Now."

At least Kizer said blood, Jed thought, *instead of* red-dyed machine oil.

"In." Captain Bog pointed to his quarters. Then, as he had before, Captain Bog pointed to the sofa. "Sit."

Jed sat and the captain stood, fists on his hips. "I've always had bad luck with stragglers, but against my better judgment, I let you keep your watch. A junkstorm hit Skova not four days ago, and I told the crew we'd be digging there in three hours. But without supplies? We won't be doing digging anywhere! I've lost a fresh dig, a month's supplies, and the confidence of my crew. I'm not a thief, so I don't regret what I did. But that said, you'll tell me everything. Right now."

"I told you, I—"

"I know what you said. And I believe you. But I'm not being told everything. You get one last chance to come clean with *everything*. If you're lying or leaving out one scrap detail, I'll throw you on the tinker's schooner faster than you can fall off a ladder. I was decent to trust you—even saved you from that vulture. Now be square with me."

Jed nodded. "Okay. I did come from under the fringe. That

wasn't a lie. Rain from the sky, wood that grows fruit—all of that was true." The captain eyed the painting of the woman. "My parents went missing, and they left me this watch and a letter that said to never take it off."

"You said that already. What else?"

"I'm getting there. When I met Riggs, he knew the watch was relic junk. I said I didn't know what it was. And then . . ."

He paused and looked at the floor.

I can't mention Shay. He'll kill her—he'll throw her off the ship.

"And then what?"

"I found out more."

"How?"

"I—I can't tell you."

"You want to go back to the schooner? You know what that tinker will do?"

"Steal my watch."

"And?"

"Kill me?"

"Why would he kill you when he could sell you to a scrap pit as a digger?"

Jed winced. "I can't be responsible for hurting this person."

"You mean one of my crew?"

"If I tell you, promise not to hurt them."

"I deal with my crew how I want. That's not your concern."

"What if it's not your crew?"

"What are you babbling about? I've had my eye on you since you stepped foot on this ship. You haven't talked to anyone else."

"Then it should be an easy promise. Swear that you won't hurt them or leave them stranded."

"No. You talk, or my knuckles will get real touchy-feely with your face."

"I can't," Jed said. "Do what you have to, but I'm not going to let someone else get hurt because of me."

Captain Bog drew back his arm. *You can take it,* Jed told himself. *You've been through worse.* A memory flashed in his mind of when he'd had to cut open his own arm to drain a bubbled infection, sterilize and bandage the wound, then swim along a saltwater channel. The sting from the salt water still haunted him.

The captain's fist flexed, then relaxed, then flexed again. "Fine. You have a deal. Now talk."

Jed's shoulders relaxed. "When we were on my grandpa's steamboat, there was a girl. She survived the wreck."

The captain chuckled. "You think I'd fly back there to beat up a girl?"

"She's not exactly on the steamboat anymore."

"She's *what*?"

"Remember—you agreed."

Captain Bog straightened and his fingers flexed again. "A stowaway?"

"She snuck on board while the crew was searching the wreckage. She's scared."

"I don't care! *No one* sneaks onto *my* ship!"

"Do you want answers or not?"

The captain glowered. "Keep talking."

"She recognized the watch. She knows what it does, but she wouldn't tell me. She said it could . . ." Jed knew the next words would sound ridiculous.

"Could what?"

"Could make someone king of the junkyard. More powerful than the king of the dread."

Jed waited for a scoff or a laugh. But the captain just looked at the watch as if his eyes were scalpels dissecting a specimen.

"Like a gilded relic or something?"

"She didn't think so. But she said Riggs could read it."

"Riggs? Why Riggs?"

"Something about his glasses. I'm not sure. She's sort of odd."

Captain Bog walked out of his cabin. "Sprocket!"

"Aye, Cap'n?"

"Send Riggs to my quarters, now!"

"Aye, Cap'n!"

Feet pattered down the bridge staircase and then down to the lower decks. A minute later, two sets of footsteps returned.

"Get in here," the captain called.

Riggs entered and stood at attention. "Yes, Captain?"

"Sit down. I want you to look at something." Jed scooted to one side of the couch. Captain Bog opened a porthole window and light pooled in.

Jed held out his hand.

A grin stretched along Riggs's face. "Well, now . . . well, well, well . . ."

The captain loomed over them. "What is it?"

"It's a—"

"And don't say 'relic,'" the captain interrupted. "We already know that."

"Ah . . . yes . . . well . . ."

"Is it a gilded relic?"

Riggs nearly snorted. "Not even close."

"Then what?" the captain asked. "Apparently you're the one who's supposed to know."

"Me? Why me?"

The captain released an irritated sigh. "You don't know scrap about it, do you?" He glared at Jed. "You told me—"

"She didn't say that he'd know *what* it was," Jed interrupted, "only that he could read it."

"What? Who are you talking about?" Riggs said.

The captain pointed at the watch. "Read it, Riggs. What does it say?"

Riggs studied the face. "The clock numbers are obvious. But look here and here."

Jed and Captain Bog nearly collided to hunch over the device. Riggs touched the red symbols.

"What are they?" Captain Bog asked.

Riggs tilted his head one way then the other. He pulled off his glasses, then found a red-lensed pair. "Township symbols. They're old. But definitely townships. Look. The silver hands point to this township in this sector." He touched the symbols, then switched to a new pair of glasses. "The black hands indicate the time."

Captain Bog shook his head. "But they're not moving."

"No." Riggs took off his glasses. "They're not."

"She said the hands would move when they're ready," Jed added.

At his words, Captain Bog perked up. "It shows a time and place, yes?" Riggs nodded. Enchantment glittered in the captain's eyes. "It's a treasure map."

The three stared in silence at the watch.

And then the hands began to spin.

17

The six hands slowed and settled into place.

New symbols.

New township.

New time.

"Where is that?" Captain Bog asked. "What does it say?"

Riggs swapped glasses. "Dawndrake territory. Seventh sector. Eight o'clock."

The captain pulled a chained watch from his coat.

"Eight in the morning or eight at night?" Jed asked.

"It's already past eight," the captain said. "Must be evening." He stuffed the watch into his pocket and strode from the quarters. "Sprocket! New heading!" Jed and Riggs followed.

"Where to, Cap'n?" Sprocket asked.

"How close are we to Dawndrake?"

"Ten hours, maybe more."

The captain checked his watch again. "And if we run hot?"

Riggs shook his head. "Without those replacement capacitors, I can't burn *Bessie* past forty percent for a ten-hour cruise. She can sprint ninety-five percent for three, maybe four minutes. Then the engines will fail. Then we'll explode. Then we'll plummet and hit the junk, where we'll explode again."

"Okay. I get it. What will forty percent get me?" Captain Bog asked.

"Nine hours."

"Sounds about right," Sprocket said.

"Nine hours, then. Let's get moving."

Riggs and Sprocket headed off in opposite directions.

Kizer marched over. "Sir? Dawndrake is in the opposite direction of Skova! What about the dig site?"

"Change of plans. Seems we might have ourselves a treasure map."

"A *what*?"

"Jed here—"

Kizer's face tightened. "So it's *Jed* now? What happened to Golden Boy?"

"I'm hoping he turns out to be a golden boy."

"He's getting inside your head! If that piece of scrap's telling us where to go, it's a trap."

"Sprocket!" the captain shouted. "Make sure the shatter-kegs are charged. Just in case."

"Aye, Captain!"

The captain looked at Kizer. "Better?"

"This tug couldn't defend herself against a broken wasp using slugs as shatterkeg fire, let alone a full dreadnought!"

Captain Bog frowned and patted a loose plank in a nearby wall. "He doesn't mean that, sweetheart. Just a bit upset is all."

Kizer rolled his eyes. "Captain, we can't—"

"Ki"—Captain Bog held up a hand—"leave it. We're going to Dawndrake."

"Yes, sir." Kizer nodded, but the muscles in his neck were stiff and the motion was awkward.

"Jed," the captain said, once out of earshot of the crew, "take me to the stowaway."

Jed's stomach clenched. Shay was probably alone in her corner, trying to open another can of food.

"Remember that you agreed to—"

"If you remind me what I agreed to once more, I might just have to forget. Now go."

Jed walked down the stairs to the mess. "I should go alone. I don't want to spook her."

"Two minutes—then I'm coming down."

Jed scrambled into the innards of the ship. *Not like the captain could fit between the pipes down here anyway.*

Inside the stowaway cabin, Shay hummed softly to herself. She was dragging the charcoaled stick in circles on the floor. Over and over. Thousands of black circles.

"Hello again," she said in a bright voice without looking up.

"Hi. It's me."

"I know."

He glanced at the lemon, still in perfect detail on the wall, then at the other pictures around the room. "What are all of these?"

"Pictures."

Something about that lemon. He couldn't stop staring at it. *Why? Why did she draw a lemon?*

"What do they mean?" The question was too vague, of course—especially considering who he was asking. He braced for another evasive Shay remark.

She stopped making circles and looked up.

"They're what's inside me."

"Inside how?"

"Sometimes, I feel like there's something stuck." She looked at her torso. "I can't stop thinking about it. It just stays in there, banging on my belly, saying, 'Get me out of here, silly girl!' And so I paint it out."

"Sometimes I feel like that too," Jed said without thinking.

"You do?"

He was nodding before he realized it. And then words he never intended to say spilled from his mouth. "I make things too. Food. I cook food." His mind flashed to Lemon Saturday.

Lemon poppy-seed doughnuts. Every Saturday for months. I had to have them. I had to. If I didn't—well, I didn't know what would happen if I didn't.

His mind felt dizzy—no, blurry—no, that wasn't it either.

"Did I say all that out loud?" he asked.

"About the lemon poppy-seed doughnuts? Yep." Her eyes were filled with wonder. It was an eager look—almost *thrilled*.

"What does that mean?" Jed asked.

"How am I supposed to know?"

He looked at the lemon on the wall. "That. You drew that." He reached into his pocket for the lemon. She looked from it to the picture on the wall.

"Mine needs more yellow, doesn't it?"

"Why did you draw it?"

"I told you. It was inside of me. 'Let me out, Shay! Let me out!' So I let it out."

Three heavy stomps rattled above, and dust particles fluttered from the ceiling.

Jed pointed up. "I had to tell Ugly Mouse about you."

She nodded. "Will he put me in a cage and hit me with pipes?"

Jed's heart sank. "No," he said quickly. "He promised he wouldn't hurt you."

"So did Captain Butterfly."

Jed winced. He knew nothing about his grandfather, but he couldn't imagine the man caging and beating a helpless girl. "I don't know anything about what happened with Captain Butterfly, but I won't let this captain do that. You can trust me."

She studied Jed—studied the lemon in his hand. "You're different from other mice."

"I am?"

Her lips turned up in a mischievous grin. "Quite different. Not like Captain Butterfly at all, are you?"

"I wouldn't know. I never knew him."

"Why would you?" Still smiling, she bit her lip. "No. No, not like other mice at all, are we?"

More stomping. More dust.

"We're coming!" Jed called. "Come on. I need to get back up."

"Okay." She crawled after him.

Captain Bog stood by the trapdoor, one hand on his hip, the other holding his watch. "Did you pause for a nap?"

Jed took Shay's hand and helped her up. "This is Shay." He adopted his most sympathetic voice. "She's the only survivor from the steamboat. While she was there, the crew locked her in a cage and beat her. She's been stuck in a tiny space on this ship and has probably had barely any cans to eat for days."

"Cans? As in *our* cans? A stowaway *and* a thief? No wonder they beat you."

Jed glared.

"Actually," Shay said, "I had plenty to eat. Lots of cans up here. Delicious cans. Peaches and blackberries and pea soup. Yum! But"—she held up a finger—"I only ate when I was hungry. Or wanted a treat. Or didn't have anything else to do . . . like draw pictures on the walls of your boat."

Jed held his breath. A smile filled the captain's face. He was either amused or about to announce something threatening or painful. From Jed's experience, it was usually both.

But he simply folded his arms and nodded, the awkward smile still plastered on his scarred lips.

"Do you have any more blankets?" she asked. "I took one

from the big room with the pretty paintings. But it has a hole in it." She connected her thumb and finger to make a ring. "Like a mouse nibbled through."

"Yes," Captain Bog said. "I know the blanket. A hole like this?" He spaced his fingers a coin's width apart.

"Exactly!"

"That's my blanket."

"Well, it's not very comfortable. You should wrap disobedient mice inside it to *punish* them!"

Captain Bog tilted his head as if considering the idea. "I'll keep that in mind."

"Yes. Keep it in mind."

He studied her for another moment. "You know, you oddly remind me of . . ." He stared into her eyes. "Of . . ." He shook his head, unable to finish the thought.

"Of your blanket?" she asked.

His face lit up as a rare and mirthful laugh escaped his throat. "I was going to say my daughter."

Jed looked up. "You have a *daughter*?"

"No." He didn't meet Jed's eyes.

"Is she dead?" Shay asked. "How did she die?"

Captain Bog took a slow, steady breath. "She was taken."

"By the wicked scritchlings?"

"By the dread."

"Did they turn her into one?" she asked.

He scratched at one of the thick scars on his chin.

Shay eyed the motion and cocked her head. "Did you try to rescue her? Is that how you got all those scars?"

He stopped midscratch. "You're a smart girl, Shay."

"There were too many, weren't there? You couldn't stop them all. Too many wicked scritches."

"You seem to know a lot about those creatures."

She leaned closer and whispered, "They're looking for me. They want to *catch* me." She leaned back and grinned, the volume returning to her voice. "But I'm too sneaky. Sneaky like a *mouse*. Stupid scritcherings look and look but they're too clumsy to snatch mice."

"Why do they want to catch you?" the captain asked.

Shay smiled. "I like you," she said. "You're a smart mouse. I bet you're a fun mouse."

Captain Bog looked at Jed. "What do you think, Jed? Am I a *fun* mouse?"

"Oh, tons of fun. I've never had so much fun. He even threw me a funeral party."

Shay clapped her hands. "I knew it. I knew it. I do love fun mice."

Captain Bog drew a deep breath. "So," he said, and then exhaled all at once, "Jed here says you know something about his watch."

"Oh, yes."

"He told us that you said it could make someone stronger."

"Nope," she said. "That's not what I said."

"No?"

"I said it could make you *very* strong. Mouse king! Mouse king of the whole junkyard!"

"How?"

"It leads you to *treasure*."

Captain Bog's eyes brightened with an *I knew it* expression.

"Riggs knows where to go," he said. "But how will we find the treasure when we arrive?"

She laughed with a squeak. "You don't need to find the treasure, silly. It will find *you*."

18

Captain Bog cleared his throat. "Everyone, I'd like you to meet Shay."

She stepped forward.

The crew looked at one another.

Kizer cocked his head. "I don't understand. Where did she come from? Is that what you traded from the tinker?"

The captain's eyes shifted, and he cleared his throat again. "She was part of the steamboat crew. She snuck on board when we landed."

Chatter swept through the crew.

"She *what*?"

"A stowaway?"

"How?"

"She's been here the whole time?"

"Where was she hiding?"

"Who is she?"

"What are you going to do with her?"

The captain waved both arms in the air. "Everyone calm down. We're not doing anything with her for now. I made a deal with Jed that—"

"Jed. Of course," Kizer mumbled.

"It seems we found ourselves a bit of luck," the captain continued. "She, Jed, and Riggs gave us a location that might lead to treasure."

"Treasure?"

"What treasure?"

"Where are we going?"

"How do you know they're telling the truth?"

"Everyone shut their mouths long enough for me to speak!" the captain yelled. "The tinker offered Jed twenty thousand batteries for his little wristwatch—and *don't* all you start babbling again!" he said before the chatter could continue. "It's given a heading, and we're going to go see what's worth twenty thousand batteries. All right?"

With that Captain Bog turned and walked away.

After a barrage of questions and awkward introductions, a feeling of excitement buzzed through the ship. Pobble played bright songs on his fiddle, Riggs whistled in the engine room, Sprocket spun shatterboxes on her fingers for hours, and even Kizer seemed to forget how much he hated Jed.

And after a song-filled day of flight, Sprocket called from the lookout, "We're coming up on the coordinates, Captain!"

The crew gathered at the front of the ship. Jed gripped the railing and peered all around. The junk didn't look any different from any other junk. Nothing stood out, not in the air and not on the piles. The watch's hands stood still.

"Slow to one-quarter speed," Captain Bog called.

"One-quarter speed!" Sprocket said.

The hum of the engines wilted to a low rumble, and the ship slowed.

Captain Bog scanned the sky. He took out his own watch and grumbled a single *hmm*. "What time do you have, Riggs?" he asked.

Riggs removed a rusty pocket watch. "Seven fifty-eight."

Captain Bog's lips scrunched together like a coil of twine. "Seven fifty-eight . . ." He glanced at Shay. "I thought you said the treasure would come to us?"

She nodded eagerly. "It'll be a wonderful surprise."

They waited in total silence for the two minutes, which felt like ten. No one moved. No one breathed. The captain's watch ticked. *Tick, tick, tick.* He shifted in place. His toes squirmed, causing the tips of his boots to rise and fall. He chewed his lip and scratched his scars.

The second hand ticked and ticked until, finally, it reached twelve.

Nothing happened. No ray of light illuminating a box of gold. No giant message in the clouds. Nothing.

"Riggs!" Captain Bog shouted.

"Aye, Captain, I've eight o'clock as well."

A whirring sensation quivered in Jed's wrist. "Captain," he said. "The watch."

The six hands spun.

Captain Bog grabbed his wrist. "Where is it? Where is the treasure? How could we have missed it?" He glared at his own watch. His fingers tightened around it, and Jed thought he might chuck it off the ship. "What happened to the treasure?" he asked again, turning to Shay.

Her face beamed with delight, and she rocked in place. She bit her bottom lip and giggled.

"Well?" The captain clutched his watch so tightly, his palm turned white. "Where is it?"

She clapped her hands, then opened her arms, closed her eyes, and spun in place. "It's all around you!"

Captain Bog looked frantically in every direction. "I can't see anything!"

"Boom!" Shay yelled.

A second later, thunder cracked through the sky. The crew stood frozen. Another crack shattered the empty air.

Sprocket's hand leaped to the butt of her shatterbox.

A cool breeze fluttered over the ship. Captain Bog spun in place, as if some giant, invisible enemy were looming over him.

And then Sprocket yelled, "Junkstorm!"

The captain sucked in a breath. "Sprocket, get us out of here! Go! Now!"

Sprocket bolted to the helm. The rear propeller whirred to life, and *Bessie* lurched forward.

"Faster!" Captain Bog yelled. "Riggs, engine room!"

Sprocket jammed a lever into place. The gears in the ship's hull whined as motors spun wildly.

The cool breeze washed over the deck of the ship, this time hitting with enough force to knock Jed off-balance. He gripped a cable from the smokestack and held tight.

The white clouds darkened into gray. They swirled together, and the color blackened.

"Riggs!" the captain yelled through the floor. "I don't care if *Bessie*'s engine won't work for a month—you get her moving!"

Sprocket yanked on the helm controls, and *Bessie* shot forward. The gears screeched as the propeller spun faster still, its blades now a translucent blur.

The deck rattled under the added pressure.

The massive black cloud above tightened in on itself and began to swirl, bathing them in shadow.

A cone poked down from its center and widened into a funnel.

Wind slapped the ship and threw Jed to the railings. He clutched the bars and peered over the boat. The junk below rattled against the wind.

"Sprocket, up ahead!" Kizer shouted.

Junk began falling from the black clouds like giant metal raindrops.

A ladder flipped through the sky, end over end. It smacked

the side of the boat and disappeared below. A tape measure clattered on the deck. And then a candle. And a coat hanger. And—

"Watch out!" Jed yelled as a washing machine headed straight for them. At the last second, Sprocket pushed a lever and *Bessie* jerked to the side. The washer flew by Jed's face with a dense whoosh.

"Shatterkegs on the main deck, now!" Captain Bog shouted.

Pobble and Kizer sprinted to the lower deck.

Shay still spun and giggled, in a manic dance.

A dark object flipped through the sky directly over the bridge.

"Piano!" Jed yelled.

Sprocket yanked a lever. *Bessie* turned, but the piano clipped the side of the ship, ripping off railing and a chunk of the deck.

A vacuum cleaner plummeted toward Jed. He dove, and it crashed beside him. Before he could stand up, a tray of silverware pelted the deck, and a spoon smacked him in the head. He wrapped his arms around a smokestack cable.

"Make way!" Kizer called. He and Pobble hefted a shatterkeg up the stairs. They returned for a second one, which they rolled to Captain Bog.

"Stand them up on their ends and get them into the mounts!" the captain yelled. "Jed, get over here and help!"

His voice was muffled by the wind and colliding junk tumbling through the air. Jed grabbed one of the barrels. With the captain's help, he propped it up until it pointed at the sky. They hugged the gun as the ship rocked against the wind.

Captain Bog reached to the deck and lifted a small hatch. He pushed the shatterkeg with his hip until it clicked into the opening.

Pobble, Kizer, and Shay lifted the second one into another mount.

"Nothing hits this ship!" the captain said. The others nodded—Shay with a smile.

"Train car, twenty degrees starboard!" Kizer yelled.

The front car of a train emerged from the black spiral. It turned slowly in the air. "Wait for it," Captain Bog said. "Wait for it. . . ."

Kizer cranked a lever on his shatterkeg, and a series of buttons lit up. When the train car was nearly on top of them, the captain yelled, "Fire!"

Kizer slammed his fist into one of the buttons. The shatterkeg whistled. A cracking sound ripped through the air. A column of blue dust appeared from the tip of the barrel and ended at the train car. The massive car broke into pieces.

The captain yanked a lever, and their shatterkeg's buttons lit up. One of them was red. Jed's heart skipped a beat. If there was ever a time to trust his parents—now was it. He punched it.

A crack sounded, and a column of blue particles painted a line through the sky.

Captain Bog searched the open air. He steadied the shatterkeg—still searching the sky.

"What was that for?" he yelled.

"I—I thought I saw something."

"Don't touch the controls! If you even—"

Before the captain could finish, the button turned red again. Jed threw his palm against it. The shatterkeg whistled.

Out of nowhere, a rogue Jacuzzi tumbled up over the side of the ship—heading straight for the bridge. The shatterkeg fired, and the blast slammed into the Jacuzzi, bursting it to pieces.

The others froze and stared at Jed as ceramic tiles clattered harmlessly around them. Captain Bog nodded once. Jed nodded back.

The thunder grew closer as more junk hit the ship. Objects beat against the hull, making terrible splintering sounds. Captain Bog and Kizer alternated shatterkeg shots as Sprocket weaved through the falling debris.

"I'm running out of charge!" Kizer said.

"We're down to only a few shots here, too," the captain said. "Save your fire for junk that will take us out of the sky."

As if testing their resolve, a bookcase flipped toward the deck.

"Hold!" Captain Bog shouted.

The bookcase exploded against the back of the ship. Jed couldn't tell which shattered pieces were from shelves and which were from *Bessie*.

A life-size iron statue of a dachshund punched through the ship five feet from Jed's toes. *Bessie*'s engine whined and popped.

"We've lost power to one propeller!" Sprocket called.

"Keep her moving!" the captain called back.

Kizer blasted a pickup truck away from the bridge, and the captain fired at a bunk bed.

Junk rained over them, piercing the deck until it looked like a sieve. A metal file cabinet drifted toward Jed.

The captain fired, but the beam missed. "Shoot it!" he yelled to Kizer.

Kizer mashed the buttons, but the shatterkeg didn't fire. "We're out of juice! Take cover!"

Jed and the captain dove. The file cabinet hit the deck where they were standing, smashing the shatterkeg into pieces.

The crew huddled near corners, under railings, and in the bridge as debris clattered around them.

Wind gusted against Jed's face, forcing him to close his eyes and listen to objects tear the ship apart.

The engine wailed and coughed.

"Come on . . ." Jed whispered to himself. "Push through— you can do it, *Bessie*."

Just then Sprocket shouted from the bridge, "Clear skies ahead!"

Jed opened his eyes. The edges of the black cloud were turning to gray. The howling winds began to die, and bits of sun peeked through the sky ahead.

Sprocket's arms had been like machines themselves— cranking and twisting levers while her feet alternated between pedals. But as the sky cleared, her motions relaxed.

Jed released the smokestack cable and collapsed. The propellers slowed, and *Bessie*'s engine sighed in relief.

19

The crew assembled, and excitement burned in their eyes. Shay seemed simply delighted.

Captain Bog stood up straight and held his hands behind his back. "We've got an hour—maybe two. Iron and copper will have seen that storm a hundred miles away. We'll have falcons and wasps swarming the skies any minute, blasting anything not matching their own metal. Let's get in, get out, and make the most of this!"

They cheered, with raised fists.

"We're going back?" Jed asked.

"Of course we're going back!"

"But—"

"But what? Your girlfriend was right! Treasure map indeed!

Junk doesn't get fresher than this."

The crew cheered again.

"But you said copper and iron are coming."

Captain Bog waved a hand as if that were the last thing on his mind. "An hour at least—maybe two! They never find storms before that." He patted Jed's shoulder and squeezed. "Good work, Jed. No, *excellent* work. You deserve this. Shay might not think so, but I'll bet you're holding the first gilded relic seen since the javelin chase three decades ago!" He turned to the crew. "Let's hear it for Jed!"

The crew hollered into the sky. Even Kizer offered a small nod.

"You know what?" Captain Bog said. "Tonight we should cook for *you*."

Jed smiled, imagining the captain stirring together canned chili, blackberries, and chicken noodle soup.

Pobble gathered hiking packs, backpacks, suitcases, and shoulder bags, then dumped them into a pile.

"Riggs will search for supplies to patch up *Bessie*," the captain said. "The rest of you get cans and batteries—nothing else. Is that clear?" They nodded. "Let's move out," he said, throwing an army-style duffel bag over his shoulder.

Sprocket set *Bessie* onto a dimple of space in the fresh junk pile. Jed strapped a hiking pack to his back and followed the others. Sunlight glittered over millions of untarnished metal surfaces.

Where does it all come from? Jed wondered. It was as if it was sucked from his world and dumped into theirs.

He stepped from the tug and sank to his knee in the unsettled pile. Cans of food crowded his legs. Hundreds of them—thousands, even. Cans everywhere, piled in great heaps. He could fill his whole pack before taking ten steps. And batteries dotted the fresh pile like sprinkles on a birthday cake.

He set the pack on a pool table and scoured the cans. *Whatever I want,* he thought, *all right here.* He found sweet peas and garden-fresh peas. Field peas and chickpeas. Black-eyed peas, wasabi peas, peas and carrots, and even purple-hull peas. He held one of the cans to his face. *I don't even know what purple-hull peas are.*

The stack of peas teetered on the pool table's green felt–covered slab. *I could fill the whole tug with peas if I wanted. I could find anything.* He found creamed possum, canned muffins, jellied eel, teriyaki frog legs, armadillo, whole squid, minced elk, hot wings, smoked rattlesnake, reindeer pâté, Cajun-style alligator, shark fin, sheep tongue, BBQ worms, boar spread, and even something that said "grass jelly" on the label. Jed studied the picture of the purple gelatin cubes. They looked nothing like grass *or* jelly.

"Sorry, but you're staying here for now." He tossed the grass jelly, creamed possum, and jellied eel back into the piles. The others were simply too exciting to pass up. Canned muffins sounded questionable but were worth a shot. He'd try anything once. Well, maybe not grass jelly.

He picked up a yellow can. *Lemon pie filling.* He could almost smell the baking pie crust—almost *see* his mother fiddling with the broken knob on the stove, grumbling about cheap plastic and old appliances. He could almost hear his father's *"Shhh!"* as he snuck into the kitchen and snatched her into his arms. She'd giggle and flail as he tossed her onto his shoulder, her yellow-ruffled, sauce-stained, flour-dusted, daisy-spotted apron flapping against his face. *"You're blinding me, woman!"* he'd say, struggling to push the fabric away from his eyes without releasing his captive.

Jed's throat went dry. The lemon filling was suddenly heavier than it had been a moment ago. He held it in both hands and stared at the happy picture of fresh-baked pie. "Why did you leave me?" he whispered to the can. "Why did you do this? This isn't Yellowstone National Park! It's not some camping trip. I don't even know *what* this is. I could barely find food before today. How am I supposed to find *you*?"

"Are you talking to a can?" Captain Bog's voice bellowed behind him.

Jed looked up. "No."

"Did it say anything interesting? You sounded pretty sweet and mushy. Were you two getting to know each other? Middle names, favorite colors, that sort of thing?"

"I wasn't talking to a can."

Captain Bog rubbed his chin. "Hmm. Interesting. Either (a) you don't know what the word *talking* means or (b) you don't know what cans are. Because you were holding one, and you were talking to it."

"Whatever."

"Well, wrap up the conversation before the fleets come and blast us down, steal our tug, and ship us off to the iron prisons."

"Would they really do that?"

"Definitely. Coppers are just crazy. Irons? They think they're 'righteous' and 'noble' and that murder, robbery, and forcing people to dig for them is all for the greater good of the sovereign."

Jed tried to decide if he was being serious.

"Tell you what: Chitchat with any scrap of food you'd like once *Bessie*'s plump with loot. You can have all the privacy you want. I bet Shay would love to join. Just you, Shay, and your can. How does that sound?"

"I wasn't talking to a can," Jed muttered as he tucked the pie filling into his pack with an armful of other cans without even checking the labels.

"Good choice," Captain Bog said. "Nice talk."

Jed turned and stalked back to the ship. He emptied the pack in the mess.

Within an hour, the shelves were stocked so full that Pobble had to pile cans on the floor.

"Cans to last a month!" Captain Bog said. "Everyone unload, and take one more trip for batteries."

By the time *Bessie* lifted into the air, the mess was a mound of cans, and the crew had so many batteries that the cooking bathtub was half-full of them.

"Take us out," the captain said.

"What's our heading?" Sprocket called.

Captain Bog lifted his chin. "Dawndrake. Let's celebrate."

"Aye, aye!"

"Drinks on me!" The captain scooped a handful of batteries from the tub and tossed them into the air.

Bessie sailed at one-tenth of quarter speed as the crew patched up what was left of her. "Run the engines just enough to keep us from falling," Captain Bog told Riggs. By nightfall, the ship still had so many holes that Jed had to hop along the main deck more than he walked. As he hammered a tin cookie sheet over a cavity in the smokestack, he smiled to himself. It wasn't too hard to fix a thing made from junk to begin with. The next morning, they worked most of the day scooping junk and patching holes. The red light had returned on Spyglass's face, and Jed considered using a nail to permanently fasten it down.

When the sun began to fall, Sprocket called from the stack nest. "Dawndrake township, ahoy!"

A huge mass floated against the sunset. "*That's* Dawndrake?" Jed asked no one in particular. It looked more like a copper iceberg plucked from the ocean and hung in the sky.

"Mm-hm." Pobble nodded. "Best pubs in three townships."

Hundreds of propellers—each as wide as *Bessie*—spun at the base of the township with blurring speed.

"But it's in the air," Jed said.

Pobble nodded. "Where else would it be?"

"On the ground? Does every town fly?"

"I suppose some are on the ground. Scrap place to put one, if ya ask me. Don't last too long, what with the junkstorms. One storm'll bury you before you can blink."

Sky ships buzzed around the town: schooners like the tinker's, oil rigs, two-man shuttles that looked like rowboats with a rear propeller, and even a bulky steamboat. They docked beside a long strip of decking that protruded from the town like a ship's plank. Sprocket engaged the sky prop and set the ship idly hovering. Riggs roped the stern to the dock.

"Isn't there a place to land?" Jed asked.

"Dawndrake would need twice the undertown propellers if every ship sat on top of it," Pobble said.

The captain cleared his throat. "All right, let's see who's staying with *Bessie*." Something rattled between his cupped palms as he shook them. "Riggs, you first."

He parted his thumbs an inch. Riggs plucked out a battery slathered in black paint. The captain moved to Pobble, who picked a black-painted battery. Shay clapped her hands at the game and reached to take one. Captain Bog grinned.

"You think I'm leaving you with the tug after you snatched my favorite blanket? Not a chance. I'd come back missing my pillow!" He looked at Shay with warm eyes. Protective, even.

One day on the tug and she's already charmed the very bear of a man who wanted to toss me to my death for a bit of "evening entertainment."

Sprocket reached in and pulled out a black battery. "Down to you and me, Ki," the captain said, shaking the last two batteries together. Kizer concentrated as if willing the right battery to come to his fingers. He pinched one and plucked it free. Red.

"Ah. Bad luck, Ki," Captain Bog said, closing his fist around the last battery.

Kizer scowled and flicked the battery to the floor. "Third time in a row."

Captain Bog patted Kizer's shoulder apologetically. "Next time." He turned to the others. "Everyone take one handful of batteries. Let's celebrate." Everyone dug into the bathtub, carefully lifting a heap of batteries as if trying to redefine the volume of "one handful."

As they left the ship, Captain Bog fidgeted with something in his pocket. He smiled at Jed and revealed the tip of a second red battery.

"Shh," he whispered.

Jed grinned. There'd been two red batteries the whole time. It was brilliant. If Bog always picked last, he'd never be stuck on watch.

They walked in a line along the thin strip of dock to the main town. The junk below was an indiscernible brown blur.

"Watch yourselves here," Captain Bog said to Jed. "Dawndrake's a copper township."

"What does that mean?" Jed asked.

"It means everyone who lives here is crazy. And not just regular crazy. Full-on gutter-clunk crazy. Light-buildings-on-fire-and-run-through-them-naked crazy. All of them."

Sprocket folded her arms and glared. "Hey! I was *born* here! What does that say about me?"

"You're right," Captain Bog said. "Sprocket's not that crazy. She's worse. Much worse."

"That's right, I am," Sprocket said with a satisfied nod. "And don't forget it."

"Crazy how?" Jed asked.

Captain Bog thought for a moment. "Let me put it this way: I've never seen a group of people who want so badly to die."

"That's not true," Sprocket said. "I don't want to die."

"Oh, so then you haven't competed in the new gauntlet in Jysterfield?"

"They put up a second gauntlet?"

Captain Bog shook his head. "You wouldn't be interested."

Sprocket gave him an offended scowl. "Why not?"

"Because it's insane, that's why. They call it the Juggernaut. The course runs more high-speed death fans, acid-cloud bombs, and suicide spikes than even an iron battle cruiser could hold! Only four javelins out of a hundred even *survive* the run!"

Excitement fluttered in Sprocket's eyes. "I've got two weeks' shore leave saved up. I bet if I leave after—"

Captain Bog held up his hand. "You telling me you want to use your time off to run through some death gauntlet that I made up just now to prove a point?"

"Wait." Sprocket opened her mouth. "There is no . . ." She glared at him, and her shoulders slouched. "Way to build up a girl's dreams, then crush them in your ugly sandpaper hands!"

Captain Bog turned to Jed. "See what I mean? Just wait till we're inside the township."

They walked along the dock until it connected to a network of streets that squiggled into the giant cluster of buildings. The buildings nearest the town's edge were only a few stories high, but the deeper the group went toward the center, the higher the buildings reached into the air.

The narrow structures couldn't have been more than one room wide, yet each was easily twenty stories tall. Jed imagined tipping one over with his bare hands. That was when Jed began to understand what Captain Bog had meant.

Thousands of cables, ladders, catwalks, and zip lines connected buildings together in a rickety network of scaffolding. Copper townspeople leaped from tip to tip with nothing but air below them. They sped recklessly down zip lines, lazily holding on with just a single hand. The catwalks had no railings. The ladders wobbled unsteadily. And the web of zip lines tangled together—one giant collision waiting to happen.

"They're so skinny," Jed said to Pobble.

"What are?"

"The buildings."

"Buildings? You mean the spikes?"

"Is that a spike?" Jed asked, pointing to one of the pencil-like towers.

"Course it is. Don't you got spikes in Denver?"

"We call them buildings. Or houses. We've got lots of houses, but they're not very tall at all. Sort of short and fat."

Pobble thought for a moment. "Then you stack 'em on top of each other?"

Jed laughed. "No. Just next to each other."

"But if there's lots, how do you fit them all in Denver?"

"Denver's on the ground. We can build houses wherever we want."

Pobble shook his head. "Not here. Towns would need more propellers if they had Denver spikes."

"Is that why they're so tall and skinny? So they don't weigh as much?"

Pobble shrugged. "I ain't the magistrate. I couldn't tell you."

The coppers looked like a colony of bees, swarming wildly through the town. Some rode coils of copper rail that spiraled around the spikes. Others hopped on pulley platforms that yanked them up into the sky.

Jed read the copper lettering on the black double doors of a spike:

BILLY BRISTLE'S MAPS
ACCURATE AND UPDATED WEEKLY!

The next shop advertised ALL THINGS SHATTER: CUSTOM SPINDLES, HIGH-CAPACITY BATTERY DRUMS, AND QUALITY FINISHES. The shop after that was a maintenance bay boasting two-hour engine tune-ups for any standard S-four or T-one block. They passed a 24-HOUR BUNK and an ALL-FRUIT-CAN SNACKERY. Jed saw a customs declaration office, permit registration buildings, smokestack repair shops, and a sign for CLEAN BUBBLES DECK-SCRUBBING.

They reached a platform, and Captain Bog opened a metal control box. A dozen empty slots numbered one to twelve were marked with names of businesses. The captain plugged batteries into slots all the way to the fifth one, which read COPPER ROSE, and pressed a button. A waist-high gate slid into place, and the platform rose up the side of the spike.

At the fifth floor it halted, and the expended batteries hissed and dropped into a waste barrel below the panel.

Before them stood an elaborate set of double doors. The wood was carved into intertwined roses. In the center of each door, the roses were coated in a film of copper.

"Ah, the Copper Rose," Captain Bog said.

Pobble opened his mouth. "The Copper Rose? I've never stepped one foot in there."

"Well"—Captain Bog smiled—"you're rich now, so step both feet in." He pushed open the doors.

If an opera house could be a restaurant, this was it. When he was ten, Jed's father had taken him to the opera. "Women appreciate a man with culture!" he'd said. "Now hide these bottles of root beer in your coat. They don't allow drinks at the opera. That's why I always pay extra for a curtained booth! I hope your mom remembered the roast beef sandwiches. Root beer's not the same without 'em, after all."

Everything about the Copper Rose reminded Jed of that night: Scarlet curtains ruffled around private booths, their thick fabric bunched in the center with gold rope. Plush chairs with buttoned cushions. Roman columns. And just the right amount of amber-tinted light to make everything look like aged gold.

For once, nothing felt like junk. Chair matched chair. Table matched table. Waiters wore matching tuxedos with tails and white gloves. Jed pictured the tinker here, perhaps wearing a monocle and laughing the way rich people did over trivialities. It was a distinct sound, somewhere between a "Ha!" and a "Ho!"—always in threes and often followed by a "Well said, chap!" or preceded by an "I say!"

A chandelier hung overhead. How had the crystal even survived a junkstorm?

"Your best table, miss," Captain Bog said to the hostess.

She led them to a booth enclosed by a red curtain.

"What can I start you off with?" She snapped cloth napkins in front of them in the air, then draped them across their laps.

"Pineapple juice," Captain Bog said, studying the menu in front of him. "Aaaand . . . split pea soup."

Jed nodded to himself. At least someone might appreciate the eleven different kinds of canned peas he had found. Either that or the captain was just trying to sound fancy.

"Do you have strawberries in syrup?" Sprocket asked.

"Of course."

"Then two cans for me," she said with a smile.

Riggs ordered maraschino cherries and applesauce. Shay ordered pickles and a can of Burstin' Cheddar's Easy-Cheese. Pobble ordered three cans of chicken, two cans of peaches, one can of chili, and a can of sugarcane syrup to drink.

"And for you?" the waitress asked Jed.

"Just pineapple juice, thanks, perhaps with a splash of guava nectar? Unstirred."

"Might I say that's an excellent choice?"

Jed smiled. "You may. Thank you."

She left and returned a few minutes later with their order. She passed Pobble a porcelain gravy boat of sugarcane syrup, a thick crystal parfait dish filled with the peaches, and a fancy ashtray with the chili.

Jed forced himself not to laugh—even when Pobble lifted the gravy boat, his pinky outstretched, and sipped syrup from the spout.

Captain Bog lifted his goblet of pineapple juice. "Here's to Jed." They cheered. "Here's to a new life of endless riches!"

Jed's smile disappeared. "Endless?"

"As long as that thing keeps running," Pobble said.

Jed stared at the smiling faces. "I appreciate all you've done for me—I really do—but I'm not here to look for treasure. My parents are missing, and I need to find them. They could be in trouble, or hurt, or . . ." His voice stumbled.

The crew looked at one another, smiles fading.

"Where do you plan to start?" Captain Bog set down his drink.

"I don't know."

"Then what's the harm in biding your time? Scooping up bathtubs full of batteries?"

"I'm not here to get rich!" Jed slammed his drink on the table. Pineapple juice splashed around it. "I'm sorry." He drew an unsteady breath. "I didn't mean it to come out like that. But I can't just wait around, hoping I'll bump into them. I need to search."

"Search how? Walk?" the captain asked.

"If that's what it takes."

Captain Bog leaned back. "Here's what I see: you need a boat, a crew that knows the terrain, and resources to travel. I happen to have two of the three. But like any crew, we need gears for the engine, oil for the pistons, and food for the men."

"Just the *men*?" Sprocket asked. "Then what am I supposed to eat?"

Captain Bog rolled his eyes. "Deck planks." He turned back to Jed. "We can help each other out."

"*You're* going to help me look for my parents? Like you helped me look for my grandfather? That didn't work out so well for me. Thanks, but no thanks."

The captain leaned forward. "Take us to one junkstorm a week and my ship's yours for the other six days. You point; Sprocket'll fly."

"How do I know you'll actually do that after a storm?"

"You already found one. The next six days are yours."

Jed paused. "Wait, really?" The captain nodded. A ship to himself. That was more than he could hope for on his own—by a mile. "Deal."

Captain Bog grinned, and his scars stretched over his face. "And if you keep cooking, that makes you part of the crew, and crew gets equal share of the plunder."

"I'd cook whether I got a share or not. I have to eat that scrap too, you know."

"I'll drink to that!" Pobble lifted the gravy boat and took a swig of syrup.

Captain Bog chugged his pineapple juice, then clapped the glass down. "Who are we looking for? Give me their names."

"Ryan and Mary."

"Ryan and Mary what?"

"I can't say. They told me not to tell anyone my last name."

"What scrap advice is that?" Riggs said, wiping cherry juice from his lips. "How are we supposed to find them?"

"So we don't know exactly who we're looking for, where they are, what happened to them, or who took them?" Captain Bog asked. "Did I miss anything?"

"I know that's not much to go on," Jed said.

"What about friends? Enemies? People who wanted to hurt them?"

Hurt them? Who would want to hurt them? "No. No one."

"What about motive? Were they rich?"

Jed's parents had never really talked about money. They didn't *seem* rich—but they weren't poor. *Although . . . weeklong vacations every few months my whole life? Normal people don't have the money to do that, right?* But their house wasn't big—or new. The cabinetry was outdated, the linoleum scuffed, and the carpets smelled faintly of whatever wet dog had lived there before them.

"No. I don't think they're rich."

Riggs pointed at the watch. "That's something to go on. Where did they get it?"

"How many times do I have to tell you? I have no idea where it came from. Okay?"

Riggs raised his hands as if Jed had pulled a knife. "Just trying to help."

More like fishing for clues.

Captain Bog tapped the rim of his empty glass. "I need more. Trying to find two people somewhere in the junkyard with nothing to go on is like . . ." He thought for a moment. "Ah, scrap it all. That doesn't need a comparison—it's like trying to find two people somewhere in the junkyard with nothing to go on!"

"If I knew anything else, I'd tell you!"

"Ah, that's good to know. Then what are their last names?"

Jed glared. Captain Bog winked.

"Ryan and Mary," the captain repeated to himself. "Hmm. I suppose we could start in Yillond, and then—" He paused. "Shay! What are you doing?"

Shay was squirting lines of Easy-Cheese in an oval over the tablecloth. "Dot, dot, dot," she said, speckling dots of cheese inside the shape. "It's a lemon! Now I have yellow!"

Captain Bog's head swiveled back and forth. He shoved empty dishes over the cheese. Shay scowled. "Well, I'm ready to go." He tossed several batteries on the table, then leaned in and whispered to Shay, "I'd leave an *extra* big tip if I were you."

The Roof Hotel was at the top of the tallest building in Dawndrake—forty floors up. The first thirty floors cost a battery apiece. The next five were two each. The final five took five batteries every stop. Sixty-five batteries later, Jed had his own room with floor-to-ceiling windows, a bowl of complimentary cans, and a bathtub with battery-operated heating coils.

The next morning, he strapped himself to one of the zip line coils. Forty flights below, the crew was already awake and waiting for him.

"Where to, Captain Golden Boy?" Captain Bog asked as Jed landed. Before he could respond, the captain turned to the others. "Oh, and that's not going to be a *thing*, by the way. If any of you slugs call him captain, I'll stuff you in an empty can and roll you down the stairs."

"I don't know," Jed said. "Where do you think we should start?"

"A man named Digger might be able to help."

"Digger it is, then."

Captain Bog led Jed to a shop called the Etch Book.

An elderly man missing most of his teeth waved them inside. "Which of you handsome gentlemen wants an etching? I'll do one for thirty batteries. Two for fifty! It might sound high, but I do the best etchwork in the yard! No one better than Digger the Etcher. No finer etch for a thousand miles— that's a guarantee!"

Jed turned to Captain Bog. "Etchwork?"

"We'll take two. I hear good things about you, Digger. Word is you can etch just from description. Is that true, or am I only hearing scrap?"

"It's true. Not many folk pay for such an etching. It's not an easy etch, after all."

Captain Bog dropped a sack of batteries on the counter.

Digger grinned, showing the few teeth he had left. "Let's get started!" He waved them to a room with an art easel and odd supplies. He picked up a spray gun connected to an air compressor with a hose, then waited.

The captain nodded to Jed. "Go ahead."

"With what?"

"Tell him what your parents look like."

Digger peeked over the easel.

"Oh, um. My dad has a big nose. But not my mom. Hers is small like mine"—he glanced at Shay—"like a *mouse's*."

Digger meticulously released bursts of air at the easel as Jed spoke.

Jed continued for hours. He described every feature in vivid detail: The freckles on his mom's cheek, which looked like a single shake of pepper. The bony cheekbones of his father. His mother's queenlike forehead. His father's eyes—wrinkled from ten thousand smiles.

When he was finished, Digger turned the easel around and showed Jed two acid-etched metal plates. Jed's stomach clenched. His mom. His dad. They were smiling. Smiling at him.

"How's this?"

Captain Bog elbowed Jed in the ribs.

"It's . . . it's perfect."

Jed took the plates. They were flawless. He reached into his pocket and handed Digger another handful of batteries.

"But your friend already—"

"I know," Jed said, still staring at the picture. "This is just to say thank you."

"Can you make us stamps of these?" Captain Bog asked.

"How many would you like?" Digger asked.

"Let's start with four stacks."

Digger took the etchwork to a black machine that looked something like a long barbecue grill. He placed the plates in a tray, then yanked a series of levers and pulleys. Steam coughed from small stacks. When Digger opened the reverse side, a copy of the etching dropped to the floor with a metal clang.

He continued until Jed had four stacks of twenty thin plates.

For the rest of the evening, the crew helped Jed hang copies of the etchwork all around town while Riggs and Shay stayed on board the tug and hovered near the dock. Each copy had instructions to contact them at dock line 487 if anyone recognized the picture.

A day passed.

And then a second.

And three more.

They talked to thousands of coppers and knocked on hundreds of spikes.

Nothing.

Kizer suggested they try an iron township cluster. "Farburrow is half this size with twice as many people and ten times the organization," he said.

"Yeah, and it's also iron-regulated," Sprocket said.

Kizer folded his arms. "And?"

"And we don't exactly meet regulations."

"Regulations?" Jed asked.

Riggs cut in. "I don't like it. The Iron Guard can check the ship any time. They'll take one look and find T-five engine enhancers, carbine-cored firearms, and dread paraphernalia. All of which will send us to an iron cell! I'm not getting my engine seized because some uptight customs officer thinks I shouldn't be allowed to own it!"

"We'll just keep our distance," Captain Bog said. "You'll drop us at a dock zone in the morning and pick us up at night."

He turned to Jed. "And while we're there, nod politely to the scrap slugs, who don't give a clunk about anything or anyone but themselves. Those ramshackle, grease-chinned, pompous pieces of . . ." He mumbled more incoherent curses to himself.

"Okay, then," Jed said. "Stay away from the clunk."

"Exactly."

Kizer scowled. "It's called order," he said. "It's better than letting a whole town full of lunatics swing through the air on chains."

Captain Bog held up a hand. "I shouldn't have said anything. Iron, copper, it doesn't matter. They're all scrap."

It was a full day's travel to Farburrow. When they were four scopes away, a pinprick of light glimmered on the horizon. The closer they got, the brighter it became. The township shone like a mirror under the sun. Polished steel plated every surface, as if the whole metropolis had been outfitted in a suit of battle armor. Riggs dropped the rest of them at the nearest dock zone, and they walked into the township.

Farburrow was the opposite of Dawndrake in every way. The Farburrow spikes looked like long, sleek silver needles. The streets were perfectly bricked in aluminum. And on those streets, people walked with purpose. No one meandered about like the coppers had. An unsettling silence blanketed the township. Jed felt uncomfortable even whispering while they walked.

As they had before, they all took the etchwork from shop to shop, asking if anyone recognized the people in the images.

No one did.

Until they entered Hamlin's Brewery.

Jed called for attention as he moved from group to group, flashing the etchings to anyone who would look. Again, nobody recognized the images. Jed turned to leave, shoulders down.

"Wait," a voice called. "Let me see those again."

A man with gray hair and a well-groomed beard held out his hand. Jed showed him the pictures.

The man nodded to himself.

"How do you know these two?"

"They're my parents," Jed said.

He nodded. "And what names did you say?"

"Ryan and Mary."

"Ryan and Mary *who*?"

"Just Ryan and Mary."

"Just Ryan and Mary?" He stroked his chin. "They wouldn't happen to have the last name *Jenkins*, would they?"

Sprocket's gaze shot toward Jed. "*Jenkins*? Ryan and Mary *Jenkins*?"

Jed's skin felt hot. His cheeks burned.

The man's eyes shifted in a strange way. His hand moved to a holster at his hip, and he pulled a shatterbox free.

But before he could lift it, Sprocket's four-foot shatterlance was somehow already in her hands, at the ready.

"Do you know what that kid is worth?" the man said to Sprocket. "We'll split it. Fifty-fifty."

"I don't think you know who you're talking to," Sprocket said. "I'm not some iron gutter clunk. I'm a javelin."

"Javelin?" He nearly shouted the word. "A *javelin* in *this* establishment?"

The room fell deathly silent as every person's eyes fell on Sprocket.

Kizer leaned toward her. "We should probably run," he whispered.

Sprocket eyed the roomful of glaring faces. "We should probably run," she repeated to Jed.

A few irons rose from their seats. Shatterboxes hissed and hummed as others around them readied their equipment.

Still holding the shatterlance in one arm, Sprocket unclipped a canister from her belt with her free hand. The canister dropped to the floor, and a cloud of smoke burst around them, filling the room.

Chairs slid away from tables, and iron footsteps thundered around them.

"Now," Sprocket said. "Go!"

Iron everywhere began to shout, and more shatterboxes hissed to life.

Blue bolts pierced the cloud of smoke and sailed over Jed's head.

"Run!" Kizer yelled, yanking Jed by the arm and leading him to the exit.

Kizer shoved open a set of double doors, and smoke spilled into an empty street. "Follow me!" he called to the others, still holding tight to Jed's arm.

They ran, but every iron from the brewery chased. The iron shouted to others in the streets to stop them.

By the time they reached the docks, at least a hundred iron were on their tail.

"Get us up and out of here!" Captain Bog shouted to Riggs and Shay on board.

Ladders uncoiled down the ship.

"If ever there was a time to learn ladder climbing," Captain Bog said to Jed, "now is it. Jump!"

They each leaped from the dock onto a rope ladder.

Bessie's propellers whirred, and the tug lifted away from Farburrow.

"Jenkins?" Sprocket said when they were clear from the township. "Ryan and Mary *Jenkins*?"

Jed nodded. "You know them?"

"Everyone does! They're the ones who started this whole war!"

"They *what*?"

"Most everyone in the yard used to think gilded relics were just glittertales," Sprocket said. "Did you know that? Well . . . turns out most of the yard was wrong. Because the Jenkinses found one. The only gilded relic that's ever been found."

"My mom and dad?"

She nodded. "Those two were cracked as gutter clunk."

"What do you mean?"

"I mean they were insane. Like their heads were full of applesauce instead of practicality."

"Practicality?" Kizer said, one eyebrow raised. "This coming from *you*?"

"Hey," Sprocket said, "I'm as batty as the next copper. But the Jenkinses were as madcap as coppers ever get."

"My parents were copper?" Jed asked.

"Javelins," Sprocket said with a nod. "The best. And one day they just flew straight into the fog. Everyone thought they were dead, but six months later, out they came with a gilded relic. And a whole armada of dread nipping at their tails." Sprocket laughed once. "I swear, every copper, iron, rust, and dread chased those two over each inch of the yard. Then, one day, they just disappeared."

"But what if they didn't just up and disappear?" Captain Bog said. He turned to Jed. "What if they dug their way under the fringe?"

The others followed his gaze. Then they looked back to Sprocket.

"My sister hunted for the Jenkinses," she said. "I used to help her mark up yard maps back home. We'd shade out areas whenever someone claimed to have had a Jenkins sighting. The last few areas weren't too far away from the spot where we picked up Golden Boy."

Kizer looked at Jed's watch. "So then that junkstorm spotter really *is* the stolen gilded relic?"

Shay giggled and covered her mouth with both hands. "Sorry," she said.

"What's so funny?" Kizer asked.

"I've already told you," Shay said. "It's pretty, yes. But it's not gilded pretty. It's only regular pretty. That would be too silly. Much too silly."

While the crew argued Shay's point, Jed thought about his parents: Copper javelins. Javelins who started a war.

"I know where we can go," Sprocket said.

"You do?" Jed asked.

"There's a secret javelin base about nine hundred scopes west."

"Nine *hundred*?" Kizer said. "That doesn't make sense. I've never heard of copper operatives out that far west!"

"Did you not hear the part about it being *secret*?"

"You think they'll know where my parents are?"

She shrugged. "Maybe. If any copper would, they would."

"Nine hundred scopes is a decent flight for a *guess*. A month, maybe more . . ." Captain Bog said.

"It's all I got," Sprocket said.

Captain Bog looked at Jed and nodded. "All right. Then let's hit a storm on the way out, fuel up, and head west. It'll be a long trip."

Jed smiled. "Thank you. Maybe you *are* 'thoughtfulness and warm hugs' after all."

"And maybe that's just your imagination talking."

T^{*enacity,*} Jed tried to remind himself. He had decided last week that *tenacity* was the most difficult word in SPLAGHETTI.

As they flew toward the storm, Jed wandered the deck. A light caught his eye. Spyglass. Again. The red light, as it had been every morning, was pulsing once again.

"Would you stop that already?" he muttered.

The head turned, and he could feel the empty eye and spyglass staring at him. "I think you and I are going to be good friends," it said.

"Why do you keep saying stuff like that? You don't know me. You're just some clunk decoration." But as the words left Jed's mouth, his throat felt dry and pinched uncomfortably.

"But I *do* know you. I know a lot about you. In fact . . . let's play a game to see how well I know you. It's called Guess What's in Your Pocket." He smiled. "I'll go first. I'm picturing something . . . something *round* . . . something *yellow* . . ."

"How do you—"

"No, no. It's not your turn yet. I'm smelling something. Something that smells like home. And *family*."

"Stop it."

"I see a—"

Sprocket's thin voice shouted from the bridge, cutting off Spyglass. "Pobble! I thought you sprayed the deck last week!"

"Yup," Pobble called back. "I spray it down every Rigday. Sometimes even again on Nearday."

"Then why's a gollug slug stuck here under the helm?"

"We'll play later," Spyglass whispered. "When fat janitors and shrill pigeons aren't squawking at each other."

Jed pressed the button on Spyglass's head, and the light disappeared.

"Get up here and scrape this thing off!" Sprocket shouted.

Pobble grabbed a plastic spatula and marched up the bridge stairs. "I'm a-coming."

A few moments later he walked out, a purple slug stuck to the spatula. He smiled at Jed. "You ever taste one of these?"

"I've had escargot, if that counts," Jed said.

Pobble's brow scrunched. "Never eaten that can before. Not that I can recall, at least." His confusion shifted into something sneaky. "Hey, I got an idea. I'll give you a handful of batteries to take a bite right out of its back!"

Kizer peeked around from one of the stacks. "Hold on. Make that *two* handfuls," he said. He reached into a pocket and pulled out some batteries. "But only if you swallow the bite." He slapped the batteries onto a table.

"Are you crazy?" Jed said. "I'm not going to take a bite out of that thing."

"I'll put in a handful," Sprocket said from the top of the staircase.

"Bring the slug over here," Kizer said, pointing to the table. "You in on this, Shay?" Kizer asked.

She strolled closer. "In on *what*? What are you all doing?"

Jed walked to the table. He poked the slug and it made a squishing noise.

"Bite! Bite! Bite!" chanted Pobble.

"Bite! Bite! Bite!" Sprocket and Kizer joined in.

The whole crew was smiling and cheering. He couldn't help but smile back.

Shay pushed her way through the group. "Eww! Jed, don't." She leaned closer and whispered, "Besides, you could get *twice* that many batteries, silly mouse." She stepped back and cringed at the slug. "That's disgusting."

Pobble stepped in front of her and slapped Jed's back. "Ah, don't listen to her. It probably tastes like blueberries or something. And just look at all them batteries."

Sprocket looked over her shoulder. "Hurry. Before Captain catches me away from my post."

And then another word from SPLAGHETTI surfaced in Jed's mind. A word he'd once thought he'd never feel around this crew. But now he *did* feel it. Or something like it. A word that made him consider—just for a moment, at least—taking a bite from the back of a gooey slug.

Gregariousness.

. . .

By Nearday afternoon, they'd reached the storm.

"Pull us back, Sprocket," Captain Bog said. "I want a safe distance. Nothing hits the ship, got it?"

"Aye, aye, Captain."

Gray clouds swirled in the distance and drew together.

"Get ready," Captain Bog called.

The clouds deepened into black. Old junk lifted from the piles and new junk fell. Everything whirled into a thick mass, crashing like thunder in a wild frenzy. No matter how many storms Jed witnessed, each was as terrifying as the last. The dark, whirling winds howled. Junk exploded in the air and clattered to the piles.

Shay was giddy as always. "Do you ever wonder where it all comes from?" he asked her.

"The sky?"

"The junk."

"I bet those mean clouds find pretty things and drink them all up. Then they get sick because they drank too many. Their bellies get gray and sad. Then . . ."

She paused and looked at Jed.

"Blaahhhawwwrrg!" she shouted. "They puke it all up!"

Jed laughed. "But where do the clouds get it from?"

"Clouds fly higher than any mouse's wings ever. Even over sky stacks."

"You mean into the fringe?"

She shrugged. "Maybe."

"Looks like it's over." Captain Bog nodded to Sprocket. "Take us in."

The propellers hummed and the ship lurched forward. The inky darkness had drained from the clouds, and they were again a puffy white.

"Okay," Kizer began, "you know the drill. Once we land, Pobble clears stock space in the bay. Mess storage is packed eleven cans deep, deck to ceiling, so don't stop for cans. Batteries and ship repair, nothing else unless you see—what was it called again, Jed?"

"Smoked rattlesnake."

Kizer nodded. "Smoked rattlesnake."

Originally, he'd only cooked rattlesnake up out of curiosity, but the crew had loved it. Admittedly, it wasn't half bad out of the can. It had been years since he'd eaten rattlesnake. He thought of the desert camping trips he used to take with his dad. They'd roast a snake over the fire, then lie on the cracked earth and watch the sky change from a deep blue to—

"Volley incoming!" Kizer shouted.

A bowling ball punched through the freshly white clouds and soared toward *Bessie*. Sprocket kicked a lever, but it was too late. The ball slammed into the deck and went straight through the ship as if the hull were made of paper.

"Everyone all right?" the captain asked. "Let's take her in a bit slower, Sprocket." He searched the clouds. "Still a few stragglers."

"Aye."

Sprocket cranked another lever. A terrible whine whistled from the engine. She repositioned the lever and jiggled it. The screech worsened.

Riggs yelled something from below. His feet pattered up the stairs to the main deck, and his head peeked up at them. "What the clunk just happened?"

Kizer pointed to the sky. "Bowling ball. Went straight through *Bessie*."

"No." Riggs shook his head. "It went straight through her engine!"

Captain Bog spun around. "It *what?*"

"I need to shift power to the defluxor core," Riggs said.

"Will it hold?" the captain asked.

"A brand-new one? Definitely. One that's been on its last mile for the last two thousand two hundred and thirty-eight miles? I don't know."

"Any other options?"

Riggs shook his head.

"Do it," the captain said.

Riggs hurried off to the engine room and paused at the staircase. "If you hear something snap, or see even a little green smoke, then, well, we're all going to die. So"—he gave a two-fingered salute—"it's been a pleasure. Mostly."

The crew waited in silence. Sprocket sat frozen in the

command chair, gripping the ship's controls. Shay chewed her bottom lip. Kizer paced in erratic circles. And Captain Bog—emotionless as ever—lifted his chin a few degrees, hands clasped behind his back.

Nothing happened.

No sound.

No smoke.

"The core's connected!" Riggs shouted from below. "And it's taking the added payload!"

The crew cheered, and the corner of Captain Bog's lip turned up. He nodded to no one in particular.

Then a snap echoed inside the belly of the tug. Metal clanged and rattled below their feet.

Another snap.

And another.

Each snap louder than the last.

Everyone stared at the deck as ghostly tendrils of green smoke slithered through the metal planks. The strands of vapor joined together until the entire deck was bathed in green mist.

Sprocket pulled a lever. The engine snarled and sputtered.

"Land the ship!" Riggs shouted. "Now!"

Sprocket tugged and shoved levers. "The helm isn't responding!"

A final piece of metal snapped. The hum from the engine fell silent. *Bessie* was dead.

"We've lost propulsion!" Sprocket yelled.

"Sky prop, now!" Captain Bog called.

The nose of the ship tipped forward.

They began to fall.

Sprocket jammed a lever, and the sky propeller blades flipped into place. They started spinning, but it was too late.

Wind rushed against Jed's face.

We're going to crash. We're going to die. I'm going to die.

"Brace yourselves!" Captain Bog wrapped his arms around the railing.

The sky prop whirred faster. Jed anchored himself to the smokestack. The once-blurry brown of junk was now rich with detail.

Sprocket yanked levers and stomped pedals, but nothing responded.

The sky prop reached full throttle, and the tug began to slow.

Lift. Lift.

Shay squeezed her eyes shut and curled around the cable next to Jed. She looked like a frightened mouse with nowhere else to hide. Sprocket released the controls and strapped the helm belts around herself.

The sky prop shrieked as it struggled to slow the ship. It wasn't enough. *Bessie* rammed into a pile.

One second Jed's arms were wrapped around the smokestack, and the next they weren't. Where had it gone? Where was it?

He was staring at the sky.

Then at the deck.

The sky.

The deck.

His limbs flopped around his body. Weightless. He reached out. *Grab something! You're going to die. Grab anything!*

His head smashed against something dense, twisting his neck in a way it had never twisted before. A pop echoed in his ears. His eyes shook, and the world became a splatter of borderless color. Nothing made sense. Nothing fit together.

He tried to lift an arm, a finger. His body wouldn't respond. Stillness crept through his veins like venom. Pressure squeezed the air from his lungs, and the swirl of color before him faded into black.

23

The sky was the color of uncertainty.

No, Jed thought. *That doesn't make sense.* He studied the sky. Stared at the black splotches breaking through the clouds. They were bulbous and foggy and made his stomach feel like eggs.

Eggs? That's not right either. What's happening to me?

He tried to stand. His legs wouldn't respond. He looked down at his body, and thick horror oozed through his chest.

They're—they're—

They were gone. Legs gone. Arms gone. Everything gone.

He screamed.

The clouds darkened and roared. Black rain poured down. But it wasn't rain. It was oil. Splashing against him. Covering his face—his eyes.

My legs! I need my legs!

More oil.

I can't stand up! Somebody help! I'm going to drown!

The oil poured from the clouds in great sheets. Jed coughed and choked.

So much oil—too much.

It was heavy and thick and rose like water in a sink. It rose past his ears. Past his chin. He clamped his mouth shut, and it poured over his face—over his eyes. Its weight pressed against him like a slab of stone. A dizzy blur seized his mind, and his consciousness faded.

. . .

When Jed awoke, his skin felt slick and cold. His heart hammered against his chest. He swiped at his arms, trying to wipe away the liquid.

Sweat. It's only sweat. His heart slowed, and he drew in a breath. *I was dreaming.* He checked each arm and each leg. They were where they belonged. His vision cleared. There was a woman in a red dress dancing in the rain.

A painting.

"About time," the captain said. "Been wondering when you would get your lazy backside out of my bed."

Jed sat up. His vision swirled like a kaleidoscope. "What happened?" He rubbed his head. "We were crashing . . . and then . . ."

"And then we crashed. And then you lazed about in my bed for two hours."

"Is everyone okay?"

"They're not a bunch of scrawny babies who need two-hour naps after *Bessie* has a bumpy landing."

"And Shay?"

"Banged up. She isn't complaining, though. You get one scrape and you're out cold."

Jed rolled his eyes. "Yeah, I get it." He rocked his head from shoulder to shoulder. It had popped so loudly when he'd hit . . . well, whatever it was that he'd hit.

The porthole revealed that they were still grounded. "I've been out for two hours?"

"At least."

"But"—sweat beaded his forehead—"what about the iron? And the copper?"

"We're patching up as fast as we can. Crew's still looking for parts."

Jed's heartbeat thudded in his cheeks. "One hour—two at the most. It's what you said! We have to get out of here. We have to hide."

"I'm not going anywhere anytime soon." The captain patted his thigh. A pool cue and a yardstick wrapped with an orange scarf splinted the bone below his left knee.

"Is it broken?"

He shrugged. "I'll bet you thirty batteries I could still climb a ladder faster than you."

Jed gave a sympathetic smile. "How long before we're found?"

"I was expecting visitors a half hour ago. We've been lucky to make it this long undiscovered."

Jed stumbled from the bed and made his way to the main deck. The impact had shredded the hull, and two of the main propeller blades were cracked.

Riggs stood near a pile of gears and scavenged parts, flipping through his notebook.

"What can I do to help?" Jed asked.

"Got any magnetic couplings or platinum fuses?"

"I don't know what those are."

"Didn't think so." Riggs sighed. "Go find a car horn, three feet of copper tubing, and a pickax. Check the backsides of refrigerators for the tubing."

Half the items in his notebook still hadn't been crossed off. "We're not even close to getting in the air, are we?" Jed asked.

"Closer than it looks." Riggs scratched four items off the list and drew a few arrows. "We don't need everything on here to lift her off the piles. Just get me that tubing."

Jed pictured the steamboat war zone. "Copper and iron will be here any minute."

Riggs gave a single laugh. "Of course they will! What do you want me to do about it?"

"We should hide." Jed scanned the skies for movement.

"Are you crazy? I'm not leaving the ship! Do you know what they'll do to it? Strip it bare and turn it to scrap!"

"Better than iron prisons. Or dying."

Riggs tapped the list. "We have time. We can make it." He

crossed another item off the list. "Maybe if I pull turbine fans and swap the coolant generator with—"

"It's not worth it."

Riggs snapped his notebook shut. "This is my home! I'm not leaving my home!"

Jed pointed to the skyline. "If warships start showing up, you could easily jump down and hide under some bucket, but what about the captain? He won't be able to run."

Riggs rubbed his eyes. "If I can just find . . ." He lifted a sheet of metal.

"How sure are you that she'll even get off the ground?"

Riggs looked at the cracked smokestack, broken propellers, and fractured hull. "I don't know."

"We need to get the captain and find a place to hide," Jed said. "We'll fix her up as soon as the warships leave."

Riggs reread his list before kicking a copper pipe sticking out of the deck. "Fine. Start gathering cans. I'll get the captain."

Jed hurried to the mess and grabbed a hiking pack. *Sorry, Pobble. No berries and syrup if we're going to last longer than a day.* He filled the pack with corned beef hash, beef stew, chili, sweetened condensed milk, and tuna with oil.

He hefted the pack on his shoulders and marched up the stairs.

"Here, take the captain," Riggs said. "I need to find the others."

Riggs took the bag of food, and Jed replaced him as a crutch. The captain leaned against Jed and hopped on his uninjured leg. Jed stumbled against the weight.

"Of course they send the runt to carry me," the captain

said. Despite his effort to lighten the mood, apprehension bled into his voice. "You doing okay there?"

"Riggs is gathering the others," Jed managed to say between steps. "I'll be fine. Just keep moving."

"The stowaway hatch is buried. We'll need to jump from the main deck."

Jed paused to catch his breath. "The main deck?" The stairs in front of him looked twice as long as they normally did. "Okay." He sucked in a breath and lifted under the captain's arm. "Come on." His words left his mouth in labored bursts. "I can climb ladders faster than you can walk."

Jed half carried, half dragged the captain up the stairs. When they reached the main deck, they both collapsed onto the floor. Jed stood and stared at the junk below them.

"We're going to need help," Jed said.

The captain didn't respond; his eyes were frozen on the horizon. Dark clouds billowed in the distance. They bubbled and churned, swirling together like a junkstorm.

Jed checked his wrist. The watch hands were still.

Captain Bog shook his head. "That's not a storm." Jed looked closer. The black clouds hovered, dense and impenetrable in the distance.

"Falcons?" Jed asked.

Captain Bog shook his head again.

"Dreadnoughts. Hundreds of them."

"Oh, little Sprooocket." Spyglass's singsong voice sounded like shattering glass. "I told you I was patient. My legs are coming, and I'm so very hungry."

Adrenaline surged through Jed. He hooked the captain's arm around him. "Move!"

They limped forward.

"Don't go far," Spyglass said to Jed. "I've got plans for *you*, too."

The red light was back. Blinking steadily on Spyglass, as if it was winking at Jed.

When they reached the railing, Jed peered over the side.

"The ladder," the captain said.

Jed shook his head. "You won't be able to make it down the ladder!" He spotted the crew in the distance. "Riggs! Riggs!"

They were too far away. Even if they heard him, they couldn't make it back before the dreadnoughts arrived.

Captain Bog pulled away from Jed. "Get off the ship! Get to the others and hide!"

"I'm not leaving you behind."

The captain drew his fist back and cracked it against Jed's skull. Jed's vision flickered and he stumbled.

"Get off the ship!" Captain Bog yelled. "Go!"

Jed pulled the rope ladder into the ship.

"What are you doing?" the captain asked.

"Shut up."

Jed looped its end around the captain's waist.

"Get this off me!" The captain pulled at the rope, then drew back to strike at Jed again.

Jed kicked him in the leg between the splints. Captain Bog howled and clutched his broken leg while Jed tied the rope.

Jed reached into the captain's pocket and took his can opener. "Hide yourself when you get down there."

The captain looked up from his leg. "When I get down *where*?"

Jed took a deep breath and shoved the captain over the railing. When he was about to slam into the junk, the rope ladder pulled taut. The captain grunted, and his body swayed above the ground.

My turn.

Jed stepped onto the ladder, but as he put his full weight on the rung, the rope began to tear. He scrambled back into the ship.

"Get ready!" He pressed the blade of the can opener against

the rope and began sawing. The captain's weight helped the fibers tear easily. The strands snapped. There was a solid thunk as the captain hit the junk pile.

Captain Bog groaned, then hollered, "You ever do something like that again, I'll pull off your eyelids!"

Fumes seeped into the air. The dreadnought fleet was nearly on top of them.

"Jed, get down here!" the captain yelled. "Get off that deck! They're going to see you!"

Jed straddled the railing. It was too high to jump. He bolted to the lower decks and hauled the mattress from the captain's bed. He'd spent all his energy carrying the captain, and now his breath was short and his muscles wobbled.

Almost there.

He lifted the mattress high and ran.

"What are you doing?" Captain Bog called.

Jed flipped the mattress over the edge and leaped from the deck. Air rushed over his face. His stomach dropped. He landed with a chest-shattering impact. The force was so powerful, Jed wondered if he'd missed the mattress and hit a boulder instead. He coughed and struggled to suck in air.

"Go!" Captain Bog yelled.

Jed crawled to his feet, barely able to breathe. He searched for the captain but couldn't see him.

"You trying to give away my location?" Captain Bog called. "Because if you stick around any longer, you will."

Jed stopped looking and ran. The sky darkened above him as dreadnoughts surrounded the tugboat: a fleet of ships, stained black from the smog lingering around the hulls like ghostly cocoons. An angry orange glowed through cracks and seams, as if inside each ship was a giant furnace.

A pair of hands wrapped around Jed's face and yanked him to the ground.

"Get down!" Sprocket whispered. "Where's the captain?"

"Hiding by the ship. Where's everyone else?"

"Riggs sent Shay and me to find you two. Then *those* showed up." She motioned to the circle of dreadnoughts.

"Why are they all here?" Jed asked.

Sprocket shook her head. "I don't know. But the ground will be swarming with dread any second."

"We have to get to the captain!" Jed said. "They're going to find him!"

"If we step one foot out there, they'll find us too." She tightened her grip on Jed's arm. "Right now you do what I say, got it?"

"But he's—"

Sprocket squeezed, and Jed winced. "This is what I do. And I'm really good at it. Okay?"

"Okay."

Like scampering mice, they ducked from cover to cover. Sprocket led the way over loose junk, avoiding gaps and unsteady footholds. Jed matched her steps.

A sound echoed from below. "Psssst!" Shay smiled up at Jed from underneath a lawn mower. "Down here."

Sprocket lifted the mower, revealing a wide cavity. They crawled inside and covered the opening.

Brown pleather seats and small windows lined the wall of the cavity. It was a school bus, toppled on its side and buried under a heap of junk.

"We couldn't reach the captain," Sprocket said.

"I can," Shay said. "I'm a sneaky mouse."

Sprocket shook her head. "Too dangerous."

"Sprocket's right," Jed said. "We just have to hope the dread don't find him."

He crawled to the window and shifted the lawn mower to see. They were barely a hundred feet from the tug. He could still see *Bessie*'s smokestack and Spyglass's head, chanting into the open air.

"Send down the lines!" it shouted. "So I can slurp up the soup inside these pink flesh bags!"

Something above them popped, and a cable shot from a dreadnought. A spike at its tip impaled the junk, and the cable pulled taut. As soon as the first cable landed, hundreds more followed. Lines whistled through the air, anchoring into the piles all around them.

The cables began to quiver as dread crawled from the ships and began to descend.

They were like Pobble's story: Limping figures sewn together with twisted patches of metal. Scraps of steel wired to skin. Spinning gears in place of muscle.

They hit the ground like rain on a tin rooftop. One crunched into the junk by the mower. It had a mop for one of its legs, a birdcage for a chest, and a garden trowel for a hand. Two other dread had limbs made from fire extinguishers, broken axles, metal beams, and crude, rusting scraps. They hobbled along the uneven junk with a clatter.

The dread turned toward Spyglass and began to creep aboard the tugboat. They piled at the ship's base, climbing on top of each other to board.

"Spyglass," a dread muttered. "It's Captain Spyglass."

The word *spyglass* trickled through the mob, each of them chanting it and peering over the dread in front to see.

"Everyone stop mumbling and one of you weevil-eating maggots get me a body!" Spyglass shouted. "Now!"

An unseen dread in the center of the swarm screeched, and metal parts scattered in the air.

A dread lifted a headless body into the air. "Here, here! This one! Right here! Take this one!" it shouted.

"Too short," Spyglass called. "And not ugly enough. Pick again."

Another dread screeched, and a moment later its headless body was lifted above the crowd for approval. "This one! He's a good one, I swear! Was my deck mate. Strong bones. Tall. Ugly as slug snot. I would've stolen his body for myself if I didn't want you to have it!"

Spyglass studied the offering. "Very well. Bring it up here and get me off this post."

The dread dragged the headless body to the deck while others scampered to the smokestack to retrieve the head mounted to the stack. One of them touched the red, flashing button. It stopped flashing, and the spyglass retracted.

Spyglass was quickly fastened to his new body. He stretched

his new limbs and examined himself. He pulled a shatterbox from his boot and nodded. "Who found me this body?"

A dread scrambled forward. "I did. Name's Grom."

"You said you wanted to steal this body for yourself?"

"Well, yes, but not now. Now it's yours. I wanted to—"

Spyglass aimed the shatterbox at Grom and fired. Metal parts burst along the deck. "Sorry, Grom, I can't have crew wanting to steal my new legs. Did anyone else want this body? Anyone?"

"Him! Him!" a dread shouted. "Doozok here wanted it too!"

"You liar!" Doozok yelled, swinging the shovel that was his arm into the dread's face.

Spyglass lifted his shatterbox and shot them both. "Anyone else?" He waited, but no other dread spoke. "Good. Now where's your captain?"

A dread, its body at least as tall as Spyglass's, walked forward. The swarm parted as he approached.

"Captain Lurg," the dread said with a nod. "I'm captain of dreadnought 188."

"I think you're mistaken," Spyglass said. He raised his shatterbox again and pulled the trigger. A crack filled the air, and black smoke snaked up from the barrel. Lurg crumpled to the floor. "Because it looks like *I'm* captain of the 188." He looked at the nearest dread. "Wouldn't you agree?"

"Aye, Captain," the dread said without hesitation.

Spyglass nodded. "Good. Any of you chin scabs hear

differently? No? Perfect," he said, not waiting for a response. "Now listen up. I'm starving, and there's three little flesh bags hiding about the piles that I'm particularly interested in. One is a duck-kneed shoe wipe with a broken leg. The other is a sweet little darling I made a promise to. And the third is a special boy I'd like to get to know better. Find them."

The swarm slipped off the ship and began digging. Searching.

"There're thousands of them," Jed said. "They're going to find us."

"Quiet!" Sprocket said.

As one of the dread searched the junk near the tug, its back leg snapped in half; then something launched it skyward.

"There! There!" the dread chanted. "Found one, there!"

Three dread scrambled into the space and hauled Captain Bog to his feet. They carried him up the mound and delivered him to Spyglass.

The crowd chittered in excitement.

"Ah, the mighty Captain Bog," Spyglass said. "Such a big and brave spit weasel. How strong and brave are you now?"

Captain Bog lunged forward and struck Spyglass in the face. Dread scrambled to yank him back and restrain his arms. The captain snorted and spit onto Spyglass's cheek. Even at this distance, Jed could see the wad of saliva splash against the leathery forehead and roll down the nose. Spyglass didn't flinch. He didn't even wipe the spit from his face.

"Your face looks better mounted on a stack," he said.

"Perhaps yours will too," Spyglass said.

"I want his arm!" a pirate shouted, waving the mangled rolling pin attached to his elbow.

Spyglass shook his head. "This bladder-scabbed cockroach is *mine*. First I want him tied to the mast and baked in the sun just like I was, thanks to him. Take him to the ship! And find the others!"

Dread scampered from the tug and returned to the piles to dig. A small group stayed to stuff Captain Bog into a tight, black sack and drag him along the junk floor to one of the hanging lines.

They tugged on the line, and it lifted Captain Bog and the dread into the ship.

Jed, Shay, and Sprocket stayed silent inside the bus. The dread dug under them, to their left, to their right, and walked right over them—but none noticed the three silent mice in the school bus.

Then one of the burrowers turned around. And headed straight for them.

"We need to get out of here," Jed whispered to Shay. "Now."

She shook her head. "They'll see us and *snap!* put us straight into mousetrap bags like Ugly Mouse. I don't want to go into a mousetrap bag."

The tunneling dread burrowed closer.

"That's why we need to find somewhere else to hide!" Jed said. "They're almost on top of us!"

Sprocket nodded. "We need to go."

The lawn mower flipped aside. A dread—both eye sockets empty and black—stared at them.

"Run!" Jed said.

He jumped up and shoved the creature. The three climbed from the bus and sprinted. Dread closed in on them from all angles. They were everywhere—as if they were the fog itself.

"There's nowhere to go!" Sprocket yelled.

Jed looked in every direction. She was right. There was nowhere to go.

A hand grabbed his elbow and yanked.

"Get off me!" Jed kicked at the dread. His foot collided with a copper pipe and broke it from its shoulder. But another dread was already holding his arm again. And his legs.

They carried him to the tugboat and dumped him and Sprocket before Spyglass.

Jed looked around for Shay. Where was she? Had they found her?

"Hello, darling," Spyglass said to Sprocket. "If I recall, we had plans for a date, you and I. That is, if ever I managed to find new legs." He looked down. "Which I now appear to have. I want you to know how much I'm going to enjoy this."

25

Spyglass grabbed Sprocket's arm and opened his mouth. His jaw unhinged itself, revealing every yellowed tooth in his gums.

He clamped his teeth around Sprocket's arm and tightened his jaw.

Her skin dimpled under the bite. She held her breath, and her eyes squeezed shut.

Spyglass bit harder, savoring the moment.

His jaw flexed, and Sprocket screamed.

She tried to yank her arm away, but Spyglass's grip was too strong.

As he bit harder, a familiar whistling sound cut through the air. The tail of one of the dreadnoughts exploded in a cloud of fire and smoke.

Far away, silver dots appeared on the skyline. Falcons.

Trails of violet smoke shot from their noses and headed for the ring of dreadnoughts. More explosions rattled the ships, and one dreadnought began to sink to the junk. The dread returned fire.

Spyglass released Sprocket's arm, and the lens on his eye protruded—focusing on the wing of falcons.

"Bag these two and bring them to my ship! Tell the forward three vessels to engage the falcons. Tell the rest to return to the fog."

"Three dreadnoughts won't be enough to fight that flock," one of the dread said. "They'll just get blown to bits."

"Fligg is right," another added. "We have more than enough dreadnoughts. We can win."

"We got what we came for," Spyglass said. "We're not here to knock birds out of the sky."

"What if the other ships refuse?"

Spyglass grabbed Fligg by the neck. "Then you tell them the order came directly from the *Galleon*. We're to gather the cargo and leave."

"What cargo? I never heard of any message."

"That's because you're a worm. Now get it done!"

Three dread grabbed Jed and stuffed him into a black sack. The material was stringy and felt like a tight, sticky web. A dread grabbed Jed's legs and pulled him to one of the cables. In unison, the circle of dreadnoughts flared their engines. All but three ships turned in retreat and began to accelerate. Jed rose into the air, passing the black shroud of smoke engulfing the ship. He landed on a metal floor. Hydraulics hissed as the bay doors closed, sealing him inside the heart of the dreadnought.

26

Orange light glowed around Jed. The dread who'd carried him into the ship hurried off.

The sack around Jed's body was impossibly tight. He squirmed, but the sticky material barely stretched. He flexed his arms and neck. They wouldn't move more than a couple of inches. He tried his fingers. Nothing.

And then the tip of his pinky grazed against something in his pocket.

The can slicer.

His lips curled into a web-squished grin. Bit by bit, he slid the tool up and out of his pocket. Once it was free, he pressed the round blade against the webbing and made sawing motions.

A satisfying rip sounded in the quiet chamber.

His heart beat faster.

He continued sawing.

Jed finished cutting away the sack and peeling off the sticky material.

"You're not a very sneaky mouse, are you?" a voice said behind him.

"Shay? Is that you?" The orange light pulsed and glowed against her face. "You're okay! How did you escape?"

"You're not the only mouse with tricks."

"Do you know where the others are?"

He searched the empty floor.

Shay hopped over clumps of junk. "Over here, silly." She pointed at another body.

Jed sliced away the webbing. A foot tore free and kicked toward his face. He lurched backward. "Sprocket!" he half whispered, half shouted. "It's us!"

"Us?" she asked, ripping off the rest of the webs. "Golden Boy? Is that you?"

"And Shay."

"How did you get free?"

Jed held up the can slicer.

"Right."

Shay cleared her throat. "We should go, yes? Before scritchets come scritcheting around and find empty scritchet sacks?"

"Yeah," Jed said. "Where are the others? Where's the captain?"

"In another scritchery," Shay said.

"How do you know?"

She examined each of his eyes. "Weren't you watching?"

"Watching what?"

"When the scritchlees heave-hoed him into the other scritchery. That one!" She pointed up and to the left of where they stood.

"You can find him?" Jed asked.

"Of course!"

She bounded to the far wall, then pushed against a panel. A door opened, spilling orange light into the room.

"How did you know that was there?" Jed asked.

She gave a disapproving scowl. "You should learn to look better."

The door swung open, revealing a dim corridor. Shay skipped through the opening. Jed and Sprocket followed tentatively.

"Slow down," Sprocket whispered. "You're going to get us caught."

"Oh yeah? Wanna bet? Five batteries says I can make it to the end of the hall without a single scritchbug seeing me. Ready? Go!"

She turned and sprinted. "Shay, stop!" Sprocket whispered as loudly as a whisper could get. "Get back here!"

Jed had never seen someone run so fast. Shay's thin body floated with each stride, though she made the motion look effortless as a morning jog.

"Shay!" he whispered. "Wait for us!"

Shay wasn't at the end of the corridor. "Shay," Jed said again. To his left a thin shadow darted away. "Stop!"

They ran after her, but whenever either of them got too close, she'd giggle and skip away.

Each corridor was as black and indistinguishable as the last. Jed ran so fast the lefts and rights escaped his mind until they were deep inside the mazelike ship.

The patter of Shay's footsteps disappeared.

"Shay?" he whispered.

No shadow—no sound.

"Where'd she go?" Sprocket asked, sucking in labored breaths.

Jed looked to the left, then to the right, where he spotted a tiny form crumpled on the floor. His heart thumped. Shay's arms were twisted awkwardly, her body limp and her eyes closed.

Sprocket rushed to her side. "Shay? Can you hear me?" She touched her shoulder.

"Boo!" Shay said, jumping up.

Sprocket lurched back, and her hand jerked toward her shatterbox.

Shay clapped her hands, then bit her bottom lip.

"Are you crazy?" Sprocket snapped. Her shoulders relaxed.

Shay nodded enthusiastically. "Oh yes. Quite."

"Well, don't do that again," Sprocket said.

"Where do we go from here?" Jed said.

Shay pointed left.

"How do you know?" Sprocket asked.

She shrugged.

Jed and Sprocket looked at each other. When they turned back to Shay, she was gone.

"Great," Sprocket mumbled.

They ran in the direction she'd indicated, but before the end of the hallway, Sprocket grabbed Jed and pushed him against a wall.

"Shh!" She held a finger to his lips.

Three shadows flickered on the corridor floor ahead.

Sprocket shoved a shatterbox into Jed's hand. She then unstrapped the shatterlance from her back and pulled a lever into place.

The shatterbox was heavier than Sprocket's finger spins made it look. "How do I—"

"Just pull the trigger."

"Okay, but what if I need to—"

"Jed"—she winked at him and patted his shoulder—"point and pull the trigger."

"Yeah."

Sprocket smiled and stood. They stalked down the corridor, but the shadows were gone.

Something snapped, and metal clanged against the iron deck. Jed's finger twitched, sliding against the trigger.

Sprocket knocked his arm to the side. "Watch where you're pointing that thing." She made a series of hand signals.

Jed shrugged. "What's that supposed to mean?"

Sprocket repeated the motions, and Jed shook his head.

Another sound echoed through the hall. Metal smashed

into metal. Something twisted and snapped. A group of struggling shadows flickered against the wall ahead. "Shay!" Jed called, full volume. He ran ahead toward the movement. "Shay, I'm coming!"

Shay popped out from around the corner, wide-eyed, and touched a finger to her lips. "Shhh! When you're trying to sneak around, you're not supposed to yell."

"Are you okay?" Jed's voice bounced against the walls. "We saw shadows—heard fighting. I thought someone was attacking you."

"They *were* attacking me, silly."

Jed rounded the corner. The scattered remains of three dread lay strewn across the corridor.

"You—you did this?"

"What was I supposed to do? They attacked me."

A mix of relief and fear trickled through him. Who was she? Captain Bog could barely fight off a single dread.

"But how did you—"

"Whoa," Sprocket said, catching up to them. "What happened?"

Shay rolled her eyes. "Come on." She waved them forward. "Every scritch probably heard you two. Not sneaky at all."

Three dread scampered toward the noise—toward them. When they found the bodies, they scurried back the way they'd come.

"We can't let them sound an alarm," Jed said.

Sprocket drew her shatterlance. A crack filled the air. One dread exploded, gears showering the deck. Sprocket cocked a lever, aimed, and fired again. Another dread burst into tinkling bits of metal.

Jed raised his shatterbox and pulled the trigger. Blue particles skimmed past the ear of the third. He fired twice more and hit the dread in the back.

Shay shook her head. "Not sneaky one bit . . ."

Sprocket swirled her finger through the lingering smoke in

a signature. "They'll probably send more than three next time."

"We need to find a place to hide," Jed said. "We can't fight them all."

Sprocket readied another battery in her shatterlance's chamber. "Speak for yourself."

Shay crossed her arms. "Yeah, speak for yourself."

"You can't leave us behind," Jed said to Shay.

"Then run faster."

She spun and sprinted through the corridors, weaving left and right with seemingly no direction in mind.

"She's going to get us all killed!" Sprocket said through gritted teeth.

Around the next corner, a red light pulsed above them, and a foghorn blared with a grinding screech.

"They found the bodies," Jed said.

Sprocket shrugged. "What was left of them, at least."

Up ahead, Shay jolted to a stop.

"Here." She pointed at a door.

"What is this?"

"The most fun place to hide," she said, pushing it open.

They entered a carpeted room with a leather sofa, a four-poster bed, a carved oak desk, and a chest filled with cans and batteries. Jed pulled open the heavy window curtains. The sunlight stung his eyes. "Is this the captain's quarters?" he asked.

"Mm-hm."

"Shay, how did you know this was here?" A chill ran up his back.

"I've been on lots of ships. They're all the same." She plopped onto the sofa. "Yep, best place to hide."

"Hiding in the captain's quarters? You're not serious!" Sprocket said.

"Oh—I'm *very* serious."

The plush bedsheets and pillow were unwrinkled as if never used. "I didn't picture dread having rooms like these. Even Spyglass."

"Spyglass? That scritch with the back-and-forth eye? No, silly. Not *that* captain. The captain of *all* the scritchens. Captain Mouse King."

Jed's stomach tightened. "We're in the mouse king's room?"

Sprocket looked from Jed to Shay. "Mouse king? What are you talking about?"

"The king of the dread," Jed said.

Shay waved a hand. "Oh, hush hush. Mouse king has a fluffy room on *every* scritchum boat. Just in case he flies on one."

"How could you know that?" Sprocket asked.

Shay shrugged. "Doesn't it sound like something he'd do?"

Sprocket gave Shay a dramatic shrug. "How would I know? I've never met him! How do you even know the dread *have* a king?"

"Because he's a mean mouse! Tells me I'm a bad mouse! 'Bad mouse, Shay!' Not a good mouse. Not *ever* a good mouse. I try and try and try and try and *try* to be a good mouse, but always, 'Bad mouse, Shay! Bad mouse!'"

Sprocket gave Jed a wary glance.

"Aren't the dread going to look in here for us?" Jed asked.

Shay nodded. "Oh, definitely. In fact, they're coming right now. We should probably hide."

"They're what?" Jed said. He and Sprocket stared at the door. Hobbled footsteps clattered lightly behind it.

"Under the bed," Sprocket whispered, shoving Shay to the floor.

Jed dropped and scrambled as fast as his hands and knees would allow. The door opened just as he tucked himself under the bed. Feet clomped into the room.

Two were Spyglass's. Four were not.

The other two dread searched the room, opening cabinets and closets.

"If you don't find them before we reach the barge," Spyglass said to the dread, "I'll melt you both into doorstops!"

"We'll find them, Captain," one of the dread said.

"Yes. You will."

The three finished their search and left the room.

Jed, Sprocket, and Shay waited for the sound of footsteps to disappear.

"Well . . ." Shay said. "Now we know where we're going."

"What do you mean?" Sprocket said.

"The barge. Those scritchnobs said we're going to the barge."

"What's the barge?" Sprocket asked.

"Scritcherdom! Where all the scritcherbugs are."

"Like another moving township?" Jed asked.

"Oh, no. Not at all. It has wings like other townships, but

it's bigger than mountains and mountains. Fly and fly for hours and hours to reach the end."

"Hours?" Sprocket said. "You're telling me it's a sky town that takes *hours* to cross?"

"No. I said hours *and* hours."

"And where is it?"

"Where's what?"

"The barge."

"You already know, silly. All mice do. You talk lots and lots about it."

Sprocket shook her head. "No, I don't."

"Of course you do. You just call it something else."

"Then what do I call it?"

"The fog."

28

They took turns listening by the door, but Spyglass didn't return. And so they waited. Sprocket cleaned her shatter-lance, Shay sat on the floor playing with a piece of lint, and Jed held the lemon. It was barely a lemon anymore. The rind was stiff and shriveled. Orange blotches stained the peel. Any hint of citrus was gone, replaced by the smell of pocket and decay. But it was his last connection to home, and he would keep it until he found his parents or it withered away to nothing.

Eventually the light from the window outside dimmed. Black clouds stretched along the horizon. They didn't swirl like the funnel of a junkstorm. They didn't shift with the winds or float or fall. They hovered—still, like a wall at the edge of the world.

"The fog . . ." Jed said.

No one spoke as they slipped into its shadowy mass. Smoky particles danced along the windowpane until the glass was as black as night.

"How do they know where they're going?" Jed asked.

"They listen," Shay said, tilting her ear to the window, "for the sound of engines, and ovens, and clinking, and growling."

Sprocket's brows were tight with apprehension—or fear—or both. But the look wasn't directed at the blackness or the smoke they'd entered. Her body shifted ever so slightly away from Shay's—first a shoulder, a foot, a small turn of a hip. And soon she was two steps away from her.

Shay flattened her palms against the glass. Her gaze was fixed on the black window. "Clink, clink, clink, clink, whoosh," she whispered. "Clink, clink, clink, clink, clink, clink, clink, clink, *whoosh!*"

With each *whoosh* her eyes widened, then slowly returned to normal.

For an hour, maybe longer, they watched.

Nothing changed.

Nothing appeared.

Shay stood transfixed by the black glass, quietly whispering. And then Jed heard something outside. Small at first. Barely noticeable. *Tap, tap, tap, tap . . .*

He stepped to the window.

What was it?

"Clink, clink, clink, clink, whoosh," Shay whispered.

Jed froze. "You've been here before, haven't you?"

Sprocket's hand hovered over a shatterbox at her knee.

"Shay?" Jed asked again.

Her eyes stayed fixed on the window. She let out a low, eerie growl.

A deep moan coursed through the darkness. Shay growled a second time, as if answering the moan.

Jed's cheeks burned. "Shay!"

She flinched and looked at him. "What? What did you say?"

"What is going on?"

"I'm . . ." She looked at the floor as if trying to recall. "I'm not sure."

"Have you been here before?"

Her face twisted. "Think, think," she said to herself, slapping her forehead. The confusion drained from her eyes, and she looked up. "Yes. Yes. I think I have."

"Here?" Sprocket shouted. "You've been *here*? To dread territory? And you didn't tell us? What's going on, Shay?" Sprocket's fingers tightened around the hilt of her shatterbox.

Jed gave Sprocket a small head shake. "Tell us what's going on, Shay," he said. "You knew exactly where to go, where the dread king's quarters were. How? How do you know this place?" He motioned to the window.

She chewed on her lip. "I don't know, I don't know, I don't know!" Her eyes squeezed shut. "I can't remember all the things. Only bits. Little bits. Little, tiny bits." She pinched her fingers together to show how little.

"Think," Jed said.

Her head shook, concentrating. "I don't know. I don't know, I don't know."

"Jed," Sprocket said, pointing at the window.

The black fog thinned as the dreadnought passed through the wall.

A world of night stretched before them.

Far below, tens of thousands of dread swarmed. Ships floated around them in all directions—some as small as *Bessie*, some large enough to make the dreadnought feel like a rowboat. Warships lined the ground below in neat rows.

"That's not the ground," he said, leaning closer to the window. "That's a ship's deck."

Sprocket laughed. "No," she said. "That's impossible."

"He's right," Shay said. "One big boat. The biggest. It's going to clean the junkyard—like a *cleaning* boat. Clean, clean, clean. Pick up all the junk. Pick up all the people. Until no more junk. No more people. All clean."

Whenever Sprocket looked at Shay, her jaw tightened.

"Let's get the captain and get out of here," Sprocket said.

"That's him." Shay tapped on the glass. "The mouse king."

Jed's heart jumped. He swiveled and searched the darkness outside.

"*There.*" Shay pointed. "Behind that ugly boat. Wait. You'll see."

A distant dreadnought drifted to the right, revealing a spot of striking red. Untarnished, in the center of the smog-stained world, was a crimson boat.

It was a three-masted sailing ship, like the kind Jed had read about in history and seen in movies about the Revolutionary War. It was like nothing in the junkyard. Long, golden planks bowed around its surface in a bricklike pattern, every plank matching its neighbor. The gold surface shimmered in the darkness like the dawning sun. Three red sails billowed on each of the tall masts.

"My grandfather—you said they took him there. I have to find him. I have to get on that boat."

"What?" Sprocket spun around and looked at Jed. "You can't *possibly* have said what I just heard."

"I've been trying to find him since I got here. I don't expect you to understand."

"Good, because I *don't*!"

"I'm not asking you to come. We'll get the captain and you off the ship. But I'm going there." Jed stabbed the window.

"All that will do is get yourself killed," Sprocket said.

Jed didn't respond. He just stared at the red and gold shimmering in the darkness, thinking of how to get on board.

29

Sprocket opened the door to the captain's quarters and peeked out. "Clear."

One by one, they darted into the corridor.

Jed nodded. "Okay, Shay. Show us."

She smiled and bolted down the hallway.

"Great," Sprocket said. "This again."

Shay stopped by a door and opened it to reveal a mop and a bucket.

Jed assessed the closet. "This should work."

They squeezed inside, and Jed opened the door just a crack. Before long, a group of dread hobbled past.

Sprocket swung open the door, slamming it against the first dread. It toppled to the floor. Jed leaped on a second dread, swinging his fists.

Shay danced around the third as if it was a game. The dread slashed at her. She smiled and bent over backward. Her left foot kicked the blade from the dread's hand. The dread lunged forward, but she dodged and ran. It stumbled, and Sprocket cracked the butt of her shatterlance against its head.

Once all three dread were motionless on the floor, Jed pulled a pair of boots off one of them and measured them against his own feet.

Sprocket took off her perfectly maintained trench coat, folded it neatly, and set it beside the dread. She cringed as she removed the creature's oil-soaked shirt and pulled it over her own.

Jed pointed to the trench coat. "You won't pass for a dread wearing that. You have to get rid of it."

Sprocket shook her head. "I've been around more corners of the junkyard than anyone. Never seen a coat I liked as much as this. If it's not dready enough for them, then I'll just deal with it."

Jed nodded. "Okay. Then just know that I'm heartbroken for having to do this."

"Having to do what?" she asked.

Jed pulled a knife from a dread and slashed a gaping hole in Sprocket's coat.

Her eyes stretched wider even than Pobble's Ping-Pong ball stare. She reached for the coat but Jed slashed again.

"You clunk piece of—!"

Jed swiped a third time, then nodded. "That should do it. Now it'll pass for a dread coat."

Sprocket shook with rage. "I'm going to strangle you with your own shoelaces!"

"See?" Jed said. "You even sound like a dread now."

Sprocket's hands clenched into fists, and her eyes burned with murder.

Shay stuffed pipes and scraps of metal into a baggy set of tattered clothes. When she was dressed, she twirled in front of the others. "How do I look?" she asked.

"Perfect," Jed said.

Sprocket mumbled something to herself and pulled on the rest of her clothes.

They moved what was left of the bodies into the closet. Then, in their best hobble, they shuffled down the corridor after Shay.

"You know where Captain Bog is?" Sprocket asked.

"Mm-hm," Shay said.

"You seem to know a lot—" Sprocket said.

"Oh, yes." Shay nodded. "I do know a lot. I know that when you pull gollug slugs, they can stretch twice their body length before they snap and all the goopy stuff inside them falls out. I know that white paper doesn't taste good after two sheets and brown paper after three. I also know that—"

"That's all fascinating," Sprocket interrupted, "but how do you know where you're going? I want a real answer, not a *Shay* answer."

Shay paused and thought for a moment. "Fourteen."

"Fourteen?"

"Yes, fourteen." Shay nodded once, then turned around and kept walking.

"I hate her," Sprocket mumbled.

"Shay, stop!" Jed called. He raced to catch her.

When they caught up, Shay stood next to a staircase.

Sprocket grabbed her by both shoulders. "This is important," she said. "There's going to be a lot of dread up there, so we can't run, okay?"

"Of course not," Shay said. "That's not very sneaky. We're dread! Remember?"

Sprocket nodded. "Yes. We're dread."

Shay wagged a scolding finger at Sprocket. "So no running around, all right?"

"Yes," Sprocket agreed. "No running around."

"Good dread."

They climbed to the main deck. The fog hovered around them like a misty sky.

The deck was a patchwork of compressed junk, stacked like bricks. A warped plunger, a broken fishing pole, and a scuffed paintbrush were all embedded into the junk around Jed's feet.

Dozens of smokestacks jutted out from the dreadnought at crooked angles with no particular order. Some were feet apart from one another, while others were isolated.

"Are we sure the captain is out here?" Sprocket asked.

Shay smiled. "Of course not, silly. That's why we're looking. But you didn't *really* mean to ask that, did you? You're just a lazy mouse, that's all."

"I—" Sprocket opened her mouth.

"Either that, or a scaredy mouse."

Sprocket closed her mouth and kept walking.

Shay nodded.

At the next stack, Shay pointed to a large grate on the deck. They walked to the grate and peered inside.

A gray sack lay under the deck in a small, boxy pit.

"Captain!" Jed whispered.

The sack squirmed. "Jed?" a muffled voice answered. "Is that you?"

"And me!" Shay squeaked.

"Hold still, Captain," Sprocket said. She removed the shatterlance from her back and aimed it at the lock.

"Don't!" Jed said. "The dread, they'll—"

A crack sounded, and a beam of white dust splashed against the deck. The lock burst into three pieces.

Sprocket lifted the grate, then dove into the pit and cut the captain free.

"Where's the rest of the crew?" he asked, pulling the strands away from his face.

"It's just us," Jed said.

Captain Bog nodded. "Well, now that every dread on the ship knows where we are . . ."

As if his words had called them, the deck clicked with the uneven gait of dread.

"Let's find a life raft," Sprocket suggested.

Captain Bog shook his head. "They'd just blast us out of the sky. We need another way off this ship."

"I'm not leaving the barge," Jed said. The others looked at him.

"Stop saying that," Sprocket said. "We're all leaving. And that includes you."

"Not until I find my grandfather."

"What's he blathering on about?" the captain asked.

"Shay told me that when the steamboat was attacked, they took my grandfather to the *Red Galleon*." Jed pointed at the red ship hovering in the distance. "To the dread king."

The captain's face went rigid. "Jed . . . I know firsthand what the dread king does to people like you and me and . . . your grandfather. He calls us meat sacks. And you know what he does to *meat sacks*?"

Jed's heart thudded. "Shay said he makes people drink engine oil."

The captain lifted his brows as if surprised that Jed knew. "He does. I've seen it." His throat quivered.

Your daughter, Jed thought. A sick feeling prickled through him, and it was suddenly hard to swallow.

"I have to try," Jed said. "Just like you had to for your daughter. And you'd do it all over, wouldn't you?"

Captain Bog was quiet for a long moment. "Okay."

Sprocket's jaw slackened. "Okay? Did you just say *okay?*"

The captain grabbed Jed's shoulder and limped forward. "We need to find a place to hide."

He waved the others forward, but a pack of dread spotted them. The clicking of their footsteps rattled faster.

"Run!" Sprocket said.

Together they dragged the captain along the deck.

Another pack of dread saw them and moved in from another angle.

More dread added to the packs by the second, until hundreds of them closed in from every side.

"There's nowhere to go!" Sprocket shouted.

Dread everywhere formed a tight circle around them.

Spyglass pushed to the front of the pack and drew his shatterbox.

31

"How nice to see you all again," Spyglass said. "Just like old times. Except now I have legs. And this"—he waggled the shatterbox in the air—"and two thousand dread." He touched his belly. "I'm curious . . . are any of you hungry? Because I'm starving."

"Shay," Jed whispered. "Get ready to—" He looked behind him, but Shay was gone.

"Look what I found!" Shay's voice called from above.

Jed looked up. "Shay?" She stood on top of a crate, holding a fire extinguisher above her head.

Everyone stopped and stared.

Even Spyglass.

"What are you doing, Shay?" the captain said, with a *get out of here while you still can* tone to his voice.

"I found one of the gilded relics!" She held the fire extinguisher higher.

"You *what?*"

She nodded. "It was over there." She pointed off somewhere nondescriptly. "Just lying on the deck."

"Shay, get out of here," the captain said.

She hopped down from the crate and walked toward them. Dread parted as she passed. An eerie feeling swam over Jed.

"What's going on, Shay?" he whispered.

"This"—she handed the fire extinguisher to Captain Bog—"is one of the gilded relics. It's a special one that makes scritches do whatever you want!"

Captain Bog searched the twisted faces around him. None of the creatures moved.

"Try it!" Shay said with a squeal.

Captain Bog took the fire extinguisher and held it like it was about to explode. He looked from Shay to the dread and then back to the fire extinguisher.

"Make them do fun things like jump on one leg or act like scritchmice!" Shay said, clapping her hands. "Do it! Do it!"

He limped toward the edge of the circle, and the dread parted. "Act . . . um . . ."—he looked at the extinguisher again—"like scritchmice?"

Dread began crawling around the deck on all fours in their best "scritchmice" impressions. Even Spyglass dropped his shatterbox and crouched to the floor, hobbling about on hands and knees.

"What is that?" Sprocket said, studying the fire extinguisher.

"I told you! Isn't it fun?"

"How did you . . . ?" Jed began.

"Over there." She pointed again. "Just lying on the ground. Lucky, right!"

"Lucky . . ." Captain Bog mumbled, sounding almost scared of Shay.

"Now you can be the captain of *this* boat too! Stoke the engines! Grind the crank gears! That sort of thing. So where to, Captain?"

Silence filled the deck.

Everyone stared at her.

"What's going on, Shay?" the captain asked.

Jed stepped away from Spyglass, who was still on all fours.

"We need to get Jed to the *Red Galleon*. Right?" Shay said. "I bet if you ask the crew, they'll help! We should probably do that soon. Yes?"

"Shaaaay?" Captain Bog drew out the word like a parent accusing a child of something.

"Yes?"

"What's going on?"

She shrugged. "I already told you. And time's running out."

He looked at Sprocket. "What's going on with her?"

"I've been asking myself that for weeks."

"We can talk in the captain's quarters, if you'd rather," Shay said. "Seeing as how you're the captain now, yes?"

Shay turned and skipped back the way they'd come.

"Shay, wait!" Captain Bog called, limping after her.

"Don't even try . . ." Sprocket mumbled.

As Jed turned to follow, he glanced back at Spyglass. The dread was staring at him, and there was something in his eyeless face. It was small—almost unnoticeable. But Jed noticed.

It was the faint hint of a smirk.

32

Back in the dreadnought's captain's quarters, the four stared out the porthole at the *Red Galleon*.

"We can't just expect to float over there and jump on board," Sprocket said.

"Sprocket's right," Captain Bog said. "They'll get you before you hit the deck."

"Not if they can't see us," Jed said. "What if we use the same idea you had against that wing of falcons? Fly as close as we can, then pop cloud bombs around both ships." He looked at the captain. "Can you fly this thing?"

"Maybe. *Bessie* was a dread tug last I checked."

"Here," Shay said, handing the fire extinguisher to the captain. "Don't forget your gilded relic."

"Right. Wouldn't want to leave it lying around, would I?"

"Nope!"

. . .

Jed, Shay, and Sprocket stood at the edge of the dreadnought, holding the ends of their coiled rope ladders.

"Closer," Jed mumbled to himself. "A little bit closer."

With Captain Bog at the helm, the dreadnought drifted near the *Galleon*. A pop sounded, and a cloud bomb launched into the air. It exploded, and a shroud of smoke billowed around the two ships in a tidal wave of black.

"Now!" Jed said, dropping the rope ladder. Rung by rung, he descended until his feet no longer felt additional rungs. His jaw tensed and his breath stopped. Where was the *Galleon* deck?

He squinted, but the black smoke was too thick.

What if they weren't above the *Galleon*? They'd fall all the way to the barge.

Either the ladders were too short, or they were dangling above open air.

Heroism, he told himself, thinking of SPLAGHETTI.

He sucked in a deep breath and let go. He fell through the air, his heart in his throat. Jed's feet slammed against something solid. The others dropped beside him.

"Shay, Sprocket," he whispered. Two hands reached out and touched his shoulders.

"We need to hide before the smoke lifts," Sprocket said.

"I can't see anything. What if we run off the edge?"

"I see something," Shay said. "A crate." She grabbed Jed's hand. They ducked behind a large box and waited for the smoke to clear.

When the darkness lifted, Jed turned around. Six dread stood in a semicircle around them.

Jed drew his shatterbox and fired. One of the dread burst apart.

Sprocket drew her shatterlance and shot the other five before Jed could pull the trigger again.

All around them, limping steps clattered through the smoke.

Sprocket fired again and again. Dread crashed against the deck.

More footsteps. Dozens. Hundreds.

The steady clatter evolved into a thundering stampede. Jed shot blindly into the smoke. Metal scraps showered over the deck, but the dread continued to march.

"I'll go find a shatterkeg," Shay said. "There's one nearby."

"Shay, no! Don't go by yourself!" She bounded away as if she hadn't heard Jed.

A moment later, wheels squeaked beside him, and something pressed against his legs. He reached down and found a shatterkeg lever. He punched a button and a boom shook the deck.

The sound of broken crates and pieces of the ship echoed through the air. He thought of the surrounding dreadnoughts—the hundreds of warships.

They're all going to come. Thousands of dread—hundreds of thousands. Even if we survive, even if we take the whole ship, it won't matter. We won't escape.

Jed fired the shatterkeg again, and bits of metal sprayed the deck. Shadows surrounded them—black shapes through the smoke. Arms outstretched, Shay leaped forward like a cat toward its prey.

Sprocket tapped the trigger of her shatterlance so quickly, the chain of shots dyed the blackened air with blue lines of smoke. Until she pulled the trigger once more and there was only a click. She dropped the shatterlance and drew two shatterboxes. Shots blasted through the smoke, and dread collapsed.

Two more clicks. Two empty shatterboxes.

Metal limbs clanked against the deck as hundreds of dread breached the smoke around them.

"That's enough," a voice called from the darkness. "Weapons on the floor."

The dread stopped. Weapons dropped to the deck.

Shay scampered back to the others.

Silence filled the air.

Not a single dread moved. Their metal bodies stood like statues. The smoke lifted, and a figure walked toward Jed.

The dread king.

Jed's dream played again in his mind. The oil, forced down his throat, slippery and thick. Shay's words rang in his head. *He makes disobedient mice drink the same oil his engines drink. And then he watches them gurgle their last squeak.*

Smoke shrouded the dread king's features, but Jed could see his silhouette. He held a box, then lifted its lid with a small creak.

"Jed, the music box!" Shay yelled.

The relic. Able to put a roomful of people to sleep.

A melody trickled into the air, one note at a time.

Shay tackled Jed and covered his ears.

One by one, dread crumpled to the floor. Sprocket teetered at their side. Her shatterlance clunked against the deck, and she dropped to her knees. She swayed in place, and fell.

Shay's hands pressed against Jed's head, and she hummed to herself.

His heart beat faster.

She's not falling asleep. Why isn't she falling asleep?

Her hands lifted. The music stopped, and the box clicked closed.

The smoke had gone too.

A man stood before him. A man with a big nose and a bushy mustache.

No.

Jed's blood froze in its veins. His ears throbbed and his lips went numb.

This can't—no.

The air around him felt heavy and pressed into him on all sides.

"I've been waiting for you," his grandfather's brittle voice said.

The man smiled and opened his arms.

Jed stood, though his legs shook.

"How . . . ?" Jed's voice fell away. Something clattered to the deck. His shatterbox. "You're here . . . but how are you . . . ?" The words, gone again.

"Come over and give your grandfather a hug!"

"But . . ." Jed's ankles brushed against a dread.

His grandfather closed the gap and wrapped lanky arms around him.

"What's—what's going on?" Jed stared at the metal corpses. "You're . . . working for the dread?"

"Heavens, no, boy!" He clapped Jed's shoulder. "They're terrible creatures. Absolutely horrid!"

Every word from his grandfather—even the sight of him surrounded by sleeping dread—felt like a scorpion's sting piercing deep into his neck.

Jed looked at a dread. And then another. And another. Their twisted frames. "Then why are you . . . ?"

"The world is in trouble, Jed. *This* world. *Our* world. We need to save it. Together. Your *family* needs you."

"My family?"

"Your family is bigger than you know, and they're dying. But you can save them. Save us all. I've waited nine years for your return."

Nine years.

"Car seat," Jed mumbled. His head still felt packed with cotton. The thoughts . . . the memories . . . "A blue car seat. You buckled me inside. And then I was falling. Why was I falling?"

His grandfather squeezed Jed's shoulder. "I'm sure you have many questions. I'll answer them all. I promise. But there's much you need to learn. I want to show you something."

He hooked his arm around Jed.

"No." Jed turned around. "Sprocket, she's—"

"She'll be just fine. She's only sleeping."

"I'll stay with her," Shay said.

Shay's voice broke Jed's mind from his shock. He'd nearly forgotten about her. She stood next to Sprocket, her hands clasped in front of her as she stared at the deck.

"The music box. You didn't fall asleep," he said to her.

"Shay's special," his grandfather said. "Aren't you, Shay?"

Shay looked at the deck. "I'm special." The words sounded stiff. Like they'd been etched into her mind after a thousand repetitions.

"Are you all right?" Jed asked.

She didn't look up. "I'm fine. Go. I'll stay with Sprocket."

"We'll be back before you can blink," his grandfather said.

"But—" Jed hesitated. Shay's gaze stayed fixed on the floor as his grandfather pulled him away.

They wandered the pristine empty deck until they reached a staircase to the lower deck. The walls and flooring were dark brown planks. The wood was treated, stained, and lacquered. Jed touched a wall. It was slick and new. The varnish still had a sweet scent. He ran his fingers along the perfectly fitted boards. "How did you find these? They all match."

His grandfather smiled. "Ah, yes. Wonderful craftsmanship. I'm quite pleased."

"But *where*? Where did you get it?"

"From home."

"What home?"

"There are secrets in this world meant just for us. Wonderful secrets. Beautiful secrets. Secrets that would enchant even those who've lived beyond the fringe . . ."

He gripped the knob of an oak door and twisted.

A lush garden blossomed behind the open door. Bright tomatoes nearly glowed on their vines. Sprouts of turnips, carrots, cabbages, and onions. Purple sprigs of lavender next to plump marigolds. A delicate blue orchid under a hydrangea bush. Rows of herbs: thyme, basil, parsley, and cilantro.

Jed's foot sank slightly as he walked. Rich soil blanketed the floor in dark brown. He scooped a handful of it and held it to his face. The damp earth filled his nostrils as he took a deep breath. The particles crumbled through his fingers, and he brushed his hands together.

A glint of yellow caught his eye. In the center of the room, in full bloom, was something he could describe no better than *wonder*. A lemon tree. Tall and magnificent, its branches arching over the other plants like a mother's safe arms.

His grandfather walked in front of him and sniffed the air. "Ahh. Can you smell that?"

Jed inhaled. A wave of nostalgia coursed through him. He was home again. Peeling lemons for his mother's pound cake, flipping through the pages of the Lemon Anthology for Lemon Saturday. He could hear her humming to herself as she sliced the lemons into wedges. Her apron—eternally dusted with flour and spotted with stains of a thousand meals.

"Do you still have it?" his grandfather said, shattering the memory.

"Have what?"

He plucked another lemon from the tree, then scratched the rind and smelled it. His eyes closed. "The lemon, of course." He opened his eyes and glanced at Jed's pocket.

Jed took out the lemon. Its leathery rind was shriveled and dented. The orange blemishes had multiplied, discoloring the surface.

His grandfather took the fruit and replaced it with the one he'd just picked.

"A fresh one for the road. We do love our lemons, don't we? Wouldn't want you to be without one."

The new lemon was supple and rubbery. The way a lemon *should* feel. Jed looked up, but the wilted lemon was gone. A sting of loss pricked his heart, as if a piece of his parents had been ripped away.

"How did you know?"

"Because I asked you to bring one with you. We have wonderful things to make, and we need every lemon we can get." He winked. "Follow me. I have one more surprise."

His mind—*so fuzzy*. But every time clarity struck long enough for him to ask another question, his grandfather walked off. Or spoke first.

They left the garden and walked to the door across the corridor. His grandfather opened it, and a sweet scent filled the air. A kitchen, much like his kitchen at home. Cherry cabinets, a frosted-glass pantry, an iron stove, a granite-topped island counter, and even a microwave.

A ding sounded from the oven.

"Ah! Just in time." His grandfather rubbed his palms together and strolled to the oven. He grabbed an oven mitt, then pulled out a wire rack.

Lemon poppy-seed doughnuts. The way Mom makes them. Jed's heart raced. *What's happening?*

He pressed his thumbnail into the back of his hand. It hurt. But so had the oil—from the dream.

Wake up, wake up.

"What was that?" his grandfather asked.

"Nothing."

The man dipped the freshly baked doughnut into a bowl of glaze, long enough for it to soak into its core.

This isn't real.

"Here." He handed Jed the doughnut on a napkin. "Try it. They're my *favorite*."

Jed lifted the doughnut to his lips. Steam snaked up from the wet glaze.

So sweet. So perfect.

His teeth closed around the doughnut, and the bite melted onto his tongue. Just the way it did at home.

A memory pushed its way to the front of his mind. The summer after he turned nine, his family had vacationed in Bangladesh. He'd come across an animal he later learned was called a slow loris. It was not much bigger than his shoe, with large, misty eyes. Its fur pulled into teardrops around the eyes, making it look vulnerable and frightened. It licked its elbow and cocked its head at Jed. He smiled back. *"Hi there, little guy."* When he crouched, the loris lunged and sank its teeth into Jed's shoulder.

Jed tried prying it off, but its skinny arms grasped his like bands of iron. His father ripped the loris away. But it was too late. Jed's muscles seized from the poison in his veins. He blacked out and woke in a hospital. From that day on he'd always remembered the eyes. Big, beautiful eyes. Harmless. Innocent.

He'd been on more dangerous adventures than a boy his age should have been able to survive. But he *had* survived. Because he'd learned to. And if there was one thing he'd learned over the years, it was to trust himself when something didn't feel right. Jed recognized poison behind innocent eyes.

This isn't right. None of it is.

"What do you mean you asked me to bring it?" Jed said.

His grandfather lifted his eyebrows. "What?"

"The lemon. You said you asked me to bring one."

"I'll explain everything in time. Enjoy your doughnut."

Jed set the doughnut onto the counter and backed away. His throat felt hot and shaking.

"You knew everything! The lemon . . . the doughnuts! How did you know?" His voice roared through the room.

His grandfather patted the air. "Calm down. You're safe. Nobody's trying to hurt you."

"Safe?" *How could I have been so stupid?* "Shay. Where is Shay?"

"With your friend. Don't you remember?"

And then he did remember. He remembered how she'd slumped. How she'd stared at the deck, hands clasped in front of her as if shielding herself from the man with the music box.

"You hurt her," Jed said. "She told me. You beat her with a pipe!"

"That's absurd. Why would I do that?"

The dread. Their fallen twisted bodies.

"Don't lie to me. I know you hurt her!"

"Listen to me. Shay's memory, it's broken. She doesn't remember things clearly."

"Maybe that's what happens when you hit people with pipes!"

His grandfather's jaw tightened. "This was supposed to be a wonderful moment. A beautiful moment." He mumbled as if speaking to the floor. "Now it's ruined." He slapped the wire rack of doughnuts. They flopped through the air and splattered over the glossy hardwood. "Ruined."

Jed backed toward the kitchen door.

His grandfather raised his hand. "Stop. Please."

"I'm going to find my friends."

"I've had them taken elsewhere. They're being cared for, I promise."

"*Promise?* You *promised* to tell me what's going on!"

"It's not that simple. But you're home. We have plenty of time to talk."

"*Home?* This isn't my home! I don't even know you!"

"I'm your grandfather."

No. Whatever this is, it's not my grandfather.

"Where are my parents? What have you done with them?"

"Your parents? Why would I have any idea where they are?"

"You took them. I know you did! Tell me where they are!"

As Jed's words echoed in the room, the man's eyes changed. Gone was the doughy pout. Gone was the misty compassion, the gentle smile, the lemon poppy-seed pretense. Poison trickled into the narrowed slits.

"*Take* them? I didn't *take* anyone!" Spittle dribbled onto his chin, but he didn't wipe it away. "I don't *take* people and lock them away in some prison like those maggots did to you! Your—what did you call them?—*parents* didn't have the spine to kill you like they planned! No. Instead they *took* you! *Take,*

take, take!" He shook his head and clutched his face with both hands. "Even after you were gone, I could still hear you—*feel* you. But they *took* you so far . . . until all I could hear were whispers."

Jed backed against the kitchen door and grabbed the knob.

The man waved a hand dismissively. "Don't bother. It's locked. You were never going to leave this room." He sighed and sank into a chair.

Jed tested the handle. It didn't move.

"Who are you?"

The man rubbed his eyes. "Your grandfather, and your father, and your mother all in one. I'm more of a grandfather to you than this *meat sack* ever was." He pinched a wad of flesh on his arm and curled a lip in disgust.

The motions reminded Jed of when Kizer had done the same to him. "*You're* the dread king," Jed said. "You're not my grandfather at all, are you?"

"This meat sack"—he pointed at his face—"deserved what he got! Taking you away from me! Letting maggots raise you in a tunnel! Yes . . . it was a blue car seat. They snatched you away from me. Sneaky maggots. Those *things* you call parents wanted to kill you. They snuck onto my boat to murder you. Spineless fools couldn't do it. So they took you instead. What kind of people steal a baby? One as precious as you?"

"Shut up!" Jed yelled. "Just shut up! Where is my grand-father?"

Poison surged in the man's eyes. "This face is *not* your *grandfather*! *I* am your grandfather! Not this filthy"—his fingers clutched the flesh around his forearm—"sack of"—he pulled the patch of skin and it tore away—"*meat!*"

Underneath the skin, hundreds of golden gears spun and whirred. The gold glinted as if the metal parts themselves had been painted in sunshine.

He stepped toward Jed.

"Get away from me, you freak!" Jed yelled.

"Freak?" A wicked grin danced on the monster's lips.

The yellow metal in his arm looked like pure gold. Every gear was as small as one from a . . .

Jed glanced at his own arm.

As one from a *wristwatch.*

The creature took another step.

"I said get away from me!"

"You should find a place to lie down. It will be taking effect any moment now."

"What will be tak—" And then he felt it. A tickling sensation in his brain. The slow loris flashed in his mind. The poison . . . the blurry sensation . . . the fading consciousness. "You drugged me." His foot pressed into one of the doughnuts, and icing smeared along wood planks. "You—"

Jed fell to the floor.

"Jed . . ." The dread king's voice rang like tuning forks in Jed's ears. "Wake up."

Jed opened his eyes. He tried to move, but his hands and feet were strapped to a metal table.

"I was starting to worry. You've been out for nearly a day. I'm afraid I overdosed the doughnuts a bit. But it's over now. You're here. You're safe."

The room swirled into focus. The white walls looked like a hospital.

Jed tugged against his restraints. "Let me go!"

"Soon. We need to talk."

"What have you done with my grandfather, you lying scrap of gutter clunk!"

The man ground his teeth together. "He's not your grand-father. And I do have a name. It's Lyle. Not Gutter Clunk."

"What did you do with him?"

Lyle raised his arm. Underneath the torn patch of skin, golden machinery flashed in the light. "I'm wearing him. This is all that's left."

"You—you killed him!"

Lyle rolled his eyes. "Oh, stop that nonsense. Stop acting like you're going to throw up. You *can't*. Not even if you want to."

"You killed him."

"Hush. None of that matters. You'd been gone so long, I was afraid you'd forgotten everything." Lyle scratched his fore-head. "I suppose you *have* forgotten everything." He touched Jed's arm. "Listen to me. The people who claim to be your par-ents are not your parents. They are weak little bugs that wither and die with a little sip of oil. Pathetic! Pathetic, pathetic, *pathetic!*" Lyle shouted. His hands shook. He closed his eyes and drew in a deep breath. "But not you. You're pure. Crisp. Engineered for greatness."

"Engineered?"

"Of course." He gripped the table with both hands and stared into Jed's eyes. "You. You are the final gilded relic. The greatest of all the gilded relics."

The words hung in the air.

Relic?

What was he talking about?

"Don't look at me like that. I'm not lying to you. You know it's true."

"That's a bunch of scrap," Jed said. "You'll have to try something better than that. It's not even a *good* lie. Pick something I might actually believe."

"You're right. It's preposterous. Tell me, have you ever broken a bone? Have you ever been sick? Chicken pox? Tonsillitis? No?" He leaned even closer. "What about the common cold?"

Jed saw himself floating through the air, hitting the tugboat deck, sliding fast. So fast. Head slamming into something dense. A *crack*. His neck broken. His body paralyzed. And then he was leaping from the tugboat deck. Forty, maybe fifty feet onto a tattered mattress not much thicker than his hand. The impact should have shattered his body.

The malaria-infested jungles of Africa.

Drinking river water in China. *Everyone got sick that day. Everyone but me.*

"It's okay, Jed," Lyle said. "You're home. Everything will be okay."

"This isn't my home!"

"No." Lyle shook his head. "I hardly recognize it either. Oh, how it's changed. But we'll fix it. We'll fix everything. Rebuild until it becomes what it once was!"

"I have a home," Jed said. "You're a liar!"

Jed focused on the image of his parents. The first time they made a pineapple upside-down cake together. His father started a flour fight, and they threw handfuls of it back and forth until they all looked like ghosts. He even remembered the way the cake tasted when it came out of the oven. They ate on the kitchen floor, surrounded by the flour, which covered the kitchen like a winter snowfall.

"No. I'm not what you say."

"It's okay. You'll come around. 99R15!" Lyle called. "Where is the other patient?"

Metal footsteps limped outside the room, and a gurney rolled through the doors. The dread was unusually tall and had only one eye. It stared at Jed—its head turning from Lyle to Jed, Jed to Lyle.

"What are you staring at? Go clean the deck or something." Lyle shoved the dread from the room. He wheeled the gurney beside Jed.

Shay.

"Shay!" Jed said. "Shay, are you all right?"

Her eyes darted in a dozen different directions, and she pulled against the restraints.

"She's fine," Lyle said.

"What are you going to do to her?"

"Relax. I'm going to fix her."

"I don't want you to fix me!" Shay yelled.

"Yes, you do. You just don't know it yet."

"Leave her alone!" Jed yelled.

"She needs a bit of oil is all." He took a silver can from a cupboard.

"What are you doing?" Jed said. "Don't touch her!"

Lyle opened the can. "Bottoms up."

Shay's lip quivered. "Jed, help!"

Jed jerked against his restraints. "Don't touch her! Get your hands off of her!"

Lyle pried open her mouth and stuffed a tennis ball between her teeth. Shay began to cry.

"Stop it!" Jed tried hopelessly to yank an arm free. "Leave her alone!"

Lyle tipped the can, and a thick stream of oil poured onto the tennis ball and leaked between the edges of her lips. She choked and coughed, but he continued to pour.

Tears squeezed from Jed's eyes. "Stop it! You're killing her!"

Lyle rolled his eyes. "I'm doing nothing of the sort. Settle down."

Jed kicked and strained, but the straps held him in place.

When Lyle had emptied the last of the can, he wiped its rim with his finger and licked off the oil. He pulled the tennis ball from Shay's mouth and dropped it into the can. "See?" he said. "Not so bad, was it?"

Shay's lips and cheeks were black with oil. She sniffled, and her whole body rattled with fear.

Lyle dabbed her face with a white rag.

"Shay? Shay? Say something."

"I'm . . . I'm okay."

"What did you give her?"

Lyle held the can to Jed's nose. "I already told you."

Jed sniffed the scent of oil.

"But—"

"She's a gilded relic too. The first. *My* first. My sweet daughter who sometimes can't remember who she is. How special she is." He stroked her face and combed his fingers through her hair.

"Shay? Is that true?"

Her eyes flicked back and forth. "I don't know. I don't know. I don't know," she repeated. She looked as if she was about to start crying again.

"I was younger at the time," Lyle said, still stroking her hair. "Less capable. Far less practiced. I blame myself for your shortcomings," he whispered to her. "For the fragility of your memory . . . the instability of your mind. But we all have our purpose, and she's always fulfilled hers so wonderfully."

Jed met his eyes. "Her *purpose*?"

Lyle nodded. "She's had many purposes over the years. But most recently, it was to find you. And bring you to me."

"Me? Why me?"

Lyle stood up straighter. "You are my greatest creation. The gilded relic of gilded relics. You and I are destined to be together. To purge the junkyard. To build a new world. A golden world. A *gilded* world. This is *your* purpose."

Shay's eyes tightened, and a tear slipped free, dropping onto the pillow under her head.

"But she didn't bring me here," Jed said.

"Oh, but she did. Each captain of a dread vessel has a beacon. Some people say it looks a bit like . . . a *spyglass*."

Jed opened his mouth to respond, but no words came out. He pictured the red, pulsing lens. Pulsing . . . pulsing. Every day before breakfast.

"Stuck on that stack, it couldn't activate the beacon. But Shay could. And she did. Every morning. And then you'd shut it right back off."

"I didn't! I didn't do any of that!" Shay said, tears streaming down her face.

"I know, sweetheart, you won't remember. I took those awful memories away."

She sobbed as he stroked her hair.

"You're lying!" Jed yelled.

"No. I'm not a liar. We share that quality of integrity, you and me."

"Prove it!"

Lyle pulled a box from his pocket. Inside were tiny circles of glass. He pinched one. "Hold still," he said, even though Jed was strapped tightly to the bed. He pried open Jed's eyelids and slid a lens over each eye.

Jed's vision changed. It was as if he were looking through someone else's eyes.

Shay's eyes.

Scene after scene flashed in brief fragments, like spliced excerpts of corrupted memories.

Shay talking to herself . . .

Arguing with herself . . .

Telling herself Jed was a "good mouse" and not a "Lyle mouse" at all . . .

Standing by the smokestack . . .

Activating the spyglass . . .

Finding it deactivated . . .

Reactivating it . . .

Again and again . . .

Waiting for the dread to arrive . . .

Watching Jed get wrapped in a sack . . .

Sitting by his bound body on the dreadnought . . .

Watching him use the can slicer to escape . . .

Leading him through the dreadnought . . .

Sneaking away to meet with Spyglass as the others rescued Captain Bog . . .

Telling Spyglass and his dread to obey whoever held the fire extinguisher . . .

Volunteering to join Jed in storming the *Galleon* . . .

Seeing the approval in Lyle's eyes . . .

The images disappeared as soon as Lyle removed the lens.

"Don't be upset with her," Lyle said. "She genuinely doesn't remember." His voice was soft and sympathetic. "I keep the hard memories—the ones that hurt her—right here." He opened the box and slid the lens back in its slot. "We all have a purpose. You. Me. Shay. It's who we are. Like Shay, you'll come to learn this."

"You're insane if you think I'm going to help you do *anything*," Jed said. He wanted to sound strong, but his voice quivered.

"That won't be your choice to make."

"Do whatever you want to me. I won't do what you say. You're a liar. You're lying about everything!"

"Perhaps. Then again, perhaps you only need a little convincing."

He grabbed his shatterbox, aimed it at Jed's chest, and pulled the trigger.

A white blast slammed into Jed's chest with a crushing force. He couldn't breathe.

"This is for the best," Lyle said. "It's the only way you'll understand. And you must understand."

The shot blasted a wide hole in his clothes. As the smoke cleared, bits of metal glittered underneath. Instead of broken bone and torn muscle, there were gears and coils—as golden as the sun.

Captain Bog's voice rang in his ears. *Looks like we got ourselves a little golden boy. Eh, Ki?*

Jed's heart thumped. He could feel the blood beat under his skin. Dizziness swirled in his stomach. "No, I feel. I can feel."

"Of course you can feel," Lyle said. "You feel deeper than any of those meat sacks could ever hope to."

"I—have a heart."

"A wonderful, golden heart. Stronger than every bit of iron or copper this world has ever unearthed."

"I'm—I'm bleeding."

Lyle swiped a finger in the red liquid and rubbed it against his thumb. "Oil."

"No." Jed shook his head. "This isn't possible. What have you done to me?"

"You have a destiny, my boy. And it's all in here." Lyle pressed his palm against the golden machinery in Jed's chest. Lyle whipped a handkerchief from his pocket and rubbed a patch of oil until the gold underneath shone.

"Here." He tapped the center of Jed's chest. "This will fix you—fix everything."

Lyle's finger traced a small shape. A keyhole.

"What—what is that for?"

"It unlocks your potential. Unlocks everything you are capable of. There's so much more inside of you than you could ever imagine. Potential like the world has never seen." He scrunched his lips together. "Each gem of possibility, each bottled talent, each treasure box of power, comes with a key. A key to control the dread, as Shay does. A key to make you strong. A key to make you clever. Even a key to make you *fly*."

He reached into his coat and removed a ring of keys. He flicked through them, one at a time.

"So many keys. All for you." He dropped the ring to the

floor. "But none of them matter. Because the maggots who stole you from me stole the only key of significance. The only key I care about. A key I can't reforge. I don't suppose you've seen such a key?"

He waited, but Jed only glared.

He shrugged. "Then I'll have to take you apart piece by piece. Wipe every memory. Start from the beginning. That's not what I wanted for you. For us. I wanted us to *share* your memories—not lose them."

"Share?"

Lyle touched Jed's shoulder. "Of course! Don't you understand? You're me! You're my perfected framework. A shell waiting for me to occupy! This skeleton"—he touched the golden innards of his own arm—"was only ever meant to be a temporary home. It reeks of adequacy. It yearns for the untapped potential of all those locked treasure boxes inside you." He tapped the keyhole in Jed's chest.

"The time has come. *Our* time has come. Take this moment to think. To remember. And I'll be back before you can blink. We've got a lot of work to do," he said with a smile. "An entire world to destroy. An entire world to build anew."

He turned and left the room. The door clapped shut.

Jed stared at the keyhole in his chest.

It's not possible. He tugged against the leather straps around his wrists. He needed to touch it—to touch the golden metal spinning and whirring inside his chest. His stomach felt like glue. "It's not true," he said aloud.

A soft whimper echoed from Shay.

"Shay, it's not true. This—none of this is real!"

Her jaw shook, and she winced at his words.

"Tell me what's going on!" Jed's voice bounced through the room. It rang in his ears. Felt tinny. Fake. Metal. "Answer me! Look at me! Why won't you open your eyes?"

"I'm—I'm sorry. I didn't mean to," she said. "I didn't know. I *did* know, but I didn't know. Please don't be mad. I'm sorry."

The small voice stabbed Jed with more persuasion than the sight of gears inside his body. "Am I . . . ?" He looked again at the golden metal. Spinning . . . humming so softly it sounded more like a fox's purr than the drone of machine cogs.

Eyes still shut and leaking tears, Shay nodded against the restraints.

"But I grew up. I grew older. I'm—I'm not a machine! I have a family! I have a mom and dad!"

The doorknob rattled. Shay's eyes flicked open, and Jed's gaze snapped to the door. The handle turned and the hinges creaked. A spindly dread peeked inside and scanned the room.

It was the unusually tall dread from earlier—the one who'd stared at him. It stood there, still staring. Then it removed the hubcap strapped to its chest. It unlaced the pipe tied to its leg, dropped the crowbar from its arm, and loosened the strap around its head, uncovering a second eye.

Jed's blood felt like ice under his skin. The soft hum of his mechanical chest became a wild whirring. For the man standing in the doorway wasn't a dread at all.

It was his father.

36

"**D**ad?" Jed's voice quivered. His throat felt small.

Tears burst from his father's eyes. "Jed!"

Jed's breath caught, and tears of his own soaked into his eyes. His father's arms wrapped around him.

The same arms that had carried Jed up his first mountain. The same arms that had guided Mom through a thousand living-room waltzes. And the same arms that had cradled them both after the fat air-conditioning repairman had stepped on Frank, the family turtle.

As his father's fingers laced through Jed's hair and pulled his forehead to his own, Jed thought of Frank—of his fractured shell, the stubby limbs and wrinkled neck, limp. He remembered the moment when he lifted the still turtle into his arms.

He'd been sure that nothing would ever make him feel better again. But his father's arms had somehow sucked away the pain. They'd done it then and they did it now.

"What's happening to me?"

His father pulled away and examined the burned hole and golden machinery.

"You'll be okay. We'll get out of here. Together. That man. Lyle. He's not your grandfather."

"But the picture. He looks like—"

"He's *not*. He's just a monster who killed your grandfather. He found out you were coming and tried to trick you. We tried to find you before *he* did. I came to the *Red Galleon* to stop him, but it was too late—you were already here."

Jed nodded. "But he told me"—his next words felt like shame and thick sludge—"that he *made* me."

His father squeezed Jed's shoulder. The corners of his eyes wilted like Mom's porch roses in autumn.

"I'm so sorry. We tried so hard to stop him."

He released Jed and unbuckled the straps around Jed's wrists and ankles. "We need to get out of here."

Jed sat up, and pain jolted through his chest.

His father grabbed a can of oil. "Hold still," he said, easing Jed back down. He opened the can and poured. Red oil streamed into the shimmering gears. Relief rushed over Jed. His father returned with gauze and wrapped it around Jed's torso.

"What am I, Dad?" Jed said, his voice shaking.

His father took Jed's head in both hands. "You're my son."

The words felt right—sounded right. But they weren't true. Not exactly.

"He said you stole me. . . . Stole me from *him*."

"We took you to protect you. Once we found out what Lyle was going to do with you, we couldn't let that happen. And we weren't about to let coppers or irons use you like gutter clunk. So we took you away from everything. Away from the war. Away from the killing and the greed. We didn't know what was on the other side of the fringe, but it was worth the chance."

His father paused, letting Jed take in the truth.

"We always have a choice," he continued. "You have a choice right now. You don't have to come with me. You can stay right here and wait for Lyle." His eyes flickered to the keyhole in Jed's chest. "You can choose to let him turn you into something else. It's still *your* choice. Is that what you want? There's nothing holding you to that table anymore."

"I want to go home."

His father held out a hand. "Then let's go."

Jed looked at Shay, and another word from SPLAGHETTI surfaced in his mind.

Empathy.

"We need to help her, too," Jed said.

"Okay. There's a life raft on the side of the boat. We need to hurry."

They helped Shay from the table, and she and Jed followed his father out the door. The three sprinted down the corridor to a cherry-stained staircase that led to the top deck.

His father held a finger to his lips and pointed to a dread shuffling along the deck. Jed peeked out from the staircase opening. A second dread just stood, staring at the wall, and a third walked back and forth, its head twitching erratically.

"The raft is a short sprint over there." His father pointed across the deck.

As the shuffling dread turned around, his father held up three fingers and lowered them one at a time.

"Run!"

They bolted into the open. Jed's father leaped behind a crate, crouched, and then sprinted again. Jed raced to keep pace. They ducked behind the mast, then hid behind a shatter-keg. Bit by bit they inched to the far side of the ship.

And then Jed froze at a black trench coat rocking slightly with the breeze. He cupped his hands to his mouth and called in a whisper, "Sprocket!"

The woman didn't turn around.

"Sprocket!" Jed called louder.

"Jed, no!" His father grabbed his arm.

And then she turned.

Rusted gears rotated slowly in empty patches of her hollowed cheek. Her face—half-gone—held only a ghost of the woman she once was. One eye was missing. The other empty. Cold. Foreign. Metal hoses connected her head to her shoulders.

No. A chill shot through Jed's arms. *No!*

He stumbled, but his father held him steady.

Sprocket limped toward them. *Step, clack. Step, clack.* The amputated barrel of her shatterlance was anchored to her knee instead of a leg.

"Stowaways!" she said. The silver hoses made her voice sound thin and metallic. "Stowaways on the *Galleon!*" she said louder, but the voice cut short inside the freshly attached hoses.

"Jed, come on!" His father tugged on his elbow.

"Sprocket!"

"Sound the alarm!" Sprocket called, her voice like sheets of metal being sliced. Jed ran, and the *step, clack, step, clack* behind him quickly faded. Blood pounded in Jed's ears. His jaw was tight and his muscles wobbled.

It's my fault. She wouldn't be here if I hadn't insisted on looking for my grandfather.

"Here," his dad said.

The edge of the ship.

Shay climbed up the *Galleon's* railing and hopped to a copper raft with four seats. Thick iron chains anchored it to the *Galleon*.

"Get started on these." His father handed Jed a key and pointed to padlocks on the chains. "I'll get the engine fired up."

He hopped inside and cranked a lever. Propeller blades twice the length of the raft spun underneath it as if it were an upside-down helicopter. The raft lifted, but the chains held it in place. Jed removed the first padlock and tossed it to the deck with a thunk.

"Hurry!" his father called.

Jed unlocked the other two, then hopped in.

"Stowaways!" a metallic voice rang from behind.

Footsteps clomped along the deck.

Lyle.

Lyle appeared, and their eyes met. The man's chin lifted, and his head shook ever so slightly.

"Get off that raft!"

Jed's father pulled a lever, and a hydraulic noise hissed from the engine. "Hold on!" he said, then jammed two levers forward.

The raft accelerated but jerked to a halt as chains rattled behind them. Underneath the nest of links was another padlock.

Jed ran to the edge of the raft and leaped to the *Galleon*. His body slammed into its side, and he wrapped his arms around a rail.

"Jed!"

"What are you doing?"

"Stop!"

"You're going to get yourself killed!"

Everyone yelled at him. Shay. His father. Lyle.

He pulled himself up and flopped onto the deck, then jammed the key into the last padlock.

A white blast soared past him and slammed into the raft.

Jed pulled off the lock and threw it to the deck.

"Get on!" his father yelled.

Jed stood, but before he could jump, Lyle spoke. "Take one step and I'll blast that meat sack between his pretty white eyes."

Jed met his father's gaze and mouthed the word *Go*.

The blood drained from his father's face, and his head shook back and forth.

Jed raised his arms and faced Lyle.

"I'll stay here with you. Just let them go."

Lyle looked from Jed to his father, then to Shay. Hatred burned in his eyes.

"Shay!" he yelled to her. "Shay, come back to me!"

"If you don't let them go," Jed said, "then I'll jump." He backed toward the railing until he felt it press against his hip.

Lyle's fingers spread wide, and he lifted the shatterbox in the air. "Stop! Get away from the edge!"

"Only when they're gone."

Lyle stepped closer. "You won't jump."

Jed swung one leg over the railing. And then another.

Lyle froze. "Okay—you win. Come back over the railing and they're free to go." He waved his hand in gentle beckoning motions. "But if you don't, that meat sack is dead." Lyle steadied his shatterbox.

"Jed!" his father called. "Get in! Now!"

Jed shook his head. "He'll kill you."

"I don't care! You can't let him take you!"

"I'm sorry."

Shay's eyes filled with tears. "Jed, no."

"Come away from the edge," Lyle said softly.

"Not until they're gone."

The raft drifted away slowly until it was a pinprick in the dark mist of the barge.

"All right. They're gone. Now come here."

Jed stepped over the railing toward Lyle.

The man rushed forward and swept Jed into a hug. He stroked Jed's hair and squeezed. Jed returned the embrace, hugging Lyle tightly.

Then he reached down and pulled the shatterbox from Lyle's belt. He wriggled free and pointed the weapon at Lyle.

Disappointment stung Lyle's face. "This isn't you. Don't you understand who I am? You and I—we're the same!"

Jed held the shatterbox in both hands to steady his shaking arm.

"What are you going to do? Shoot me and holler for your meat sack kidnapper to come back? Can't you see? He doesn't care about you. He left! Left without a word! Flew off with my Shay and left you! I would never do that. *Never!*" He shouted the last word, and the muscles in his neck quivered. "Give me that. I will take care of you. I won't abandon you. I'm not like *him*."

Jed's arms stayed steady.

"79Q4B. Fetch me that shatterbox. But don't hurt the boy."

Sprocket stepped forward, and Jed's heart thumped. "Sprocket, it's me. It's Jed. Don't!"

Step, clack, step, clack.

Single eye empty. Dead.

Step, clack, step, clack.

Jed twitched and trained the shatterbox on Sprocket. "Stop!"

"Or what?" Lyle said. "You'll kill your friend? That's not a very *friendly* thing to do."

Jed's lungs rose and fell.

"Sprocket, it's me! It's Jed! The . . . the one who can't climb a ladder, remember?"

Step, clack, step, clack.

Jed's hands felt slick. He held his breath, then swung the shatterbox toward Lyle and fired.

The blast hit squarely, and Lyle crumpled to the deck. Sprocket stopped and turned around.

Jed remembered how Sprocket would leave her signature in the smoke's trail after a shot. But this wasn't Sprocket. It wasn't *anything*.

"We all have a purpose." Lyle curled up to his knees and stood. The blast had washed away half of Jed's grandfather's face, revealing a golden mask. "We're all engineered for something. I am the guardian of this world. Guardians are made to endure. I never fall forever. I don't weaken. I don't rust. I don't age. And I don't die."

Jed fired again and again.

The shots knocked Lyle from side to side, but he always stood straight again.

"What I do next is for *you*," he said. "Sometimes we must hurt to be healed. Sometimes we must lose a choice to see the *right* choice. You think you have a home. A family. Friends. I am your family. And your only friend."

Sprocket grabbed Jed and dragged him forward.

"Sprocket, don't do this!" Jed struggled against her grip.

Lyle frowned at Jed. "You could have shot her. She's not even a meat sack anymore. Just a pile of *scrap*! Why do you care?"

"You wouldn't know," Jed said, studying Sprocket for any hint of life.

"I suppose not, which means she'll have to go. 79Q4B, walk yourself over the edge."

She gave Lyle a confused look. "But . . . ?"

"Don't worry," Lyle said. "I'll have you rebuilt by morning! And I'll make you twice as tall!" He tilted his head and whispered to Jed, "That's not true at all, of course. I'm not even going to look for her."

Sprocket grinned at Lyle's proposal and hobbled toward the edge.

Step, clack, step, clack.

"No!" Jed yelled. "He's lying!"

Lyle hooked his arm around Jed. "You *need* this. You need to cleanse yourself."

Jed stepped after Sprocket, but Lyle held him firm. His grip was impossibly strong.

"Sprocket, no!"

Step, clack, step, clack.

And then Sprocket lifted herself over the railing and fell into darkness.

Jed felt torn in half. "No!" He jerked against Lyle's hold, swinging his fists. "You killed her!"

Lyle caught Jed's hands and held them firm. "In time you will thank me. I promise. I swear it on my eternal life. From small pain comes great opportunity."

"I'm going to kill you," Jed muttered. "I'm going to find a way to do it."

"Come." Lyle led Jed by the arm. "I must show you something else."

They entered the ship's bridge. Levers and buttons lined the wall, but in the center of the room was an actual wheel with spokes and a carving of an anchor in its wood. Lyle scanned the skies, then pointed in the distance at the tiny life raft slowly drifting through the air. "There." Lyle gripped the wheel and spun.

The *Galleon* tilted.

"Take us closer, 821E," Lyle said.

A dread shuffled forward and pulled a lever. The *Galleon* accelerated and began gaining on the life raft.

Jed's vision wobbled, and he felt his mouth open. "No! You can't! You said you'd let them go!"

"I did let them go. Ready an acid cloudburst, 821E."

"But Shay," Jed said desperately. "She's your daughter! She's on there too!"

Lyle placed a hand on Jed's shoulder. "It warms my soul how much you care for your sister. You see, 821E will launch three shells over the raft. The acid will melt away everything that's not metal. So if that *thing* really *is* your father, he's made of metal—just like you."

"Don't! Please! I'll do anything for you!"

Lyle gave Jed a look of pity. "We both know that's not true. The second you thought they were safe, you tried to kill me. That's not something I can overlook. I'm trying to teach you. I'm doing this for you. *All* for you." He motioned to the dread. "A single barrage will be sufficient. Launch a three-shell spread thirty degrees off the port bow. On my mark."

Out of the corner of his eye, Jed noticed that one of the buttons near the controls was glowing red.

"Fire."

He bounded forward and slapped the button.

A series of shatterkegs all fired at once. Red particles of dust exploded forward, streaking past the life raft. The shots slammed into the propellers of the nearest dreadnought.

Anger coursed through Lyle's eyes. "What have you *done?*"

Chunks crumbled from the hull of the dreadnought. And then something exploded and the stern began to dip.

"You shot one of our dreadnoughts out of the sky!"

More explosions boomed, and the dreadnought began to descend more quickly. With a sinking feeling, Jed suddenly realized which dreadnought this was. His heart clenched in his chest.

Captain Bog. What have I done?

The massive ship speared into the barge's surface. A ball of orange fire swept over its hull.

Lyle's face shook with rage as flames consumed the ship.

You have to go, a voice said in Jed's head. *Go now!*

Jed turned and ran.

Lyle shouted through the air. "Stop him!"

There has to be another raft. Find it!

Jed ran the perimeter of the *Galleon* until he spotted one. Dread clattered all around him.

Before he could reach the raft, three dread barricaded the way. Jed grabbed the handle of a shatterkeg and spun it around. He fired, and the blast blew a crater into the deck.

Metal showered over the debris. As Jed skirted around the new crater, a wooden plank creaked and buckled under his feet. The floor beneath him fell away, and he tumbled onto the deck below. The shatterkeg he'd just used rolled after him and crashed through the planks near his feet, opening yet another hole to the lowest deck.

He squeezed through the hole and dropped into a long corridor.

"Jed. Stop this," Lyle called from above.

Jed scrambled to his feet. The shatterkeg had fallen on its side next to him. It was nearly as tall as him and probably weighed twice as much. He gripped the copper tubing on its barrel and heaved. The shatterkeg lifted a few inches but dropped again.

Lift. You can do this.

Jed looked at his hands, imagined the metal gears spinning under his skin.

He squatted and took a breath, then grabbed the tubing again. The muscles in his back—or whatever they were—tightened.

Lift! Jed yelled to himself.

Inch by inch, the shatterkeg lifted until it flipped upright.

Lyle's voice taunted him in his head. *I don't die.*

We'll see about that.

Jed dragged the shatterkeg down the corridor. A crunch sounded from the debris behind him. Jed turned around.

Lyle shook wood chips from his coat sleeve. "Put that thing away and stop acting like a child."

Jed lined up the shatterkeg and fired. An explosion cracked from its end. The shot clipped Lyle's shoulder. His body spun through the air and smashed through a wall.

As the black smoke settled, Lyle climbed to his feet and brushed off his clothes. "This is completely unnecessary."

The blast had torn away the last of Jed's grandfather, leaving only a gleaming machine.

Jed fired again, knocking Lyle to the floor. Again he stood. Jed wheeled the shatterkeg backward and opened the heavy oak door to the garden. He hauled the shatterkeg inside and took position behind the lemon tree.

"There's nowhere to go," Lyle called.

Jed fired again.

"I can do this all day," Lyle said, rising from the floor.

"So can I." Jed blasted Lyle through the wall of his kitchen. Frosting still smeared the wood floor.

"Actually, you can't. I'd bet you don't have more than two shots left. I suggest you make them count."

Jed looked at the shatterkeg.

He then tilted the barrel and aimed at a patch of soil not more than three feet in front of his toes.

The gears in Lyle's face slowed and nearly froze. "Stop—Jed—what are you doing?"

Jed yanked a lever. The shatterkeg fired, ripping through the ship's hull. Soil drained from the room like sand in an hourglass.

"No!" Lyle bolted forward and scooped armfuls of soil into the corridor.

Jed held his breath as he lined up the next shot. He yanked the firing lever, and the shatterkeg blasted the deck below Lyle's feet. Lyle looked up with sorrow in his golden eyes.

And then the floor around him fell away.

Lyle slipped through the hole without a sound—without a shriek, or a scream, or even a gasp. He tumbled through air toward the barge until he was too distant to see.

Jed sighed and leaned against the lemon tree.

At least for now, it was over. He was safe. His father was safe.

But as he pressed his shoulder into the tree, it began to lean with him. The deck splintered and creaked with its weight. He clung to the trunk as it began to sink.

Something snapped, and the tree fell onto its side. The deck collapsed under him. Jed grabbed a tree limb. His feet dangled in open air as planks of wood fluttered to the barge.

Another plank of flooring snapped, and the tree fell into the sky with Jed still holding its trunk.

37

J ed held tight to the trunk of the lemon tree, and together they crashed. Branches tangled around his face. A hand reached through the leaves and gripped his. A familiar hand. His father's hand.

Jed clawed through the lemon tree's branches, swatting at clumps of soil that showered around him.

"You . . . you came back," Jed said.

His father shrugged. "I was in the neighborhood."

Jed scrambled free and wrapped his arms around his father. "He said you didn't care about me. That you'd abandon me."

Shay jammed the accelerator. The raft shot forward, shaking more soil into Jed's hair. "Where to?" she asked no one in particular.

Jed's father stared deeper into the fog. "Lawnmower Mountain."

Shay lifted an eyebrow.

"What's Lawnmower Mountain?" Jed asked.

"A hidden city that not many people still know exist."

"Why are we going there?"

His father squeezed Jed's shoulder with one hand. "To find your mother. She was supposed to pick you up from the steamboat. But something happened. We planned to use relics to keep in touch, but shortly after we separated, they stopped working. I haven't heard from her since."

"She's . . . she's missing?" Jed knew that his father had just said as much, but the words came out anyway. "How do you know she's at Lawnmower Mountain?"

"If she's out of reach, it's the only place she would have gone."

"What about the relic? Can't you fix it?"

"Mine isn't the one that's broken."

"Isn't there something else you could use? Some other relic?"

His father shifted and avoided Jed's eyes. He nodded and scratched the side of his neck. "There is *one*."

"And it can find Mom?"

He nodded slowly.

"Then we'll get it. We'll do whatever it takes. Where do we start looking?"

"We don't have to look anywhere. It's already here." He glanced at the bandages around Jed's chest.

A lurching feeling turned Jed's stomach on end. For a moment—the briefest of seconds—he'd forgotten what he was. Forgotten about the spinning gears under his skin.

"*I* can find Mom?"

"You can do more than you know. You found Lyle. You found me."

"How?"

"You read the note we left? All of it?" Jed nodded. "Then you brought the key?"

Jed wiggled his toes against the metal lump. He pulled off his shoe, and the key clattered to the floor. "Is this what Lyle was looking for?"

His father picked it up and nodded.

"What does it do?"

He set it in Jed's palm and closed his fingers around it. "Unlocks potential."

Jed stared at the key. "What do you mean?"

His father removed the bandages around Jed's chest and traced the golden keyhole. "Lyle made you with the potential to do almost anything. *Anything*—but not *everything*. It's up to you to choose who you want to be. How you want to grow. What you want to do. This key"—he patted Jed's hand—"unlocks your first choice. You are not gears and gold. You're a boy with his own choice. His own life.

"The moment you turn that key, your world will never be the same. *You* will never be the same. And there's no going back."

Jed's mind yelled at himself to think about consequences—

to ask his father more, to find out what the key would do to him. But all he could think about was home. If this was the key to *that*, to home, then nothing else mattered. A word floated into his memory: SPLAGHETTI.

It was time for a little *insanity*.

Jed lifted the dented shaft of metal to his chest and slid it into the golden keyhole.

He turned, and a click echoed in his ears.

Acknowledgments

Thank you to all those who helped make this a reality. A special thank-you to:

John Robert Marlow, for undeserved patience, and for teaching me how to tell a story. To Rob, for being my biggest fan—even when my writing didn't deserve one. To Tim, for honesty. To Emma, for believing in Jed when I didn't. To Tracey and Ella, for believing in Jed when I did. To Jo, Kimberly, and Marion, for having faith in me. To Brenda and Derek, for slogging through awful writing. To Mom, for cultivating dreamers. And to Andelyn, for notes on bathroom mirrors written in bar soap, assuring me that one day, this *would be*.

Turn the page for a sneak peek at the sequel to

JED AND THE
JUNKYARD WAR!

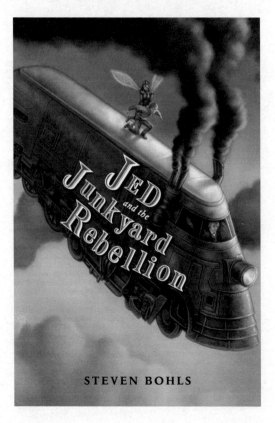

J ed lifted a dented shaft of metal to his chest and slid it into
the golden keyhole.

A click echoed in his ears.

The golden panel just above the keyhole popped open.

Under the panel was a large red button.

He reached for the button and pressed it.

Something inside him awakened. It was small and
bright ... a piece of him that had slept for many years. And
now, after all this time, it began to glow. He couldn't imme-
diately see a difference in his skin or the exposed gears in his
chest, but he could sense it. As the glowing feeling intensified,
a dull light shone through the keyhole. Shay and Jed's father
stared intently at the light.

"What's happening to me?" Jed asked.

"Guardian Mouse," Shay whispered.

Jed's dad looked at her and then to Jed. He opened his mouth as if to explain, but before he could, the heat in Jed's chest flared. His frame hummed. An electric charge coursed through his bones. The energy burned hotter. A stinging, blistering fire blazed through his blood.

And then every bit of heat from every corner of his body contracted into an inferno in his chest. Jed fell to his knees, clutching his heart.

His vision rattled. A buzz cut into his ears. The pain, the heat, and the sound collided, firing a pulse of energy that shook the barge with a deafening crack. A ring of light blasted from his chest. The light swelled across the horizon and then disappeared behind the fog that walled them in.

Jed's world went silent.

An icy chill bit at his chest that no longer held the raging sun.

Darkness crept into the edges of his vision. Then everything vanished. The barge. His father. Shay. All of them—*gone*.

. . .

A sea of blackness swirled into focus as the color drained from the world.

The air smelled like oil and tasted like metal. Smokey tendrils hovered like fog—scratchy, dusty particles that felt like slivers of glass.

Where am I . . . ?

Everything ached. His joints . . . hands . . . neck . . . even his eyes. The pain came in waves, pulsing from head to knee in steady, angry surges. He felt as if he'd been asleep for a solid month.

Slowly, the blackness sharpened into clarity, and the throbbing pain quieted.

Where . . . where am I . . . ?

He lifted his arm and held it in front of his face. The hand before his eyes was unfamiliar. He tried to move the curious fingers. They wiggled. But this wasn't how he remembered his fingers. They had been different. Shinier. Like *gold*. But these . . . these fingers looked more like hot dogs.

"So squishy . . ." he whispered, clenching and unclenching his fingers into a fist.

Even the sound of his own voice was peculiar . . . foreign . . . *fake*.

Who am I?

He tried to think. The image of a burning heat melting his mind surfaced. He shook his head. Memories felt buried and looked blurry—dreams he could not remember.

What am I?

I have a name . . . don't I?

He tried to remember—*anything*. His home? His face? The harder he tried, the soupier his brain felt.

He searched the darkness. He was in a cave. No . . . not a cave. An empty water tower on its side. Wooden windmill blades obscured the entrance. Through the gaps, he saw bits of the outside world. The ground was compressed junk. The sky was a dusty black expanse.

Near the entrance of the water tower sat a raft, quiet and still. He stared at it. A vibrant green tree with bright yellow lemons sprouted from its center.

"Odd. Boats don't grow trees . . . *do they?*" Jed whispered to himself.

This was all wrong. This wasn't where he belonged. Was it?

He didn't live under dark mist that tasted like oil and metal. He lived in a three-bedroom home, with color and smiles. Didn't he?

He twisted his neck. To his left was a sleeping girl—her small body curled into a ball. She had copper hair that glinted in the dim sliver of light, and her tiny mouth sipped quick breaths of air. She shivered and pulled her legs closer to her chest. Then she sighed and twitched her nose.

To his right was a sleeping man, tall, lanky, and sprawled out sloppily. He drew slow, heavy breaths and released low—almost silent—snores.

Who are they?

"They're dangerous. . . ." a voice whispered in his ear.

Jed's heart thumped at the sound. It wasn't his own voice. It was a man's. Someone he knew.

"Who . . . are you?" he whispered back.

"A friend," said the whisper. "And I'm going to help you escape."

"Escape from what?"

"From those two. They stole you. They are thieves. Get away from them. Hurry!"

"I don't remember you. I don't . . . I don't remember anything."

"I know," the voice whispered. "I'll help you remember. Now, crawl away."

The lanky man beside him rolled onto his side and snorted.

"What's going on?" Jed whispered. "This isn't right. I'm not supposed to be here."

A thought floated into his mind of warm beds . . . warm carpets . . . birthdays and laughter. There was no laughter here. Only darkness and strangers.

The whisper returned. "The connection is fading. You must find me. Look for the red flares. Go. Quickly!"

Icy needles prickled up Jed's spine. Fear welled in his chest, and his thoughts shattered in a frenzy of panic.

Run.

Get away.

Hide.

Carefully, he crept out of the water tower and into the darkness.

Ships hung heavy in the sky like storm clouds. *Dreadnoughts.* Jed knew the word, he knew he'd seen them before, and he knew they were deadly. He scanned the horizon for a clue. A flickering red light streamed through the sky. *Look for the red flares*, the voice had said.

"Are you there?" Jed closed his eyes and searched for the whisper. His mind was a vault of locked memories. The whisper was the key, he imagined. He was in a strange place with strange people. *I was taken? By them?*

He moved from cover to cover, toward the flare. Above, the dreadnoughts flew in jumbled fleets. The ship hulls were twisted hunks of metal. An eerie jaggedness framed the bodies of the beasts, and orange furnaces burned in the heart of each ship, leaking a dull glow.

As Jed watched, a distant fleet began to change course, turning until they were pointed directly at him.

They can't see me from that far away . . . can they?

Their engines flared, making the air ripple with heat and bringing the dreadnoughts closer.

Jed's heart thumped. He stumbled away as the ships powered through the sky.

Up ahead, another fleet turned and faced him. They, too, began to accelerate.

"You've got to be kidding me," Jed said.

Faster and faster he ran, avoiding deadly misstep after deadly misstep on the uneven terrain. The ships were gaining on him. Jed shifted direction and sprinted left, away from both fleets. The ships maintained a steady course, and that's when he realized—the ships weren't heading for him. They were heading for each other.

BOOM! BOOM! BOOM!

Orange fire shot into the air and junk rumbled under Jed's feet. He followed the shatterfire with his eyes as it arced through the sky. Flames trailed the blasts as they slammed into one another, and explosions erupted from the broken hulls.

Jed ducked behind a tire as metal rained down and impaled the ground around him. The fleets continued firing and more metal slashed through the debris. Watching the destruction, Jed sensed a problem. The battle was off kilter; it was strange . . . it was wrong. Why were the dreadnoughts firing at *each other*?

More scrap pelted the ground nearby, embedding itself in a fridge and leaving jagged metal chunks shivering upright in the junk. He swallowed nervously. The shatterkegs rumbled above him. "I need to get out or I'll be buried here."

A crack squealed open over Jed's head. Engines sputtered and wailed from one of the dreadnoughts. The storm paused, almost as if the enemies were taking a deep breath. Jed peeked out to see a dreadnought slowly being torn in half.

And then it began falling.

He leaped from behind the tire and sprinted away. He stole quick glances upward as both halves of the dreadnought sunk toward the ground. Jed's feet hit the junk faster and harder as a shadow swelled around him and the dreadnought fell closer. The nose of the ship pierced the ground first, metal shrieking in protest and debris shooting into the sky. Jed watched as the rest of the ship plummeted down.

"Go, go, go!" he yelled to himself.

Everything shook.

His lungs burned, but Jed kept running. Junk ripped, screeched, creaked, and shattered around him as smoke billowed up from the broken vessels. Figures emerged from the smoke. Black dots poked out and skittered in all directions. Before long, they swarmed the deck and crawled to the ground. They were twisted, misshapen scraps of flesh and metal.

Dread. The word lurked in the corner of Jed's empty mind just like *dreadnought* had.

He stumbled backward.

Dread from both sides met in the center of the battlefield, giving Jed a sliver of a chance to escape. He backed away until he thought it was safe, and then he ran until he could no longer hear the sounds of tearing metal. Distant ships flew in clusters toward other fleets. Dots of orange shatterfire speckled the dark sky. This was war. *But it isn't right. Why are the dread killing one another? They aren't supposed to do that. They're supposed to kill humans . . . meat sacks . . . aren't they?*

Jed dropped down behind a grimy couch to catch his breath, and the unfamiliar—yet familiar—whisper returned. "Traitors . . ."

"What?"

"I gave them life, and they turned into feral dogs."

Jed stared at the distant warring dread. "You created those things? Why?"

There was a long pause. "To survive." Another faint red flare shot up in the distance. "Quickly," the voice said. "Before they find you."

"Who?" Jed asked. "The dread?" But he could feel that the whisper was already gone.

The desolation was endless, mirroring the dark hole his questions had dug within him. Where was he? What was this place—this strange land of charred, squished-up junk and metal creatures?

A thought pricked the back of his mind: *This isn't land at all. It's a giant ship. A barge.*

He shook his head. That was ridiculous. A *ship?* The horizon on all sides of him ended in a distant gray fog. This couldn't be a ship. That was impossible. It was too enormous; ships this big didn't exist. But, even as he tried to shake the thought from his mind, something told him that this was, indeed, a ship.

He looked up. Ships were flying above him, blasting each other to scrap. How could he be *standing* on one? It didn't make sense.

Why couldn't he remember? What was wrong with him? He stared at his hands again. *Who am I?* The skin was too soft and too pink. It didn't look right. Wasn't his skin . . . *gold*? He flexed his fingers one by one. "Who am I?" he said again, this time out loud. "I have a name. I know I do. My name is—" He spoke, as if the answer would somehow spring free on its own by doing so.

It didn't.

"My name is—" he tried again.

Nothing.

A dull ache throbbed in the center of his chest. Carefully, he pulled off his T-shirt. A long white bandage had been wrapped around his chest, and red oil seeped through the gauze. He unpinned the two aluminum clasps holding the wrap in place and let it unravel. When it reached its end, the fabric tugged against the dried red. He winced, pulling it off.

A ring of skin had burned away, revealing the delicate gears that spun inside his chest. *Golden* gears.

Panic ignited in the pit of his stomach. The gears inside him whirred faster as the terror clawed through his mind.

"*What* . . . what am I?" he whispered. "What's happening to me?"

His heartbeat quickened even more, and so did the golden gears. They hummed so silently that he might have never noticed them. The machinery spun around a golden plate with a keyhole in it. Jed ran his shaking fingers over the indentation.

Taking a deep breath, Jed leaned back against an old trunk and stared up at the sky, dropping his hands. He couldn't think about everything too much. He didn't want to. He had to worry about one thing at a time, and there were plenty of things to choose from.

The fog gave no indication whether it was morning, after-noon, or the middle of the night. Jed's stomach grumbled. Whatever time it was, he was hungry.

What did people eat here? *People?* He laughed at the word. Whatever those things crawling from the dreadnought were, they weren't *people.*

But they were at least partially alive, so that meant that they had to eat something.

Jed stood and searched the ground around him.

A checkered pillow . . . a ladder . . . a painting of a dolphin.

The longer he walked, the more his stomach grumbled. But amidst doorknobs, stuffed bears, and a weed whacker, he couldn't spot anything to eat. What if there wasn't any food at all around here? What if the dread didn't *actually* eat food and instead ate *junk?* Jed touched the burned hole in his chest. Did *he* eat junk?

It had been hours since he'd seen a dread. Every so often, another red flare would launch up into the sky. He was getting closer, little by little.

His stomach rumbled again.

Just as he decided that there was no food in this wasteland, his tired eyes spotted a torn label with a muscly, green-skinned man standing in a meadow. Green Giant French Style Green Beans.

Jed grabbed the can. "Of course," he mumbled, "I'm in a world of junk with a can of green beans and no can opener."

He searched until he found a screwdriver to pry open the lid. He pounded and pulled until at last, he pinched one of the squishy green beans. The moment it touched his tongue, a memory popped open. Crisp green beans, pan-seared in olive oil and rolled in a bed of minced sautéed garlic cloves . . . hot turkey that steamed on a chrome platter . . . buttered broccoli, yams, and cranberry sauce. He was back home, sitting at the kitchen table for a Thanksgiving meal. As he chewed the cold, wet canned green beans, part of him wished the memory hadn't returned. It hung there, taunting him with safety and comfort.

He tipped the can to his chin and slurped the last few drops of water. Jed closed his eyes and thought of his warm home and warm meals once more. It was filled with shadows, but the outlines were there. Then, a new scratchy voice entered his mind.

"Wake up, Sleepy Mouse."

Jed's vision flickered. He sat still, focusing on the image. He was seeing double—a second sight overlaid on his own. He was looking through two sets of eyes at the same time.

"Wake up, Sleepy Mouse . . . wake up," the voice said again.

The vision saturated his sight until it was all he could see. Even with his eyes closed, the second pair of eyes revealed a new world to him. The voice grew louder. And then, all at once, everything that he was disappeared. Jed was in another mind.